CW01628353

To Rome with Lust

KD GRACE

Published by Xcite Books Ltd – 2014

ISBN 9781783755929

Copyright © KD Grace 2014

All rights reserved. No part of this book may be reproduced, stored in a retrieval system, or transmitted in any form or by any means, electronic, electrostatic, magnetic tape, mechanical, photocopying, recording or otherwise, without the written permission of the publishers: Xcite Books, Suite 11769, 2nd Floor, 145-157 St John Street, London EC1V 4PY

Printed and bound in the UK

This is a work of fiction. Names and characters are the product of the author's imagination and any resemblance to actual persons, living or dead, is entirely coincidental

To Rome with Lust is dedicated to that wonderful sense that so often gets neglected, the sense of smell. I am very happy to raise my glass in salute to olfactory ecstasy!

Thank you, with all my heart!

Thank you, Renee and all of the lovely Ladiez at Sh! Not only are you a fount of information, fun, and encouragement, but you're an endless source of inspiration to me. Hugs and kisses and my deepest gratitude.

Thank you, Lucy Felthouse, for cracking the PR whip, when necessary, and for staving off more than one panic attack for this neurotic writer. Thank you for boundless encouragement. I couldn't have done it without you, EP!

Thank you, Kay Jaybee, for being my 'terrible twin', for being your fabulous self, and for all the inspiration and encouragement you give me. This writing journey has been so much better because of you.

Thank you, Raymond, for standing by me when I get a little bit insane and loving me anyway. Thank you for believing in me and being proud of me and easing the journey. There's no one I'd rather have by my side. Volim te mnogo!

Chapter One

Liza thought she had only dreamed such an exquisite scent. She'd certainly never smelled anything so sexy while she was awake. It was all very strange. Her dreams had always been the only part of her life that was olfactory-free. She sat in the business lounge at JFK airport dozing, blocking out the noise and the smell of the busy shuffle. But *this* smell was different. This smell was just too delicious to ignore. It intensified, then faded, and she snuffled and inhaled and shifted in her seat.

Delays due to heavy thunderstorms meant the place was packed with passengers awaiting a spate of flights going out at nearly the same time. Luckily, her flight wasn't delayed. She was just there early, thanks to Carl. After an unplanned night alone in a hotel room, she couldn't get out of New York City fast enough – not after what she'd seen … and smelled. But she didn't want to think about Carl. Time to move forward.

She had just slipped back into that space between wakefulness and sleep when the scent wafted over her again. There was no denying it was the primal smell of male. It was the smell of desert lightning, of sage and juniper and thick, dark night. It was the smell of sex – or at least the intimations of sex or what sex might be like with a man who smelled so irresistible.

Jesus, was she really going to have sexy dreams right here in the airport? What next? Would she be rubbing herself against the sofa while all the businessmen and the tourists pretended not to notice? Surely it was only because of the sex she'd expected to get last night, but didn't. Surely it was just her angry unconscious inventing an olfactory fantasy, but God, the man smelled good – better than anyone she'd ever smelled, and she smelled everyone! She inhaled again and her deep intake of scent came out sounding like a sigh. Her lips parted just enough to take in the fullness of the experience. She could almost taste that hypnotic smell of masculinity. Her nipples chafed against her bra until they dominated the front of her sweater with an achy tetchy fullness that matched the tightening she felt between her thighs. It was as though the man stood right over her. She could smell expensive fabric weighted and warmed with the heat of his flesh. His crotch, where the delicious scent was purest, was so close that her mouth watered. The scent was heavy, thickening, male – driven by passion. Letting the dream take control, Liza shifted, uncrossed her legs, and leaned forward to draw in his scent, wanting nothing so much as to touch, to caress, to experiment on ways to arouse from her dream man more of that delicious scent.

There was a soft grunt, a startled gasp, and a large hand came down heavily on her shoulder. There was a desperate clearing of a throat and a slightly accented 'Pardon me.'

She opened her eyes and found herself nose to crotch with a very expensive suit not quite able to disguise a very nice package. Her fingers were fisted in the edges of the front trouser pockets, reeling their wearer ever closer and closer to her salivating mouth. She yelped and practically shoved the guy, who might have fallen if not for the hand resting on her shoulder. 'Oh my God! I'm sorry, I'm so sorry,' she gasped. 'I was dreaming.' Her face burned and her pulse did a drumroll in her ears as she raised her eyes up and up and up the length of the well filled-out charcoal suit to meet rich caramel eyes looking down at her from beneath thick midnight lashes. The scent hit her in waves, making her giddy, making her want to sniff like a dog in heat, making her feel wrong-footed and out of focus.

'Must have been some dream.' His eyes sparkled and he offered her a half-smile. His warm hands fell to cover hers and disengage them from his pockets. 'I can't tell you how sorry I am that I woke you, but I'd really hate it if your dream got us both kicked out of the lounge.' His thumbs brushed over the backs of her knuckles before he released her. 'Is it all right if I share you sofa? The lounge is really crowded.'

'Yes! Of course, please.' She shifted and rearranged herself, resisting the urge to fold her arms across her perky nipples. It was even harder to resist the urge to pant and sniff. My God, if an aphrodisiac could be inhaled, his scent would *so* be that aphrodisiac. She felt moist and swollen, splayed in the crotch of her panties, too tender for the weight of her body against the sofa.

'Are you all right?' The man's eyes had darkened with concern. 'You seem in distress.'

'Fine! I'm fine,' she said with enthusiasm that made her sound like a dork. 'Just outrageously embarrassed.'

'Don't be. You made my morning and gave me something I'll smile about for what'll be a very long, very tedious flight. You sure you're all right?'

'You smell amazing,' she blurted out before she could stop herself, then she felt the flash-fire burn rise to her cheeks again. Jeez! Could she sound any more stupid?

He raised an eyebrow and cocked his head. 'Thanks. Eau d'generic hotel soap,' he said.

'No, it's not the soap, I mean I can smell that too, but …' What the fuck was it with her? She practically attacks the guy – who handled an embarrassing situation very graciously all things considered – and now she informs him she's been sniffing? 'Never mind. I … like I said, I was dreaming.'

He leaned forward in a wave of scent that made her dizzy with lust. 'No, please, don't be embarrassed. I'm very interested in all things olfactory. And I'm really flattered that you like the way I smell.'

'I'm sorry. I have a sensitive nose.' She forced a laugh. 'I guess maybe I'm a little closer to my animal roots than most people. I … I pick up on scent … way more than most people do. Bit of an evolutionary throw-back, I'm afraid.'

His smile was practically edible. 'Humans are mammals. Mammals live through their sense of smell. We've just gotten lazy and forgotten how to do that. Real scent is hard to come by in a world that's been deodorized, sanitized, and scrubbed. Apparently you remember.'

Oh, she remembered all right. She remembered so much more than she wished she did at times. She could feel his dark, rich gaze against her, feel his scent bearing down on her, now spiked with the cinnamon nip of curiosity. She knew what was coming. She waited for it.

'So,' he leaned still closer and everything in her felt giddy and humid. 'Tell me what you smell?'

God, she knew he was going to ask that. She should have kept her damned mouth shut. To ask her to describe his scent was like asking her to describe what she thought sex with him would be like, and with a scent like his, she could imagine it would be pretty fucking amazing. On the other hand, if he stayed leaning close like this, she'd have a few more seconds to sniff and enjoy before he suspected her of total nutterdom.

'Don't be embarrassed. As I said, the sense of smell and the way we humans use it is of special interest to me.'

She leaned in and inhaled deeply through her nose. After all he had given her permission to sniff. 'You smell like summer lightning … at high altitude.' She inhaled again and closed her eyes, hearing the catch of his breath. 'Beneath that, you smell like evergreen and the earth around tree roots.' His breathing accelerated. She leaned still closer, and the slip and slide of fabric on fabric informed her that he'd done the same until they were nearly touching. She inhaled again. 'You smell like a rainstorm on the wind just before it arrives, but that's because you're skeptical, and I don't blame you.'

For both of them, simply breathing had become a challenge. Her belly muscles trembled and tensed way down low; in her panties, the clench and release, clench and release had left her swollen and pouty. She opened her eyes just a slit, then closed them again, but there was no mistaking the shape of his growing erection. Her own scent spiked all honey-butter and nutmeg.

'What else?' he breathed. 'Is there more?'

'Your curiosity smells of cinnamon and there's a bit of irritation – tart, tangy, almost like lemon.' Her eyes fluttered open at the same moment his did.

'Oh it's not you,' he said quickly. 'I mean I'm not irritated with you. It's this trip. I didn't plan to take it and now I find out … wait a minute. You can smell emotions?'

'Kind of,' she said, trying not to look at his

erection, as he shifted to rearrange himself a little less conspicuously. Then she couldn't resist. 'What about me? Can you smell me?' Jesus! Why did she ask such a loaded question?

He squirmed again, which did nothing to hide his needy package. A blush rose to his cheeks. 'Maybe … Possibly.' He inhaled a shaky breath through his nose like he was afraid of what he might smell. 'The more we talk … the more I smell.' His eyes fluttered shut again. 'You're … not wearing perfume.'

'I never do.' She eased herself closer, resisting the urge to rest a hand on his thigh. 'It interferes with other smells.'

He nodded, as though he completely understood. 'You smell like the sea, but you also smell like honey and butter melting over hot bread.'

Did she just whimper? Oh God, please say she didn't just whimper and shift her bottom against the sofa. Surely she didn't do that.

This time he inhaled boldly, pushing forward on the sofa, his eyes closed, suddenly making no attempt to cover the heavy strain against the front of his trousers. The cinnamon scent of him spiked and became more peppery. 'Jesus, I can't believe we're doing this.' His voice was little more than a whisper between parted lips, lips that Liza would only have to lean into to touch with her own. 'I can't believe I can smell all that. I'm probably imagining it.'

'No you're not. You're not imagining it,' she whispered back.

He was suddenly breathing as though he'd just ran a marathon, each breath through his nose, each breath followed by a gulp, almost as though he were eating the scent of her.

'People are looking. We should stop.' She barely

got the words out before he leaned in just a tiny bit further and, in his enthusiasm, his lips brushed hers. Everything spiked in a sharp stab of scent that went straight to her pussy, as they both gasped and sat back, eyes wide, fingers pressed to lips.

The delayed flight to Paris was called over the intercom immediately after one to Frankfurt and, in the jostling and shifting and gathering of belongings, no one paid any attention to them. She wasn't sure it would have made any difference even if they'd suddenly been centre stage. Their gaze locked on each other, cheeks flushed, chests heaving, they sat caught in a moment so tight, so full that its breaking apart was inevitable. It was ridiculous. She was seconds away from coming, and his cock was about to burst his trousers. And his lips, God his lips, she could think of so many places on her body she wanted those lips.

'I have to know,' he gasped. 'Surely you want to know too.' Then he did the unthinkable. He curled his fingers into the back of her hair and pulled her to him. This time their mouths met with a clash and a gasped swallow of oxygen that transitioned into parted lips and darting tongues and an absolute explosion of scent. If he had smelled amazing by himself, if his scent had sharpened hers to the cutting edge of orgasm, then the mixing and blending that happened when they touched, when those two scents came together was shattering. 'I've never smelled anything like it,' she breathed.

'Me neither.' He bit her lower lip and tugged and their blended scent became darker, spicier, with tones of earth and sea, pepper and honey, and God the guy could kiss!

She came first with a guttural grunt of an orgasm that began deep in her pussy and washed over her like a riptide. She tried desperately to hide it, but he knew it. He felt it, she even thought he smelled it, and he tightened his fist in her hair, breathing her into his open mouth. Both his hands then slid to her shoulders in a grip that was almost painful as he pulled back. His eyes locked on hers, and his whole body convulsed, and again, and again, his deep mocha gaze holding her tight as pupils dilated and eyelids shuddered.

For a moment they sat stunned, staring at each other, struggling to catch their breath. He looked shell-shocked, and she must have looked the same. 'I'm sorry,' they both said at the same time as they mirrored each other in a nervous laugh.

Then the intercom called the flight to Rome. 'That's my flight,' she gasped, awash in a wave of embarrassment. She babbled something about duty free and gifts, sounding like a total idiot. She grabbed her bag and her laptop and fled, feeling certain everyone was watching, feeling certain everyone knew exactly what they had done. It didn't matter though, at the end of the day, she'd never see the man again. And she'd never smell him again. That saddened her.

Chapter Two

As Paulo settled into the first class cabin, he looked around, just in case the woman was there. Sadly she wasn't. As the attendant announced they were waiting for a connecting flight from Atlanta, he did a little investigating and, sure enough, there she was back in coach. She sat on the aisle not far from the bathrooms, checking her BlackBerry. Just seeing her again, even from a distance, got his cock's full attention. Christ! Had she really made him come, made them both come just by describing the way he smelled, by making him describe the way she smelled? His business was scent. How could he have missed the incredibly rich and outrageously sexy scents right under his nose? Of course he knew the scent of a woman aroused. But he'd only ever experienced that scent up close and personal when he was on top of said woman, fucking her hard, or when his face was buried between her legs. Sadly, these days that didn't happen very often, in spite of his circumstances. He loved the scent of a woman, he loved the scent of sex, but this woman had taken the olfactory mechanics of attraction, the smell of a couple getting to know each other, to a level far beyond anything he could have imagined.

His pulse rate picked up as he thought of the taste of her mouth. Unconsciously he licked his lips. He couldn't keep from wondering what the rest of her tasted like; her nipples, pressed against light summer cotton, her armpits with the subtle piquant salt of clean female sweat, and between her legs … his mouth watered, his cock bucked enough to make him shift and tug his jacket down for extra coverage. He could still smell the faint scent of himself even after his efforts to clean up. Fuck! It was embarrassing. He hadn't lost control like that since he was an adolescent. And yet, losing control with the lovely brunette sniffing him in the business lounge at JFK was like super-heated kink. With the beginnings of a plan forming in his mind, he motioned the attendant to his side for a short consult, then he settled back into his seat and waited for takeoff.

Back in cattle car class, Liza tried not to elbow the rotund man sitting next to her as she checked her messages one last time and cursed the fact that she was too damned stingy to fork out for a business class ticket. *High Rising* e-magazine was doing well, better than they had ever dreamed when she and Addie began the venture four years ago. Addie reminded her of that each time Liza flew. They could afford it, and Addie would know. She kept a tight fist on the purse strings. Still Liza couldn't quite bring herself to believe it just yet. Anyway, with luck the window seat would stay empty and the man would move over and give them both breathing space.

There was a message from Addie wishing her bon voyage, and there was another message from Carl. She ignored it. What could he possibly have to say that she'd want to hear, or that she'd believe? She was too preoccupied with thoughts of what had happened in the lounge to think about anything else. Escapism, that's all it had been, pure and simple escapism, and yet in all of her years of experiencing the world through her nose, she'd never smelled anyone like the man in the lounge. She regretted not asking his name, but after what she'd done, she figured she was lucky he hadn't called airport security and had her taken away. It had only been the calling of her flight that had saved her bacon. Still, what were the chances of her ever smelling anyone so hot again?

Some things in the world were honest. Some things were always straightforward and reliable. Her sense of smell was one of those things. She should have known in the beginning that Carl wasn't for her. He just didn't smell right. Funny how she had never really realized that until what had happened in the airport lounge. When she first started seeing Carl, she'd chalked it all up to some strange allergy she only ever had when she was in New York City. But it wasn't New York, was it? It had never been New York.

She'd just finished a job in DC when she'd gotten Carl's invitation to come join him at his flat in Manhattan before she flew to Rome. He gave her the key last time they were together, saying that in the future he hoped to give her something a little less symbolic, and a lot more physical as to where he wanted their relationship to go. Funny he'd thought of it as a relationship. Funny she'd let him. Funny she'd almost let herself believe it, in spite of all of the warning signs that she should have seen months ago. Carl Blain was tall, blond, and well-muscled – and outrageously sexy. He was filthy rich, and unbelievably charming. He had broad shoulders, a great ass, ocean blue eyes. The man was a fucking cliché for one of the plethora of billionaire novels flooding the bookstores at the moment. He had taken over Blain Holdings after his father's death and had acquitted himself well from what *The Wall Street Journal* and *The New York Times* reported ad nauseum. He was the rather ruthless darling of the business world and everything he touched turned to gold. Six months ago he had allowed her to follow him around for a week on a story for *High Rising*. Almost from the first time they met, he'd asked her out, but she refused to date anyone she was working with. The minute the story was published, he asked her out again, and he hadn't taken no for an answer.

It was then she started taking the allergy medicine. It wasn't that Carl Blain stank. Of course he didn't. He smelled very sexy by the standards of the average female nose. God knew Liza had smelled a few men whose natural scent did everything but set off her gag reflex. Carl Blaine wasn't one of those men. Carl Blaine didn't smell bad to her. Carl Blaine simply made her sneeze. Repeatedly. She wrote it all off as something in the city, after all, New York wasn't the cleanest place on the planet. It probably had its unique pollens and leaf molds like every place did, and then there was the pollution. Surely there was just something in the air that made her sneeze. It was the simple matter of popping a few allergy tablets whenever she headed up to New York to spend time with Carl. And frankly, the temporary dulling of her overwhelming sense of smell was a welcome relief in small doses.

In truth, their long-distance relationship had suited her just fine. And really, how could she blame him for fucking someone else when she had managed to put him off repeatedly. It wasn't that she didn't want sex. She longed for sex, she ached for it, so badly, in fact, that she considered herself a serial masturbater. And as much as she'd hoped that the allergy medication would allow her to enjoy sex with Carl, she just couldn't get past the discomfort. Sex was supposed to be fun, right? Yet her nose wouldn't quite let her forget that Carl, for all of his sex appeal to every other female on the planet, just didn't smell like someone she wanted to fuck. Damn it, she had tried. She really had. Carl was great arm candy, and Addie had told her that her semi-regular trips to New York could almost pass as the social life she didn't have time for. Besides, from the strictly mercenary point of view, getting an exclusive on Carl Blain and Blain Holdings for *High Rising* hadn't done the magazine any harm either. As for the sex, well there hadn't been any. And even though Carl had handled her excuse of getting to know each other before they got intimate well in the beginning, it was clear the last time they were together that the man wasn't up for much more abstinence. It hadn't been a great ending to a date. She had practically pushed him off the sofa after he'd all but climbed on top of her mid-kiss. She thought it was over when he'd finally settled back in the chair across from her, cursing roughly under his breath, his cock dangerously straining the seam of his designer trousers. Instead he gave her the key to his flat with the not so subtle hint that he expected them to share his bed in said flat the next time she was in New York, and she had resigned herself to the fact that she could put him off no longer. It wasn't supposed to be like that, was it?

She wouldn't have known the half of what Carl got up to if she hadn't run out of allergy tablets and not realized it until she got off the plane at JFK. She figured she could get by without them until morning, surely. In her excitement to see him before she headed overseas, she'd managed a seat on an earlier flight. She'd never been to his apartment before, and she thought to surprise him by being naked in his bed when he got home. She was the one who got the surprise.

She could smell sex almost the moment she got out of the elevator at Carl's building. But then she had always been able to smell where sex had recently happened as easily as she could smell desire on people. She'd learned to block most of those powerful scents from her mind otherwise she would never have been able to go outside her room. The closer she got to Carl's door, the stronger the smell became. She pulled out her BlackBerry and checked to make sure she had the right address. His flat was at the end of a long corridor. By the time she got there, it was obvious the scent could be coming from no place else. She stifled a sneeze, then another one. For a long moment, she stood unmoving in front of the door, key poised in her sweaty, outstretched hand. She sneezed again and the scent rammed its way into her sinus cavity. Her pulse hammered in her ears. She fought back the urge to run. Surely she was just tired. Surely she was imagining things. Maybe one of Car's neighbours had gotten kinky and had sex in the hallway. Maybe the mail man or a delivery man had done the dirty out here with a satisfied customer.

Liza knew the smell of Carl after he masturbated. She had never told him. It excited her that she knew that little secret about him. One of the fantasies she'd had when they were together was watching him masturbate. In fact that fantasy had been more of a turn-on to her than the actual thought of sex with him. But this smell was different.

She stood in front of the door with every excuse she could think of running through her head. Her rational self, the part that listened to her olfactory Spidey senses, knew what was going on, knew that she should walk away. But the wishy-washy, overly polite part of her just couldn't bear leaving and not letting him know why, and besides, maybe she was wrong. Hopefully she was wrong.

Boldly, she stepped forward and shoved the key

home. As the door opened to a flat filled with clean lines and ultra modern chrome and leather furnishings, all the clean house smells were instantly overwhelmed by the hot, wet smell of messy sex. She reeled as though she had been slapped. She was halfway down the hall before she could hear the grunts and moans over her heart pounding in her ears, and when she turned the corner into the kitchen, she got the total sensory overload. A woman with big blonde hair lay back on the marble counter-top, exposed fake tits not bouncing, black dress shoved over her hips, her expensively stilettoed feet resting on Carl's shoulders. Carl was humping and shoving and straining between her spread thighs, bare ass cheeks clenching and relaxing in the hypnotic push and shove of each thrust. 'You like that don't you, baby,' he said. 'You like my cock in your tight little cunt.'

For a moment, Liza stood lightheaded and nauseated from the thick olfactory fog that coated her like oil. She was just going to turn and leave. Even then she didn't want to be a bother. She was just going to walk out and politely break it off in a text. But then, she sneezed and she sneezed again, and again.

'What the –' It was definitely coitus interruptus as Carl pulled out, and the blonde slid from the countertop, nearly falling off her stilettos before she caught herself and stood tugging at her skirt.

'Jesus, Liza. What are you doing here?' He struggled to tuck his cock, which now pointed accusingly at her.

'I took an earlier flight,' ah-choo, ah-choo, ah-choo. 'Sorry for –' ah-choo, ah-choo '– interrupting.' She made her way to the door in a storm of violent sneezes with him calling after her, cursing in his efforts to cover himself.

Over her sneezes, Liza could hear the woman's

shrill voice. 'Carl? Who is that? Carl? Who is she?'

She was safely tucked in the cab halfway to JFK before she stopped sneezing. It was then that she realized the big reveal wasn't so much that Carl was having sex with someone. If she'd listened to her nose, she would have known that before she ever walked through the door. The big reveal was that, even in the immaculate, dripping-money apartment, she could smell at least four other women who had recently made their contribution to the olfactory soup that was Carl's place. She strongly suspected that this particular flat was Carl's fuck pad, not his home.

That he'd led her to believe their relationship was exclusive was what really pissed her off. That he'd put just enough pressure on her to make her consider that he might be a good choice for a life partner pissed her off even more. Neither of them were getting any younger, he had said, and neither of them really had time to look. Whether he was looking or not, he certainly had no problems finding a fuck when he wanted one.

'A wake-up call,' she said out loud. 'That's what it was, a wake-up call.' Just then a flight attendant approached the man sitting next to her and pointed out an empty aisle seat several rows back. He excused himself and gathered his belongings as she shuffled into the aisle to let him out. She settled back in with a smile. Not exactly first class, but three seats to herself was the next best thing.

As the attendant announced that all electronic devices should be switched off, she shoved her BlackBerry back in her bag, still wishing she had gotten the name of the man in the lounge. No doubt she'd be masturbating to thoughts of him for ages to come. In fact it was a long flight to Rome, and she was pretty damned good at stealth orgasms, and now she had the space to indulge in comfort. As the plane left the ground, she was amazed that she felt no more than she did about what Carl had done. Was there really so little between them that she could so easily shove thoughts of him out of her head for someone who smelled better, for someone who smelled divine, actually, for someone who didn't make her sneeze?

Chapter Three

It wasn't that Paulo didn't have work to do. He never slept on planes. For him long flights always meant much-needed extra office hours, but he couldn't get the woman with the very talented nose off his mind. He knew that scent sometimes lingered long after what had left it was gone, and he wasn't sure if he could still smell the faintest traces of the woman or if he only wished he could. Why the fuck had he let her leave without getting her name? Everyone else around him slept. The plane was dark and quiet. When Paulo had convinced the attendant to offer the fat man crammed in next to his mystery woman a better seat – one farther away from her – he wasn't completely sure what his plan was, but as the flight wore on and it became more and more evident that he wasn't going to get any work done while thinking about her, he got up and eased his way down the aisle, past the curtain, and into the coach cabin.

Almost everyone was asleep or engrossed in a film with their headphones on. No one noticed as he padded down the aisle. She was toward the back several rows in front of the restrooms and the galley. It was with a sudden spike of his pulse that he saw her. She dozed against the window with an airline blanket draped across her lap, her thick, dark hair hanging loose around her shoulders. Yes, he could smell her. He was almost certain of it now. There was still a hint of the sea about her with a base note of honey and butter. He stood watching her, letting her scent wash over him, wondering how he could ever miss something so obvious. It was like seeing a different facet of the woman who was already beautiful with her dangerous curves, ripe cherry lips, and china blue eyes. Add to that her luscious scent, and she was too tempting to resist.

As he watched, she opened those china-blues, sniffed, blinked, and sniffed again. Then she turned in her seat and looked up at him. 'I thought I smelled you,' she said. Her smile was sleepy and warm as she patted the seat next to her. 'I didn't know you were going to Rome.'

As Paulo slipped in, her lids fluttered and she moaned as she inhaled his scent. She had already lifted all the armrests to form a love seat of sorts, and he moved right on over next to her. He wasn't sure exactly what he planned to do, but now that she'd invited him, it definitely involved letting their scents collide. His cock hardened at the thought. All around the coach cabin shades were pulled down. People slept curled and corkscrewed in whatever position the minimal space allowed them. It was an ideal situation. He sniffed, then he inhaled deeply, locking onto her essence. He wasn't as good at picking up scent as she was. But her scent he was sure of. Strange, but before he met her, he thought himself gifted in the olfactory department. As he settled next to her, he resisted the urge to bury his face in her lap and sniff. He wondered if she had tried to clean herself as he had, or if she had left that mouthwatering scent between her legs, slickening her panties, rubbing against her. Perhaps she'd even taken advantage of the long, boring flight to pleasure herself. That thought took his breath away and made his cock jerk in his trousers.

'Thought you might like some company,' he managed. 'I know I would.'

He barely finished his sentence when she pulled him under the blanket, giving him no time to speak before she kissed him. Her tongue lapped at his bottom lip before inviting itself right on into his mouth like it belonged there. 'Oh, God,' she groaned, 'you smell so good.'

'Tell me what you smell?' he whispered, 'Tell me.'

'Lose the jacket,' she demanded. 'I need to smell more.'

With an awkward move that nearly knocked her off the seat, he shrugged his shoulders. She shoved and tugged until the jacket dropped onto the floor. She surprised him by sliding her face into his ticklish armpit and breathing him in as though the hollow were an oxygen mask and she were in need of air. Before he could squirm too much her fingers went to work on the front of his shirt, unbuttoning until she could slide her hand in to cup a pec and pinch a nipple, which caused his cock to surge and his ass to clench just as she buried her face in the opening she'd made, breathing as though she would hyperventilate. 'What do you smell?' he asked again.

'Sex. I smell sex like I never smelled it before: fire, hot, earth steaming after a tropical rain. Lightning, always I smell lightning on you. I smell desire like pepper and cloves and star anise. I smell desire all over you.'

'Yes, you do. All over me.' He slid his hand up under her sweater and, to his delight, she had removed her bra. Her breasts were full and warm, goosefleshing in the cup and stroke of his fingers. The valley between was moist with the dew of her sweat and the scent of interrupted sleep. Her nipples and areolae pressed into his touch impossibly stiff and demanding, a demand he couldn't resist. He shoved her back against the window and pushed up the sweater. She struggled only briefly until his tongue circled the stippling tenderness and his lips sealed and tugged. He felt the expansion of her ribs as she sucked breath. With one hand she fisted his hair, holding him to her while the other pulled the blanket over them so they could lick and suck and nip in privacy.

The blanket trapped the tide pool and honey scent of her pussy and, for a moment, he thought he would come just from the smell. A split second later, he realized as her abdominal muscles clenched solid then convulsed, and she jerked against the seat, banging an elbow on the window with a soft curse, that coming was exactly what she was doing. And God, it took all the control he could muster to keep from following suit. Instead he slid his hand up under her skirt, shoving and wriggling and easing her thighs open until he found the moist gusset of her panties. He scrunched it aside and thrust two fingers into the slippery hot swell of her, still gripping, still quivering, still quaking in the aftershocks. There he lingered, fascinated by the feel of her orgasm, coupled with the intoxicating scent of arousal and release and need that blossomed again almost immediately. A thumb stroke against her distended clitoris caused her to jerk so hard against the seat that she nearly bucked him off. But he held her in place, his fingers stroking and darting in a fresh flood of fragrant heat while his greedy mouth suckled and licked as much of her breast as he could manage.

'Sit up!' Sit up now,' she hissed, wriggling out of his grasp and quickly propping her head against his shoulder, his hand still pressed to the swell of her, his mouth still wet with saliva and tingling with the taste of her hot skin. They pretended to be asleep as an attendant passed by, though no one could possibly believe anyone breathing as hard as they were and smelling as sexed as they did was actually sleeping.

When the attendant disappeared into the back of the plane, Paulo turned enough that he could see her eyes shining in the darkness, then he pulled his slippery fingers from her pussy and brought them under her nose. She sniffed and whimpered. 'That's what you do to me,' she managed. 'All I have to do is smell you and I'm wet.' The second whimper was guttural as he licked the exquisite taste of her from his fingers. Before he could catch his breath, her hand went to work on his fly. She wasn't gentle, and he didn't care. With trembling fingers, he unwrapped the blanket that had been left on the extra seat and covered his lap. Then he straightened her blanket over her bottom and fingered his way back between her legs, wishing like hell he could get his head down there, bury his face and his mouth in that delicious nectar. He caught his breath and nearly bit a hole in his lip as her mouth sheathed his cock in tight, white heat. Her tongue snaked and curled up the sensitive underside, lapping the abundance of pre-cum that now made yet another damp patch on his boxers. While one hand curled around his hip, the other cupped and stroked his full sac. He could hear her sniffing, and as he deepened his stroking and spreading and scissoring between the swollen gape of her labia, her moan vibrated down the length of his erection, and he nearly lost it again. This time the attendant simply pretended not to see as he passed, and Paulo didn't even try to dissuade the woman in his lap from her very delicious task. But her mouth wasn't where he wanted to be. The tight grip and release, grip and release of her around his fingers made it impossible not to think about burying his cock in her slick, hot depths.

As though she'd read his mind, she pulled away, wiped her mouth on the back of her hand, and nodded to the restroom just two rows back. He knew he'd never get his cock stowed, so he didn't try. He just tugged his shirt out over the top of his trousers, took her hand, and led her toward the restroom, his dick bouncing as they went. The minute they'd shoved their way in and locked the door, he sat on the lid of the commode and dug in his trouser pocket for the condom he was hoping he'd need. She watched with her skirt up and her undies dragged to one side, her fingers darting in and out of her wet slit as she thumbed her cherry-ripe clit. As soon as he was suited up, she turned around, sliding her panties down over her ankles. Then she eased herself into position, squatting, fingering her swollen lips open for him. With one hand on her hip and the other guiding his erection, he pulled her onto his lap and impaled her. They both stifled a cry, inhaled, and inhaled again. The scent was high tide, summer lightning, and pepper and spice all mixed together. She bit her knuckles to hold back the sob of pleasure. He buried his face in the nape of her neck, one hand seeking out the weight of her breasts, the other sliding down to tweak her hard clit. She was slick and tight with a grip like warm velvet, and she smelled like heaven, like nothing Martelli Fragrance at their very best could ever replicate. As he strained and pumped into her, he wondered what their combined scent smelled like to her. But before he could dwell on it, she orgasmed hard, covering her mouth with both hands to hold back what, no doubt, was an animal growl. Her whole body shivered and convulsed, and her grip on his penis became unbearable. He came in jerks and spasms until there was no breath left in him, until he saw stars behind the tight clench of his eyelids. Then they both collapsed against each other.

He was still gasping for breath when she eased herself up. She turned on him, tugged off the condom, and, before he could do more than offer an astonished gasp, she shoved up her sweater and began rubbing his semen over her tight nipples and down her belly. 'I hate that we have to use a condom,' she said. 'I want your smell against my skin.' Then she reached her hand between her legs and wiped her open palm over the splay of her folds until it glistened with her juices. Holding Paulo's gaze, she did the same to him, wiping her scent over his nipples and down his belly.

For a long moment she stood over him in the tight little room, gulping back their scent. He followed suit. God, he didn't want to leave. He wanted that smell. He wanted to take it home, sleep with it, dream with it, take it to the Martelli labs and study it. But in his little fantasy, he'd have to take the woman who helped produce that delicious scent to the lab with him, and he'd have to fuck her repeatedly. After all, results of an experiment had to be duplicable to be proven. Right? Nearly head-butting her, he bent and picked up her panties, pulled them to his nose, and sniffed. 'I want these,' he whispered as she offered him a questioning gaze. 'A memento.' While she watched, he carefully wiped her pussy on them and stuffed them into his pocket. 'I want to take something of you back to my flat with me, something that won't wash away when I shower. And when I take them out of my pocket and masturbate to your scent, I'll come thinking of you arriving in Rome wearing no panties.'

She offered him a wicked pout. 'Don't I get a memento?'

With his eyes locked on hers, he pulled a pristine white handkerchief from his pocket and made a show of wiping his cock and down around his balls. Then he refolded it and handed it to her. She sniffed it deeply and stuffed it in her waistband before wriggling her skirt down over her bare bottom.

If he'd had doubts that the experiments he'd been wanting to carry out in the Martelli labs were worth pursuing, this woman with her incredible nose and their shared olfactory experience completely eliminated them. He didn't know how he was going to do it, but he had every intention of convincing her to stay in Rome and work with Martelli. But first, he'd probably need to know her name. Before she turned to leave the restroom, he pulled her back to him and gave her a long lazy tongue-kiss, whispering into her mouth as he nipped her bottom lip, 'I'm Paulo, by the way.'

'Nice to meet you, Paulo,' she said, nipping back. 'I'm Liza.'

Back at her seat, Paulo didn't sit down. 'I have a mountain of work I need to finish before we land, and you, my lovely Liza, have delayed my progress terribly.'

'Poor dear,' she said, handing him his jacket from where it had fallen on the floor.

'I'd rather stay here and sniff you.'

'And I'd rather you did, but since you've got things to do ...' she slipped a business card in the breast pocket of his shirt '... just give me a call when you're ready for another sniff.'

He groaned as she fondled his nipple pressing against the pocket. 'Give me your phone,' he said. She pulled her BlackBerry from her seat pocket and handed it to him. He entered his number into her address book and gave it back. 'I'll sniff you in Rome once we've both had a good night's rest.' He nipped her earlobe, then turned and sauntered back up the aisle to the first class cabin.

Chapter Four

'Wow!' Liza gasped as she pushed open the door to Number 14 Bernini Place. This was way more luxurious than she had expected. She knew that Martelli Fragrance owned the Bernini Building. When they'd offered her the flat while she was in Rome writing her article, she had expected a nice studio apartment and, with any luck, a good view. What she got was high ceilings, wood floors, and very expensive modern Italian furnishings in a flat at least twice the size of her mother's house in Portland. She dropped her bags at the door and took the tour. There was a huge kitchen and a dining room with French doors leading onto a mosaic-tiled patio. There was a lounge, a study, and a master bedroom with a bathroom bigger than her whole flat. The bed was big enough for an orgy and so were both the Jacuzzi tub and the shower. She could easily get lost in the closet and have to wait for a search party, and she was already fantasizing about doing Paulo multiple times in multiple rooms.

Thoughts of the mysterious Paulo, and his involvement in her total lack of panties, had her wet and clenching by the time she lugged her bags into the bedroom. She deliberately took the time to unpack, shifting her hips as she walked, feeling the delicious friction beneath her skirt. She couldn't keep from wondering if she was still sitting in the airport lounge dreaming. Things like this never happened to her. Certainly things like Paulo never happened to her.

She'd never thrown herself at a man before, and this time she went totally off the deep end. Fucking in the bathroom in an airplane! In the air! That was so cliché it didn't bear thinking about, and yet, God, it was the best damned sex she had ever had. Ever!

Still, if she were wiser, more cautious, mindful of the fact that she'd just broken up with her boyfriend … But no! She wasn't on the rebound. Honestly, it was a relief to be away from Carl. With all the distance between them he'd never really seemed like her boyfriend. She wandered into the kitchen and opened the refrigerator door to find it fully stocked. Martelli really knew how to treat their guests. She found a bottle of chilled sparkling water and poured it into a cut crystal glass, then she nibbled at a few of the delicious grapes from the fruit bowl. Finally she moved back into the bedroom and settled cross-legged in the middle of the enormous mattress to check her BlackBerry. She supposed she should actually read the messages Carl had left. They would be a little easier to take after her steamy encounter with Paulo.

There was an email from Addie asking if she'd made it to Rome all right and how her flight had been. She actually giggled out loud. The flight was amazing, she replied. She was looking forward to sharing details with her friend over a glass of wine once she got back to Portland.

The next three emails were from Carl. She skipped those. Then there was another one from Addie asking if she'd enjoyed her time with Carl. She thought about it for a second and then simply replied that it hadn't happened. She really didn't want to talk about Carl, not when her mind was still buzzing with thoughts of Paulo.

There was the tinkle of an incoming text. She figured it was Addie and braced herself for a barrage of questions about Carl. But the text wasn't from Addie, nor was it from Carl. It was from Paulo. Her heart went into free fall.

Did you make it to your hotel OK?

With a big smile plastered on her face, she texted back.

Just arrived. Staying in a flat, actually. It's amazing! You?

In limo heading home. Have your missing undergarment in my pocket. Stroking it to stimulate your delicious scent. Pretty sure you can guess what I'm stroking with my other hand.

She laughed out loud. The rush of moist heat between her legs made her quiver. She slipped out of her sweater and unhooked the bra she had put back on before the plane landed, giving both her girls a caress as she freed them.

Really, P! Sex in a limo is so cliché.

Really, L! With your scent all over me, and your memento in my pocket it's more essential than it is cliché.

Ah yes, my missing undergarment. Thanks to you I left the poor cab driver's leather back seat very slippery.

She wriggled on the bed.

Where are your hands, you naughty woman?
On my BlackBerry, of course.

Lol! Liar.

Her chuckle sounded positively filthy.

Not lying at all. Keyboard getting sticky though.

You naked?

Still wearing skirt. Nothing! Else!

OMG, woman! What you do to me! Pic?

Her heart bounced furiously in her chest and her pussy clenched. Fuck! Had he just asked her to send him a picture? Double fuck! Was she actually considering it? She nearly dropped her BlackBerry as she texted back.

You show me yours, I'll show you mine ☺

There was a long pause. Oh god! Had she misunderstood him? Had she offended him? She was in the middle of composing a quick apology when his text came through. Fucking hell! It was a picture of his very large, very thick erection resting in the cupped palm of his hand against the silky red backdrop of her panties. The text simply read:

Your turn.

This was insane. This was not the sort of thing she would ever in a million years do. Was it because she was in a foreign country with a man she'd more than likely never see again when she was done here? For that matter they might both wake up in the morning too embarrassed to even contemplate further contact.

He wasn't some backpacker passing through. Fuck! She knew nothing about him other than that he'd been seated in the first class cabin. Maybe he was married. Maybe he was a pervert serial killer. For the briefest moment a picture of Carl's bare ass shoving and humping at the bimbo on his kitchen counter flashed through her head. She caught her breath, shoved up her skirt, and leaned back against the pillows, splaying her legs wide and bent-kneed. Then she fingered open her engorged pussy lips and snapped the shot with her other hand.

A peek at it made her stomach somersault. It was just so brazen. Her pussy, centre stage, wet and wild and on display between her fingers. Christ, she was insane, but she was totally turned on by the thought of Paulo stroking his cock with her panties while getting an up close and personal of her love box in his inbox. She wiped her fingers on her skirt and quickly typed:

To Rome with Lust: Cumming soon in a bedroom near you.

There was another long pause, but she was way past thinking about apologizing as she fingered her wet spot and thumbed her clit with one hand while flipping back and forth between the two filthy photos with the other. She was damn near there when the next text arrived.

Just came on your panties.

That sent her over and she had to wait to reply until she was done orgasming. When she could breathe again, she typed with an unsteady hand.

Just came on my fingers, then wiped them on your handkerchief.

There was another long pause in which she imagined both of them catching their breath. Finally another text arrived just as she was drifting off against the mound of fluffy pillows.

Gotta go, Lovely L. I'm home. See you tomorrow?

Her heart skipped a beat. He wanted to see her in spite of what they'd done!

Have to work tomorrow. Maybe tomorrow eve?

I'll text. I know a great Italian restaurant ☺

Chapter Five

Paulo stopped home just long enough to shower and change clothes. He couldn't quiet his mind, and it wasn't only because he'd just had the sexiest twelve hours of his entire life. As was often the case, inspiration followed very closely behind really good mind-blowing sex – at least it did for him, and his experience with Liza Calendar had definitely been just that. He picked up her card and examined it again before he stuffed it in his wallet. Liza Calendar *High Rising* e-mag. Where had he heard that name before? He'd have to look up the website when he had a few minutes, but at the moment, he wanted to talk to Coraline and get her approval for what he had in mind.

'Welcome back. She's not in her office,' Jim Dryer called over his shoulder as Paulo headed toward Coraline Martelli's suite. He fell into step next to Paulo, trying not to spill his overly-full coffee cup. In spite of being born and bred in Middle America, Jim's Italian was excellent; he could drive and park in Rome with the stroppiest Romans. He knew a hundred ways to make pasta that was *bellissimo*. The man loved everything about Italy, but in the middle of the afternoon, he still had to have at least one cup of weak instant coffee. Paulo shivered at the thought. 'I need to talk to her,' he said.

'Talk to me about what?' Coraline Martelli blew in like a wind off the Med. Somehow, she always dressed to the nines without looking like a clotheshorse, and even this late in the day she had that morning freshness about her. Her PA Alessandro looked slightly less pristine: rapidly taking notes and struggling to keep up. 'Get me some coffee,' she ordered him. He glanced up, wrinkled his brow as though he'd only just realized where he was, and then headed back toward the kitchen. 'What do you want, Paulo?' she said. 'I'm not in a great mood. I hate the new line, and the marketing people we hired are idiots. How was New York, and fill me in on this woman with the nose you emailed about.'

While Jim's eyes still glazed over at the way Coraline Martelli's brain darted and shifted, Paulo had worked with the woman most of his life. She was anything but scatter-brained. The CEO of Martelli Fragrance had one of the most brilliant minds he'd ever known. She just had too much going on to always get it out in a manner that the less brilliant could understand. Not that Jim wasn't brilliant. He wouldn't be working at Martelli if he wasn't the best, but Jim still viewed Coraline as only slightly less than a goddess, and that made it difficult for him to meet the woman head to head in her own environment.

'Come into my office,' she motioned. 'Do you need Jim? Alessandro,' she called back over her shoulder. 'Coffee for Paulo too. Jim's drinking his afternoon swill.' Then with a nod of her perfectly coiffed head she walked into her suite without so much as breaking stride. Looking dazed, Jim followed Paulo.

Coraline plopped down behind her desk, pulled out a very expensive pen, and began to doodle on the desk blotter, which was the only cheap thing in the room. And probably the most essential. Coraline Martelli's very best ideas came from what seemed like her endless and mindless scribblings on numerous sheets from her blotter. Paulo had in the back of his mind that some day they should collect all of those pages, put them into a book, and publish them. People would pay good money for the ideas that came from that brilliant mind.

'So tell me about the nose,' she said again, offering Paulo a no-nonsense smile just as Alessandro delivered two double espressos and a plate of Milano biscuits.

Paulo gulped his espresso, taking the moment to do a quick edit of what he would tell Coraline and what he would keep to himself. He was glad for Jim's presence because, when she read between the lines – which inevitably she would – she'd be less likely to grill him if they weren't alone.

OK, it wasn't one of Liza's finest moments, and she'd like to have blamed it on jet-lag, but really, it was hard to sleep when the glorious Italian sun was gleaming through the windows of the fabulous apartment, and she and Paulo had just sexted their way to yet another mind-blowing orgasm. Liza could tell from the map of Rome that she wasn't but a few blocks from the offices of Martelli Fragrance and, since she was wide awake, she might as well get an early start on her research. After a quick shower, she walked the few blocks to the Martelli Building. It had been her plan to ask if Reception would call upstairs to the main offices and get permission for her to have a look-see. But then she smelled *him*. There were some things you just couldn't write off to jet lag. She was as sure as she was of her own name that she smelled Paulo. She'd recognize his scent anywhere and, from the strength of it, he had only been there a few minutes before. She sniffed her way to the lifts without being noticed and, when no one looked her way, she took the one that smelled most like him. As much as anything, she rode the lift all the way up to the Martelli Suites so she could spend a few more minutes basking in the wonderful lightning storm and desert heat scent. When the elevator opened to Martelli's main reception, the smell only became stronger, and when no one paid her any attention, she followed it. The little gasp of ecstasy that escaped her lips was purely involuntary and would have been embarrassing if anyone had been close enough to notice.

She sniffed down a long hallway past a kitchen that smelled of rich coffee made strong and made often. It was amazing how easily she could sift through all of the smells of all of the people who worked at Martelli and single out just his amazing scent. It was as easy to follow as a marked trail. It led her to a large corner office with an open door where the scent of him was damn near strong enough to make her come. The sign on the brass plaque engraved in elegant italic letters read A.P. Delacour. Her stomach did a somersault. Why the hell would the office of the heir apparent to the Martelli empire smell like Paulo – her Paulo? She walked by the office as unobtrusively as she could, and when she was certain it was empty, she did the stupidest thing ever. She looked both ways, then she walked right on in, sniffing as she went. And oh God, the room smelled delicious – like the man had rubbed up against everything, like the man had spent the night there. She sniffed her way behind the desk where the smell of him was strongest, warm and rich. On a stupid impulse she pulled back the big leather chair at the desk and slipped into it. There was a fresh wave of Paulo-scented air as the cool leather caressed the exposed backs of her thighs. She couldn't help herself, she opened her legs, and her own scent peaked with arousal that left her sniffing and sighing and breathing at that more than magnificent blending of their smells.

Her nipples stiffened to hard points against her bra and she closed her eyes and inhaled through her nose. Then she did it again and again, her hips shifting forward and back ever so slightly against the clutch of the leather. She smiled to herself as she thought about the filthy text she would send to Paulo tonight, and how she would tease him about sniffing him out at Martelli Fragrance. Strange that those should have been her thoughts instead of thoughts of self-preservation.

'What are you doing here?' At the sound of a sharp male voice, she shoved the chair back hard enough for it to hit the wall behind as she gave a little yelp of surprise.

Busted!

When he'd finished telling the story of his encounter with Liza Calendar in the lounge and again on the plane, leaving out the orgasms and the part where they joined the Mile High Club and the part where they sexted their way to … well, more orgasms, he added quickly, 'You've just said you hate the new line, Coraline, and we've talked for a long time about doing a little experimentation with pheromones and the scents of sex and sexual attraction. If anyone could help us, this woman could. That is if you could get The Mount to agree to some experimentation.'

Coraline swallowed back her espresso in a single gulp and blinked large, bright eyes at him. 'You fucked her.'

Christ! Was she really going to do this in front of Jim? Speaking of … the guy nearly fell off his chair, spilling coffee into his lap.

'Oh for heaven sake, Jim, have you never heard of sex on a plane?' she said, giving him her perfected "grow up" look. Then she handed him a box of tissues.

There was a soft knock on the door and Alessandro stuck his head in, looking slightly embarrassed. 'I'm sorry to bother you, Ms Martelli, but –' her PA looked from one man to the other, decided on discretion, then stepped into the room and whispered something against his boss's ear. Her brow rose, making her eyes look even larger under artfully done make-up, then a smile curled around her lips. 'Really?'

The PA gave a tiny little nod as though that might keep Jim and Paulo from seeing that whatever it was, the answer was yes. Then he glanced down at the note pad that Paulo was pretty certain was surgically attached to his hand and whispered some more in her ear, so quietly that Paulo was surprised even Coraline could hear it, but then the woman never missed anything.

'Astonishing,' she said, in a voice that could have passed for a chuckle. 'Have them take her downstairs,' she said softly, her lips nearly brushing his ear.'

He nodded, made a military-sharp turn on his heels, and left Paulo once again at Coraline's mercy. 'Now, gentlemen, I believe we were discussing Paulo joining the Mile High Club with a woman whose nose could greatly benefit Martelli Fragrance.'

Liza had expected to get tossed out on her ear. In fact it wouldn't have surprised her if she had been told to pack her bags and catch the next flight back to Portland. What she didn't expect was to be escorted between two guards, both built like football players, down to a sub-basement. Maybe Martelli sent the riff-raff out through the parking garage rather than the main entrance. The elevator doors opened into a hallway that was painted stark white with minimal track lighting down the center of a suspended ceiling. The place was deserted and silent except for the buzz of the lights. But it was the smell of lust with a sharp metal edge that got Liza's full attention, and beyond that she could smell sex. In spite of the situation, Liza responded to the olfactory surprise with lust of her own, pepper-spiced and smoky. She chided herself for not being more afraid, more cautious, but the nose seldom misled her and, as the two guards stopped in front of a door at the end of the hallway, the smell of sex grew stronger. When they motioned her inside, she was surprised to find the room empty except for a plain pine desk with an armless office chair behind it. They guided her to stand in front of the desk, then one of them spoke in accented English. 'Stay here, and wait for Fidelia.' They both left. And she waited, standing stupidly where the two men had left her. She was just about to move to the chair and get a little more comfortable when she noticed there were cameras near the ceiling in the corners of the room. Her pulse ratcheted up a notch.

She'd had just enough time to imagine the worst when the door burst opened and the woman who entered nearly took her breath away with her lusty scent. She wore the female version of the security uniform – a black pencil skirt several inches above her knees and a matching tailored jacket over a white blouse. Her dark russet hair was caught up in a chignon beneath a service cap. The whole uniform was just enough to be sexy and yet left no doubt about the woman's authority. She stripped off the jacket and hung it over the back of the chair, her caramel and crème eyes locked on Liza as though she were prey. Her thin white blouse did little to hide the lacy detail of the bra beneath that cupped heavy breasts into a tight, deep cleavage. The bitter chocolate and coffee scent informed Liza the woman was turned on by being in a position of authority, and she was especially turned on that Liza was at her mercy.

'Why were you in Mr Delacour's office?' She asked, settling into the chair behind the desk.

Liza's laugh was thin and breathy. 'You wouldn't believe me if I told you.' It sounded stupid the moment she said it. Her inquisitor stood and moved to pace a circle around Liza before she finally said, 'Try me.'

'It was the scent. I smelled someone I know. Look, I realize this sounds crazy, but I can recognize people by their smell. I swear it's the truth.' God, couldn't she just snivel and be done with it? Where her sense of smell was concerned honesty always made her sound like a loony-tune.

'And just who do you think you smelled in Mr Delacour's office?'

'I know this is a tremendous coincidence, but I'm actually here to write an article on Martelli Fragrance. I'm Liza Calendar. I'm the co-owner of *High Rising* magazine. I've discussed the article with Mr Dryer. You can ask him. Anyway, I just got here and I thought I'd check out the office. Then I smelled Paulo. He's the guy I met at JFK.' She forced a breathy laugh. 'I mean what are the chances? But I know what Paulo smells like, and I followed his scent to Mr Delacour's office. God, I realise it makes me sound like a stalker, but I swear that's the truth. I'm certain Paulo was there recently.'

The woman laughed out loud. 'Are you serious? Paulo was in Mr Delacour's office? Do you think I'm a fool?' She now stood behind Liza, so close that her large breasts pressed against Liza's shoulder, so close that Liza could feel the heat of her breath against her ear. But the second before Liza could panic, she smelled the salt water and loam scent of arousal. Slowly, Liza inhaled through her nose. There was no denying it, no denying the feel of the woman's nipples pressing enthusiastically into her personal space. The scent became spicy and electric as the woman ran one splayed hand up Liza's belly then up to cup her breasts in turn, while the other pulled Liza's head back to rest against her shoulder at an uncomfortable angle. 'Of course the office smells like Paulo, stupid woman. It's Paulo's office.'

'Paulo's office? What do you mean, Paulo's office?'

Without warning, she kicked Liza's legs apart in a motioned that forced her to bend forward and grab on to the desk for balance. Then she gave her a shove until Liza was sprawled over the pine surface facing the chair at the back, and the woman's scent grew stronger. With a gasp, Liza realized she was smelling something other than the woman's growing arousal. She was now smelling her own desire joining in the olfactory dance. The woman was still close behind her, her breathing quickening, her open palm resting, first on Liza's hip, then moving down over Liza's bottom to the hem of her skirt. Lisa's butter-honey scent curled around Fidelia's – wasn't that what the guard had called her?

The woman's fingers scrunched up the edge of Liza's skirt, and then she leaned down and bit her earlobe before she said in a harsh whisper, 'Augusto Paulo Delacour, Ms Calendar. If you're here to write an article, you might want to get that fact straight.'

And this time the spiking of Liza's scent had nothing to do with Fidelia's roaming hands, but the thought that she had had sex on a plane with A.P. Delacour, the man himself!

Before she could dwell on it, Fidelia spoke again. 'The boss's office is not a public play area, Ms Calendar. Ms Martelli employs me and my staff to take care of the sluts who come sniffing.' She shoved

Liza's skirt up high enough to expose her thong. 'That's exactly what you were doing, wasn't it? Sniffing?' She grabbed the elastic back in her fist and pulled upward so that the thong raked tightly along the splay of Liza's pussy, and the catch of her breath at the sudden discomfort and the sweet salt scent confirmed the fact that it was more than just discomfort she was feeling down there. The woman's growl of a chuckle told Liza that she knew it too, whether or not she could recognize the scent.

And suddenly the threat of danger that the woman, who was far bigger and far more muscular than Liza, represented was subsumed in the peppery-sharp scent of edgy, kinky lust and, as always, Liza's nose knew. And Liza's intrigued nose wanted more. Before her brain could fully register it, her body responded. It took her a few seconds to realize that the little kitten sounds that echoed off the bare walls were her own. Fidelia's deeper, big cat purrs vibrated against the back of her neck. She half expected the bigger woman to sink her teeth in. But instead, with a spike of picante sexy aggression, she tugged at Liza's thong until she had forced her up onto her tiptoes. 'Tell me, Liza Calendar,' she huffed against her ear. 'Can you smell my pussy? Because I don't really need a special nose to smell yours, to know you like being interrogated.'

'I smell you, yes.' Between her efforts to take in the intriguing scent and the fact that the woman's erotic touch had driven her pulse up, she was struggling to keep from hyperventilating. The smell of another woman aroused by her, the smell of herself aroused by another woman, and the smell of the two of them together was a scent Liza could have never anticipated, and certainly had never experienced before.

'And do you like what you smell?'

'You know I do. I can tell you know.'

Without warning, Fidelia gave her a sharp smack on one ass cheek, and Liza yelped, then opened her mouth and inhaled the thickening cream scent. 'You didn't think Mr Delacour sent you down here for me to serve you coffee did you?' She smacked the other ass cheek and it stung like hell. 'You don't get rewarded for invading the man's private space.' She dropped a smack on each buttock in quick succession, then squeezed and kneaded, but the idea that Paulo had sent her down here distracted Liza from the pain. Then it raised the stakes in the raging scent of aroused females. He betrayed her. He betrayed their secret or else how would this woman know? But then again she'd all but given herself away to the guards when they found her. Her focus returned sharply to the woman behind her, as she slid Liza's thong down around her ankles and worried two long fingers in between the pout of her labia.

'Fuck me, bitch,' the woman whispered with a hard thrust, 'You're about to come already. What do you think? Do you smell about ready to come?' She brought her thumb to work on the nib of Liza's clit, and then another smack came down on her bottom mingling pain and pleasure. And that was all it took, she did come. Fidelia gave a knowing chuckle. 'You like that, don't you? You like being punished.'

'Almost as much as you like punishing me.' God, did she really just say that? The thought that Paulo might possibly be watching what the cameras were recording had her primed and ready for multiples. This should upset her, she told herself. She should be incensed, and yet when the woman brought her hand down again on her bare bottom, her pussy gripped and suckled Fidelia's fingers.

Fidelia's laugh was harsh and throaty as she

grabbed Liza by the back of her dress and pulled her up, then turned her so rapidly that she nearly tripped over the thong around her ankles before the big woman caught her in a heavy-breasted embrace and took her mouth with a full-scale invasion of tongue and teeth. When she pulled away, breathing like a windstorm, she took Liza by the wrist and guided her hand up under the pencil skirt. 'You want to feel if you make me wet too, don't you?'

'I know I make you wet,' Liza gasped, shoving her fingers under the edge of the woman's satin panties. 'I can smell how wet I make you.' Then in a cheeky move she would have never imagined herself making, she returned the favour, a bit awkwardly at first – after all she'd never touched a pussy other than her own – but when the woman opened her legs into a shallow squat over Liza's hand, Liza found the sweet spot and gave it a pinch that spiked the Fidelia's scent to ripe apricot. Then she fingered her way into the woman's slick gash that gripped and clenched like a hungry mouth against her thrusts. The scent became more picante, more briny as the woman approached her orgasm, and it was a heady feeling for Liza to realize she was about to make the security guard come. And when she did, Fidelia moaned into Liza's mouth. Her pussy convulsed and trembled and drenched Liza's fingers with her juices. When Liza pulled them out from under the woman's skirt and thrust them into her mouth – into both of their mouths, they tongued and suckled and lapped the taste of come together.

In some remote, barely accessible, region of her brain, Liza couldn't believe what was happening, that she was performing for unknown watchers. How could she possibly be anything but horrified, and yet she was on the brink of coming again, when the woman gasped, 'I haven't finished punishing you yet.' She dragged Liza around the desk with a hand fisted in the front of her dress. As she opened a drawer and pulled out a long leather riding crop, the scent of sex peaked with an edge of cold-copper fear as Fidelia tested the crop on the desk with a loud smack. Then, with her own skirt still up far enough to expose her panties, she sat down in the chair and wriggled her bottom against the cushion patting her thighs. 'Over my knees, Ms Calendar. Time to take you punishment for sniffing around Paulo Delacour's office.'

'You had sex with her?' Jim asked as he wiped the coffee from his crotch, trying to sound matter of fact.

'Look,' Paulo said, 'it doesn't matter if I had sex with her. What matters is that she can smell those kinds of scents. She can smell emotions, feelings. I swear I've never seen anyone like her. If you're not happy with the new line, Coraline, then let's get her onboard, involve those from The Mount who are willing, and come up with a new line, one that every man and every woman will want to wear because it'll make them think of sex, because it'll make them feel like they're going to *get* sex because they wear Martelli Fragrance. Then forget the incompetent marketing firm, go with our own team. They've never let us down before, and they understand what we need.'

'You had sex on a plane,' Jim said, now brushing the pieces of tissue off his crotch. 'I mean, you had sex on a plane because she liked the way you smelled?'

'Shut up, Jim,' they both said at the same time.

For a moment there was silence in the room, and Coraline studied Paulo until it was difficult for him not to squirm. 'She's really that good?'

'She's really that good,' Paulo replied. 'And even more,' he fought back a blush and squared his shoulders, 'it was the way we … smelled together, the blending of scent, she somehow had an instinct about how it would be … our scents together.'

Jim shifted in uncomfortably in his seat, but discussing the sex Paulo had just had didn't phase Coraline Martelli in the slightest.

'None of this should really come as a surprise. There's a reason sex smells the way it does. There's a reason every body has his or her own odor,' Coraline said. 'But it's a huge leap from the mammalian biological need to mark territory with scent to making a perfume that can capture that territorial sense of our sexuality. You think she can help us do that?'

'I think she's essential if we're going to get it right. And if we don't, then there's really no point.'

She leaned over her desk toward him. 'And does this woman have a name?'

'Liza.' He let out a long, slow breath. 'The woman's name is Liza Calendar.'

Chapter Six

Before Paulo could say anything else, Jim spilled the rest of his coffee and swallowed back a loudly whispered curse. 'Liza Calendar? You … had sex with Liza Calendar?' With each word, his voice got higher and tighter. 'The Liza Calendar from *High Rising* Magazine? That Liza Calendar? She was on your flight?'

'Ah, the journalist, I remember now,' Coraline said as though it didn't disturb her in the least.'

Paulo felt as though the floor would drop from beneath him. 'Wait a minute, you know Liza Calendar?' And now, when it was fucking too late, Paulo remembered too. He remembered why the name sounded familiar. He had grudgingly agreed to be her liaison, even though Jim had set up the interview and article without telling him in advance. He'd only been half paying attention at the time, and he was more than a little miffed. A major part of Jim's job at Martelli was to take care of these sorts of things so that Paulo didn't have to.

Jim busied himself, once again wiping his crotch. 'I know her through email and couple of phone conversations while we made arrangements for the article she wants to do. I told you about her, remember? She's staying at Bernini Place.'

'Fuck,' Paulo whispered, running a hand through his hair. 'She didn't tell me. Why didn't she tell me?'

'Sniffing you out is hardly a typical pick-up, and if

you introduced yourself as Paulo she might not have made the connection that you're A.P Delacour,' Coraline shrugged. 'I suppose it could be a ploy, but I can't think why. Maybe I should just call downstairs and have Fidelia send her up, and we can question her ourselves,' she said as matter of factly as if she'd just asked the two if they were ready for more coffee.

'She's here?' Paulo gasped.

Coraline nodded contentedly.

'She's here and you sent her to Fidelia?' he came out of his seat. 'Why the hell did you send her to Fidelia, as if things aren't messed up enough.'

Coraline offered him a cool smile. 'She was sniffing around in your office, I put two and two together after Alessandro told me what was going on and thought we'd have Fidelia check her out.'

'I'm going to get her,' Paulo said without asking leave.

'Do that, Paulo,' Coraline offered a happy smile. 'And bring her here to my office. I'll have Alessandro bring more coffee and some nice biscuits. I'm dying to meet her in person.'

As he raced to the door of Fidelia's office Paulo could hear the sharp crack of leather followed by moans that could be either pleasure or pain. He didn't bother to knock, but shoved his way in on a scene that had him breathless, and his cock was instantly stiff. Liza Calendar was turned over Fidelia's lap. Her brightly coloured sundress was shoved up to expose a gorgeous expanse of rounded bottom now bearing a lattice work of red stripes that Fidelia had clearly laid with the crop, which came down across Liza's bottom just as the door burst open. She cried out, then moaned and squirmed against Fidelia's thighs. There was no mistaking the smell of arousal, and no mistaking the part of that arousal that belonged to Liza Calendar. For a second he had to lean against the door to regain control over his cock, then he spoke in a quiet, clear voice, 'That's enough, Fidelia.'

Liza yelped and bolted to her feet, nearly falling before Fidelia could steady her. The blush that crawled up her cheeks matched the colour of her bottom as she struggled with her dress. 'Leave it,' he commanded, wondering what the hell he'd said that for. She wasn't a part of the inner circle. She had no idea what was going on. He half expected her to launch herself at him in anger.

Instead she stood unmoving with her skirt gathered in her hands, her chest heaving as she gasped for breath. And at the sight of her, face flushed, bottom exposed, breasts barely covered, Paulo felt the part of him he'd always kept in tight control asserting itself. 'It hurts, doesn't it?'

She nodded, avoiding his gaze.

'Look at me, Liza. You deserved Fidelia's punishment, you know?'

As her eyes met his, she nodded again.

'Fidelia, take care of Ms Calendar's sore bottom,' he commanded.

The security guard, breasts still exposed above the top of her blouse, a fine sheen of sweat dampening her brow, pulled a bottle of lotion from the desk drawer.

'Is anyone watching?' He nodded to the cameras.

'Angelo is,' Fidelia said.

Paulo cursed under his breath. Well he'd give the bastard something to watch then, wouldn't he?

He took Fidelia's place in the chair and offered Liza his hand. 'You were sniffing around my office.'

She nodded again as he pulled her to him.

'That was naughty,' he said. 'When I found out you were sent to Fidelia, you gave me an erection in the middle of a business meeting. That's inconvenient, don't you think?'

'Yes,' she managed with a gasp as he pulled her across his knee. He held out his hand and Fidelia squirted lotion onto his palm, which he applied in circular stroking and kneading motions over and around each wounded buttock and across and between the tops of her thighs, making no attempt to hide his erection, nor to apologize when his fingers slipped down between her thighs to brush against her labia.

'You may masturbate, Fidelia. I can tell you need to,' he said, 'but stand over here so Ms Calendar can watch what you do with your fingers. She'd like that, wouldn't you, Liza?'

'Yes.' The word came out a breathy hiss.

'This is better than sniffing around my office when I'm not there, isn't it? Now you can smell just how hot you make me, can't you?'

She whimpered and nodded and ground her mons against his thigh. He returned the favour by shifting his cock against her. When he'd finished lotioning her bottom, he helped her to her feet just as Fidelia cried out her orgasm in the palm of her hand.

'And now, Ms Calendar –' he laid a hand in the small of her back and eased her, face down, onto the desk, kneeing her legs apart '– now I'm going to fuck you.'

He ran three fingers up between her distended lips, opening her, lingering to feel her slickness while he undid his fly and lifted his cock and his heavy sac free from their bind in his boxers. He cursed the seconds it took him to don the condom. He hoped the time would come when one wouldn't be necessary. But he soon forgot the inconvenience as he grabbed on to her hips and shoved home into her tight, slippery depths, breathing in the delicious scent of honey and butter and sea air as she braced herself and pushed back against him with each thrust.

Fidelia moved around close to Liza's head and tenderly stroked her hair. 'Did she smell you, Fidelia?' He asked. 'She's good with her nose. Really good.' The security guard whimpered and stuck her fingers back into her panties as they all approached orgasm together.

Breathless and feeling like his whole body would shatter, Paulo leaned down over Liza and nibbled her earlobe while he fucked her. 'I'll let you come too, Liza, though you were very naughty.' And it was almost as though she took a deep breath and convulsed out her orgasm at his permission. That thought sent him over the edge right behind her. And when he could breathe again, he whispered against her ear. 'Get cleaned up. I'm taking you to meet Coraline Martelli.'

Paulo could smell her in the lift next to him as he leaned against the wall with his eyes closed, still not able to believe what had come over him in Fidelia's office. And fuck if she didn't smell every bit as good as he'd remembered. He figured the slightly picante edge to her scent was probably nerves. He hoped she wasn't angry, but he figured she was probably too shell-shocked for her feelings to really sink in just yet. He knew he was. Except for his anger at Coraline, of course. He kept his eyes shut, trying to figure out how to handle the situation. He struggled not to slump against the wall, but he'd just had mind-blowing sex again with Liza Calendar after Coraline had handed her over to Fidelia. Now his brain was being forced into a reality check of just what that might mean. No way was he getting out of this one unscathed. He shifted stiffly to adjust as his cock reasserted itself with the scent of Liza Calendar so close to him. At that moment, she sniffed, then sniffed again, a deep inhale that was almost a sob, as though she could actually smell his cock's happy response, which in turn made his fucking cock even happier. He hunched and kept his eyes closed, for all the good he figured it would do.

At last she spoke. 'Am I in trouble?'

'No.'

'Who was watching? Who's Angelo?' she asked.

'No one important,' he replied. For a few seconds there was silence, and he hoped there'd be no more questions. Of course he was wrong.

'Why did you do that to me? Send me down there to that woman?'

He opened his eyes and looked over at her. 'I didn't. Coraline did.'

'Why? Was it some kind of a test?'

'For her part, probably. For my part, I came to rescue you and, well, I couldn't resist.'

Her jaw stiffened. 'I'm glad you all find me entertaining.' Before he could respond, the elevator door opened, and Alessandro was there practically buzzing like a very-well-dressed bee as he escorted them to Coraline's office.

Butter wouldn't melt when Coraline came to her feet and walked around her desk to offer Liza Calendar an outstretched hand. As Paulo tried not to grind his teeth at his boss, he couldn't help noticing the subtle way that Liza took in Coraline's scent, and the scent of the room around her. No one else would have noticed. But Coraline knew enough already that he was certain she had seen the little olfactory exchange, and his shoulders knotted still further. The woman never missed anything. And she was unlikely to miss the fact that the two had fucked in Fidelia's office. In fact, he figured that was a part of her plan as soon as she realized that the invader in his suite had to be Liza

Calendar.

'Ms Calendar,' Coraline said, 'it's a pleasure to meet you. Sorry about the security. My people tell me you were sniffing around, and though the investigative use of a good nose automatically raises my opinion of you and, while we think highly of people with a good sense of smell around here, one can't be too careful.' She offered a smile that had mischief written all over it. 'As for Fidelia, well I do apologize, but she sometimes gets a little carried away with her job. You don't look too much worse for the wear though, but then I wouldn't expect otherwise with Paulo coming to your rescue.' She shot him an amused glance. 'How are you finding Rome? I hope you're not too jet-lagged. If you need a tour guide, I'd be happy to arrange something.' She shot Paulo another glance.

Liza blinked twice and couldn't hold back another seemingly involuntary, if subtle, sniff about the time Paulo figured Coraline Martelli's unmissable scent of power and competence washed over her. Then she took the woman's hand and offered a warm smile. 'It's a pleasure to meet you, Ms Martelli. I'm so sorry for the intrusion. I'm usually better behaved. I only wanted to get a feel for the place and then …' She sniffed again. 'Well I ended up in Mr Delacour's office because it smelled familiar.'

And, like it or not, that was Paulo's clue. 'Yes.' He cleared his throat and straightened his jacket and the little breath he took before he spoke brought the delicious scent of her, still on his body, to his nose. 'As I've already said, Coraline, I'm very impressed with Ms Calendar's nose.' The woman standing next to him smelled like heaven and looked like trouble. Clearly she hadn't expected to be allowed into the inner circle today.

For the first time he noticed what she was wearing

rather than what her clothing had revealed to him in Fidelia's office. She wore a brightly coloured sundress that, without being too slutty, showcased well-muscled arms and shoulders, a good bit of her luscious back, and plenty of exquisite leg. He had personally helped her back into the leopard print thong Fidelia had stripped her of before his arrival. Her feet were comfortably shoed in a pair of delicate but casual sandals that laced up her calves centurion-style. They caressed her feet in soft tan leather, revealing toenails painted cherry red. His mouth watered at the thought of sucking each one of those lovely toes as he worked his way up to the delicious main course she'd sent him a selfie of last night. He'd fucked her twice now, but he wanted to do so much more to her. Christ! He so did not need to be thinking of that right now in front of his boss. But the widening of Liza's eyes and the flaring of her nostrils along with the parting of her lips in a near gasp told him she'd caught the peaking of his scent along with the direction his thoughts were leading. The twitch of Coraline's lips into a leonine smile said she knew exactly what was going on, and she knew exactly what was on his mind. He cleared his throat again in a struggle to find his voice, then offered Liza his outstretched hand, trying not to think about what that delicious mouth had done to his cock last night.

'Ms Calendar, I'm A. P. Delacour. The P is for Paulo, as you've probably guessed. And I'm sorry I wasn't in my office to give you a more genial welcome. It's a pleasure to make a proper acquaintance.'

'Though I'm sure the improper one was much more fun,' Coraline said with a bright grin. Before the look of shock could completely register on Liza's face, the woman continued like a runaway train. 'We've just been discussing the new line, Ms Calendar. Is it all right if I call you Liza, since we'll be getting to know each other pretty well in the near future? Everyone calls me Ms Martelli, but only because they're not brave enough to call me Coraline. Paulo calls me Coraline, but then Paulo's been with Martelli since he was in diapers, and he knows my bark is bigger than my bite. Well, actually it's not, but I haven't sacrificed anyone to the goddess of perfume in a very long time now, and if you behave yourself and do as I say, you won't be the next.' She waved her hand extravagantly, 'I don't care what you call me. Just be comfortable. Though I imagine you're not feeling very comfortable at the moment, and I don't need your refined sense of smell to know that. Never mind. You'll get over it. Uncomfortable things happen to make life interesting, don't they?' Liza blinked twice and opened her mouth, but Coraline continued. 'You're staying in the flat at Bernini Place, aren't you? How are you finding it? I hope Alessandro had someone make sure the fridge was well stocked. Nothing more depressing that coming in from a long flight to find an empty larder. Try the primitivo, by the way, if you're a red wine drinker. It's one of my favourites.'

Standing with her hand still resting in his, Paulo could see Liza trying to catch up with Coraline's rapid-fire welcome. She continued. 'Yes, as I was saying about the new line, Paulo has some very intriguing ideas, which you seem to have inspired, though they've been rattling around in that head of his for a while now. You've helped him put them in a much more coherent order, and I'm hoping we can talk about them once you get settled. Oh, by the way, this is Jim Dryer. I understand the two of you have been corresponding.'

Jim stood and offered his hand. The look on his

face said he was still trying to piece together what exactly was happening. Jim had no idea what went on with security down in Fidelia's office. If he ever made up his mind to join The Mount then he'd get his personal introduction to what the woman could do. But in the meantime best keep it quiet. Paulo was still reeling that Coraline had been brazen enough to send Liza to her.

'Liza, it's a pleasure to meet you in person. I'm really excited to have you here.' Jim was nothing if not intuitive, and though it was clear the only person in the room thoroughly enjoying herself was Coraline, he quickly sized up the situation and continued almost as though he'd taken rapid-fire convo lessons from the boss herself. 'Of course we weren't expecting you till tomorrow. If we'd known, we'd have made sure your greeting was a little warmer. Never mind that. It's always nice to have someone eager to get on with their work. I have an itinerary set up for you based on our email conversations. I had our discussion of that scheduled for tomorrow morning, but I have a little time now, if you'd like.'

Her gaze moved from Jim to Coraline to Paulo, then it was as though a curtain came down. All surprise, all shock, and all things bordering on less pleasant possibilities vanished from her face. She shook Jim's hand enthusiastically and offered a warm smile. 'I'd like that very much, Jim. Thanks for being so flexible.' As he motioned her from the room, she glanced over her shoulder at Paulo and then addressed Coraline. 'I'll be looking forward to talking to you later.'

As he and Coraline watched the two leave, she nodded back to the chair and he dropped into it, suddenly feeling way more jet lagged than he had five minutes ago. 'I wish you hadn't done that, exposed

Liza to Fidelia like you did. Angelo was watching the whole thing. Did you know that?'

Coraline raised an eyebrow. 'I'm not surprised. I assume you gave him something worth watching.'

He didn't offer an answer and she didn't expect one. She took her time making her way around the desk, stopping to water a muscle-bound, waxy leafed plant that looked as though it were about to crawl out of its under-sized pot. She settled back behind her desk, picked up her pen, and began to doodle without looking at him. 'She smelled you. From downstairs in Reception, she smelled you.'

'She did. Yes.'

'From all the way downstairs she smelled you and found her way to your office.'

He shifted in his chair. 'So it would appear.'

'And you smelled her?'

'Not until I got to Fidelia's office, but I'm more sensitive to her now. You know, it's all just a matter of training our sense of smell to work like it does for all our mammal cousins.'

'Don't lecture me about human biology, Paulo. I was the one who lectured you.' On her blotter, she drew a large cartoon-looking nose with a flower beneath it. 'She's not happy with you.'

'Can you blame her?'

'No, but I can and do blame you.'

'I didn't know who she was.' He ran a hand through his hair and stood to pace in front of her desk. 'Coraline, nothing like this has ever happened to me before. You know me well enough to know that. The experience was, well, it was eye-opening.'

'You mean nose-opening.'

'That too, but I never meant for anything to happen. It was just … well it was like neither of us could resist the other.'

'She's not happy with you.' She repeated, drawing a stylized heart on her blotter with what looked like a vicious dagger running through it.

'You already said that. I must look like a right bastard. I mean if I'd had any idea ...'

'If you'd had any idea, you're not sure it would have made any difference, Paulo. I know how chemistry works.' Coraline laid down her pen and leaned forward over the desk watching him pace. 'I'm not concerned about what happened between the two of you. I have a sneaking suspicion that it was inevitable, but I'm also not blind to what the woman might be capable of with a sense of smell like that.'

Before he could say anything she raised a hand. 'First, apologise to her and make it right. I don't care what you have to do. Just make it right. Any nose that good, I want working for Martelli. I'm happy to let her make a story for her magazine out of her whole experience here at Martelli, but I want her nose. I want Liza Calendar to help us with the new line.'

Paulo eased himself back into the chair. 'Even if that means allowing me to recruit people from The Mount to do what I'm thinking of?'

She took a deep breath and drew a giant question mark around the nose. 'I'm still not keen on bringing in The Mount. I've always kept the business separate from what goes on in The Mount.'

'Business and pleasure seem to be going hand in hand quite nicely in Las Vegas, Coraline. No one would ever consider shutting down the business end of Mount Vegas. Elsa and her team bring in a lot of revenue.'

'I know,' she said. 'I know you're right, and I've thought about that.' She drew a rapid series of waves and spirals on the blotter, than laid the pen down hard. 'All right. Make things right with Liza Calendar. Get her onboard, and give me a plan. Then tell me what you need from The Mount and I'll see that you get it. You know we need this line to be something stunning this year more than ever.'

Paulo felt his shoulders relaxing until he remembered how he and Liza had just parted, then the knots were back with a vengeance. 'I'll make it right,' he said.

Coraline pulled her laptop from her bag and opened it, clearly dismissing him. As he stood and turned to go she spoke with her fingers already click-clicking on the keys. 'Paulo, I don't care if you fuck her. If that's what inspires you and she's consenting, do it. I do care if you don't make it right. Are we clear?

'Yes ma'am. We're clear,' he said.

It stung that Coraline could even think he wouldn't do everything in his power to make things right with Liza Calendar. But it stung even more thinking that Liza might believe he'd taken advantage of her. He stopped by the kitchen for more desperately needed coffee, then shut himself in his office. For a long time he stood at the window looking out over the Tiber, wondering how best to approach Liza, wondering how best to test her abilities, wondering what experiments they could do to get the necessary results for Martelli Fragrance. It pissed him off a bit that he was such an opportunist, but it was the creative and imaginative doors Liza had opened that would not now allow themselves to be closed. Scent and sexuality had to be at least as closely linked in humans as they were in other mammals. How good something smelled and the response it elicited was in the nose of the beholder. And the truth was Liza Calendar elicited a whole bunch of primal responses in him. Still, all that aside – everything aside, he wanted to make things right with her. He wanted a chance to pick her brain and understand what it was like to experience the world primarily through the sense of smell. By the time he settled back in his desk, he really wasn't thinking about what Liza Calendar could do for Martelli Fragrance. He was thinking about what she did for him. With sweaty hands, he picked up his BlackBerry and texted.

I'm so, so sorry, Liza. I didn't know who you were.

When there was no immediate response, he consoled himself with the fact that she was probably still with Jim. He didn't much like that either. If she was mad at him, well Jim was very sympathetic, and Jim did have a way with women – much more so than Paulo did, actually. Jim was a flirt and a good one. Paulo somehow missed out on all that Italian charm that Jim told him he was supposed to have. It's not that he hadn't had lovers, and being a member of The Mount, he never had to sleep alone if he didn't want to. But he supposed he took himself too seriously. Jim said that too.

Well he sure as hell hadn't last night on the plane, had he? He checked his BlackBerry just in case he'd missed the text. Nothing. He paced the floor a couple more times then made himself another cup of coffee – more than anything so he could confirm that Jim's door was still shut. He looked down at his watch, went back into his office, and made a half-hearted attempt to get through his emails. The plan he'd been so meticulously putting together had become hard to focus on when his inspiration was not answering his texts. He was just about to text again, when there was a hard rap on his door and Jim let himself in. He shut the door and came to sit in the chair in front of Paulo's desk.

'Holy fuck, dude. So you really … you know … on the plane?'

Paulo glared at him. 'I didn't know who she was.' Sometimes Jim was so much like an adolescent boy. Sometimes Paulo envied him that.

'Of course you didn't know who she was. That makes it all the better.' He leaned forward, a wicked grin plastered across his face. 'What happened?'

Paulo ignored Jim's question. 'How is she?'

'Well she's not going to tell me, is she? She came across very professional, very enthusiastic about the article, just as you'd expect her to be. If she was upset, she didn't show it.'

'Did she say … anything?'

'She said she had expected Coraline's accent to be more Italian.'

So why the hell did Paulo feel like he'd just been slapped? Of course she wouldn't say anything about him.

Jim leaned forward still farther until his ass was almost out of the chair. 'I hope you haven't forgotten, Paulo, but you're picking her up in the morning at ten for a tour of the city, you know, make her feel at home?' The bastard didn't even try to suppress a snigger. 'You told me when I asked you that your schedule was clear. Just give her a nice warm welcome to Rome, and if your welcome is warm enough, she might not ask Coraline for your head on a pike.'

Paulo flipped him off.

Jim's smile was all sweetness and light. 'I'd take care of her myself, but I have a meeting in Naples tomorrow. Some of us have to work for a living.'

Paulo flipped him off again.

He only chuckled and stood to go. 'I don't know what you and Coraline have up your sleeve, but let me know when you have a plan.' He fought back a smile.

'And if you need someone to talk to about your … hard flight, well, you know I'm always here for you, boss.' He left Paulo growling behind his desk.

Chapter Seven

Please don't shut me out. We need to talk about this.

Liza stared down at her BlackBerry and cursed. What she wanted was another message was from Paulo. What she didn't want was a message from Carl. But that's what she got. She ignored Carl's text and flipped back to Paulo's.

I'm so, so sorry, Liza. I didn't know who you were.

It sounded professional, contrite, everything she would expect of a text from the heir-apparent of Martelli Fragrance. The fucking heir-apparent! She'd had sex with the big man himself! On an airplane! And she stupidly hadn't even realized it was him. He must think her such an idiot. She was lucky they didn't put her in the first taxi to Fiumicino and send her right back home.

She really needed to text him back. But it was hard to know what to say. Quickly she typed:

No worries. Neither of us knew. No harm, no foul.

But she couldn't make herself send it. It sounded cold, and did it sound bitchy? To her it sounded bitchy, manipulative. Did she mean it that way? Oh God, please say she didn't mean it that way. She didn't want to be one of those women who manipulated good men just to make them miserable. She had no context for anything like this. How could she know how to behave? Certainly she never thought she'd behave like she had in the last twenty-four hours.

She deleted the text and tried again.

You have no reason to be sorry. The apology is mine. Clean slate?

Just as she was about to press *send*, it hit her that Coraline Martelli knew they'd had sex, knew before Paulo went after her in the basement. Had he actually *told* the head of Martelli Fragrance? Anger made her stomach hurt. They knew! They all knew. He'd told them, and she had walked right into Martelli Fragrance and made a fool of herself. They were all, no doubt, laughing their asss off behind her back.

Why did you tell them? she typed, then deleted it quickly. Her chest hurt, her heart felt like it would jack-hammer its way out of her ribcage. Well, she deserved it, didn't she? She started it. What was he supposed to think other than that she was easy entertainment on the flight, and he was bored?

Another text came through and she nearly dropped her BlackBerry. 'Damn!' She cursed when she saw it was from Carl.

We need to talk, Liza. Please let me explain.

She threw the device onto the bed, then paced the parquet floor. Fucking hell, she really didn't need Carl bugging her on top of everything else! He was old news. He was the least of her problems. And anyway, she should be thanking him. Hadn't he handed her the perfect way out on a silver platter? She grabbed up the device and typed furiously.

I don't need an explanation for what you do in your own kitchen or who you do it with. I interrupted. My bad. Problem solved.

She practically jammed her finger sending it. A message came back almost immediately.

??? I'm alone and I'm not in my kitchen. Are you OK?

Sonovabitch! How the hell had she managed to send the message to Paulo instead of Carl? Pacing again and mumbling curses under her breath she shot back.

Sorry! Text meant for someone else.

She sent it off, then figured before she made a bigger fool of herself, she'd finish this up and tuck the BlackBerry away in the drawer where it could do her no further harm.

I'm fine, no worries. I apologize for my bad behavior on our mutual journey and for invading your office space uninvited. I hope it won't color your opinion of my work.

This time she sent it. It sounded a little bit cold, but at least not snippy. It sounded like the professional she was, and the professional she would now need to be around Paulo … Mr Delacour. As for his indiscretion with his boss and his second in command, well she wouldn't mention it. The laugh was on her, and she deserved it, but she would not make a fool of herself again, nor would she give him more ammunition with which to entertain his colleagues.

The morning dawned bright and beautiful and very,

very early, thanks to jet-lag. There was a gym in the building's basement, which Liza took advantage of, then she dressed and helped herself to yogurt, a banana, and some coffee. She looked at her watch. It wasn't yet seven. She had plenty of time before Martelli's tour guide arrived to take her around the city. She was told it would be someone who knew the place well and had worked for Martelli long enough to answer any questions she might ask. Jim had been a bit vague, like maybe he was still trying to decide who would be best. Maybe he would be her guide? Maybe Martelli would feel she'd be more comfortable with another American. From somewhere in the Midwest, she thought he'd said, but his Italian was almost as good as hers. She knew that Martelli roots were as deep in North America as they were in Italy. No one could actually say for certain if the office in Rome or the one in Seattle was the headquarters, and Coraline Martelli spent as much time in one as she did the other. Clearly Paulo did too. His English was flawless with only the tiniest hint of an accent and, as much as she hated to admit it, he was all the sexier for it.

The morning was just too lovely not to do a bit of exploring on her own before her guide came. She looked down at her watch. She had enough time for a walk to the Piazza del Popolo and maybe even a bit of a wander in the Villa Borghese gardens before she had to get home for a quick shower. Being a Bernini fan, she planned to come back when there was more time and explore the Villa Borghese and all its wonderful treasures. She had adored Bernini's sculptures of Apollo and Daphne and of Persephone and Hades since she was a child, and it would be lovely to finally see them for real. She changed into walking clothes and headed out the door at a brisk pace. Being near Piazza Cavour meant Bernini Place wasn't far from the Vatican, and the walk along the Tiber was lovely. The traffic was already heaving, and the noise of the city made a manic soundtrack to her walk. The route was lined with aging churches, wrought iron balconies, and numerous small cafes. She found a quiet one and ordered an espresso, which she drank while standing at the counter, chatting merrily in Italian to the heavy-set man behind the bar, who told her about his upcoming holiday to New York.

It was just what she needed to clear her head. She walked surrounded by sleepy Italians scrambling to face their busy days in the bustle of a city that was old long before there was a United States. The history, the richness, the sheer sensuality of the place, with its rich dark coffee and its unpretentious, deliciously seasoned cuisine was an olfactory feast, a story for the nose. She breathed in and walked on, sniffing and smelling as she went.

Even following her nose, it had taken her less time to get to the Piazza del Popolo than she had expected. The hawkers were already accosting the early-morning tourists with cheap souvenirs of Rome that were all made in Asia. The more aggressive of them she politely turned down, the rest she simply ignored.

The place was as beautiful as she remembered it to be, but it couldn't be fully appreciated until she crossed the square and made her way up the steps and the zig-zaggy path that led to a car park at the edge of the Villa Borghese gardens, where there was an overlook of the whole piazza.

She breathed in the dry Mediterranean air and the iron and pepper scent of the city. A quick look at her watch, and she decided to hunt down the Villa Borghese, which nestled somewhere in the middle of the extensive gardens, so when she came back, she'd know exactly where to go to see the Berninis. The paths that led deeper into the park were still shaded, the heavy foliage of the trees filtering out the sharp angle of the early morning sun. For a brief moment her Spidey nose tingled and she stopped and sniffed. The muscles below her stomach tightened as olfactory memory sent sparks of arousal to her nipples and all points south. She closed her eyes and sniffed. Surely she couldn't be smelling Paulo Delacour. What would he be doing here in the villa's gardens? As she moved on, her fertile imagination filled her head with thoughts of what would happen if she ran into Paulo in the gardens where there were so many places one might sneak off the beaten path. She shut her mind down. It wasn't going to happen even if he was in the park. Quickly she looked around her again. Their relationship would now have to be professional. It would be difficult enough knowing that every time Jim and – worst of all – Coraline Martelli saw her, they would think about her throwing herself on Paulo. And who knew what Paulo would think.

Paulo! Christ, the memory of him coming to her seat in the plane, the memory of his scent, of his touch had her stopping and sniffing again.

And suddenly the smell wasn't pleasant anymore. She sniffed, and the sour and acrid scent made her throat clench. She was just about to turn and head back into the open when, from behind a dense hedge, two men sprung. They were both wearing ski masks.

One bumped into her hard and took off in a run. But before she could do more than gasp out half a curse, the second grabbed her bag and yanked. 'Give it back, you sonovabitch!' she yelled, jerking the strap hard.

Without a word the man took a knife from his pocket. From behind a ski mask, his eyes locked on hers. Her heart dropped to her stomach and she froze.

Before she could draw another breath, he severed the strap with a quick slice of the knife, gave her a hard shove, then ran after the other man. Sharp gravel abraded her left knee and the heel of her right hand as she went down on the path, but before she even had time to panic, a familiar scent washed over her. Strong hands moved around her waist hoisting her to her feet, and she found herself looking into the molasses dark eyes of Paulo Delacour. His scent was tinged with hot metal, and he looked like he was ready to commit murder.

'Are you all right?' he said, steadying her.

'I'm all right. I'm fine.' She didn't dare say anything else for fear she would cry. She wasn't fine! She'd been violated. She was angry and scared and she felt sick all over, but she wasn't going to tell him that.

The hot metal scent spiked. 'Like hell you are. What were you thinking? Just give them the damn bag and let it go. Nothing you have in there is worth your life.' He eased her gently onto a bench and bent to look at her knee.

Through the mist of tears she struggled to keep from shedding she saw that he was dressed in running clothes, and the smell of good clean male sweat rose from him like summer heat.

'This will sting a bit,' he said, as he took his water bottle and poured it over the skinned knee, washing off the gravel. She hissed between her teeth and fought the tears harder. From some invisible pocket inside his shorts, he pulled a neatly folded handkerchief and pressed it to the wound. Then he took her hand and checked it before doing the same. 'It's not like pick-pockets to be violent. Most of the time the deed's over and done with before you know what happened. What did they get?'

'Not much,' she said resisting the urge to run her

fingers through his hair where his head bent over her hand. 'I've travelled enough to know not to carry valuables when I don't have to. I doubt they got more than enough euros for a coffee and a cheap sandwich. There was a business card and photocopied pages from my passport. Oh, and my favourite lippy. That's about it.'

'Your phone?' he said. 'Please tell me you're not wandering about in a strange city without your phone.'

She shifted her cotton shirt enough that he could see the black leather clip-on BlackBerry case on the waistband of her shorts. 'It's not elegant,' she said, 'but it's still the best way to carry the thing.'

He offered her an agreeing smile and pulled out his own device. Still tending to her hand, he called up a number and spoke to someone in volatile, rapid-fire Italian about what had just happened. The police maybe? Certainly there was little chance of catching the thieves, and even the bag she'd been carrying was cheap, completely replaceable. At last, he hung up, stood, and offered her his hand.

'Come on.' He helped her to her feet. 'Now that the danger of bleeding to death has past, my flat's not far from here.' He looked down at his watch. 'I'll grab a quick shower, then drive you back to Bernini Place so you can clean up for our tour.'

She stopped in her tracks. 'Our tour?'

The smile that turned up the corner of his lips was the kind that should be eaten off if at all possible. 'Hi! I'm Paulo,' he said in a breathy sing-song voice, 'And I'll be your guide today for your super-duper-deluxe, top-of-the-line tour of Rome.'

Once they were at his flat, he'd pointed her to the kitchen and told her to help herself to what was there, then made straight for the shower as fast as possible.

He needed a little time to regroup. The incident in the park had shaken him badly, and he didn't figure she needed to know that. Seeing the man holding her at knifepoint had terrified him and made him furious that she would fight someone for her bag. It was just a fucking bag! And yet, she was feisty. He liked that about her, even if it had made her reckless. Rome was a fairly safe city if people used common sense, and she had done nothing that should have drawn the attack. It worried him a bit. He was sure the police would find nothing and wasn't sure his detectives could do much better, but the incident was definitely more than a simple pick-pocketing. Who would want to harm her, he wondered.

He returned to find her standing on the balcony with a bottle of sparkling water in her hand. The glare of the sun made it look as though she wore a halo. He could see the shape of her spine and the details of her bra where her thin shirt clung from perspiration. He sniffed, but the distance between them was too great for him to smell her. He moved closer. 'You could have had a glass. I do have some, you know.'

'Figured you probably did somewhere,' she said without turning around.

There was a long moment of tense silence and from somewhere in the city a siren wailed.

He didn't know what to say. Funny it had been so easy on the plane and then when they texted it had felt so natural. 'Are you ready to go?' he asked.

She nodded and followed him through the flat to the garage where his car was parked. It wasn't a long drive to Bernini Place and he filled the silence by bringing her attention to the touristy points of interest while she oohed and aahed politely in appreciation. They needed to talk. God they needed to talk, but he couldn't seem to get past the discomfort of the situation they had been placed in through no real fault of their own. She left him in her own kitchen while she went to shower, and he found himself feeling not so much slighted, but more as though she were imitating him because she didn't know what to do either. But he wasn't going to leave things as they were. He just couldn't.

It was possible Liza had lingered a little longer in the shower than she'd intended. It was mostly not knowing how to react to the man in the kitchen. She had dressed in a summer skirt and a tank top and was sitting on the edge of the bed combing her hair when she was surprised by a knock on her door and the strong scent of coffee. He entered with a cappuccino in one hand and a first aid kit in the other. Without a word, he handed her the coffee, knelt in front of her, and opened the kit.

'It's all right,' she said, trying to pull away. 'It's not that bad really.'

He offered a smile and nodded for her to lift her skirt, which fell to mid-calf. With a blush, she did as he asked.

'Have you eaten?' Before she could answer, he pressed on. 'I figured you probably hadn't. While you were in the shower, I picked up some nice pastries at the shop around the corner. I'm sorry, I'm not a good host. I just –'

She sat the coffee down on the nightstand. 'Why did you tell them?' Christ, she couldn't believe she'd just blurted it out, but it needed to be said she supposed. He stopped tending her knee and stared up at her.

'Why did you tell Ms Martelli and Jim that we'd … had sex? I mean I know I started it. I was out of line. But I would have never …' She swallowed back tears. She absolutely wasn't going to cry in front of him. If he could be a hard ass, so could she.

His eyes widened and he shook his head. 'You think I told them?' With one hand on the half-opened bandage the other came to rest gently on the uninjured knee. 'Fuck! I would have never, ever done such a thing, Liza. OK, I was excited about your sense of smell. I'm in the perfume business, and your nose is the best I've ever seen by a long shot. I thought maybe you might want to work with us on a project. I was excited about how you stimulated my own sense of smell, which is pretty damned good by the way. And …' He struggled once more to focus on tending her injured knee. 'OK, I was excited about the way we smell together, about the implications.'

'About the implications?' She kicked at him with her bare foot, but his reflexes were fast. He caught her ankle before it hit the hard muscles of his stomach. 'About the fucking implications. What was I, a goddamned experiment to you?'

His thumb was making tight little circles around her anklebone, which he still held firmly. 'Hell no, you weren't an experiment. You were a fucking obsession. Once I'd smelled you, once you'd touched me and I'd smelled us together, that was it! And after we were in the lounge and what happened there, I couldn't stop thinking about you. I couldn't.'

'Is that what you told them then, that there was this chick who sniffed you and you sniffed her back and then you had sex on the plane because you were obsessed with her. Oh, for fuck sake!' She shoved him away and stood to pace. 'I promised myself I wasn't going to do this. I promised I'd not act this way. It's my fault. I started it all. How can I complain about whatever you do with it after the fact?'

He stood and grabbed her shoulders, turning her to

face him. 'I didn't tell them. I would never.'

'What then?' she said, stamping her foot.

'You obviously don't know Coraline Martelli. The woman is scary intuitive. She knew. She knew the minute I mentioned your nose. I don't know how she knew. And even then no one had made the connection that it was you until you showed up in my office. Well, then I suppose our response to each other was obvious, and she isn't above toying with people when it suits her.'

'Oh well that's good to know – that I need to watch my back while I'm here. I wonder if I should find someplace a little less upscale and a little less Martelli to stay.'

'You still don't understand, do you?' He fell into step and paced with her. 'She got it. She only half believed me until you showed up, literally sniffing around. But then she totally got it. She wants your nose, and yes, she will toy with you and badger you until she gets what she wants. Me …' He shrugged and ran a hand through his hair. 'With me it took a while. I'll admit it, OK, I was thinking with my cock. And I wasn't terribly disappointed that the lounge was crowded and I had to sit by the sexy woman who knew how to fill out a sweater. And don't even begin to accuse me of just wanting you for sex when I'm pretty sure it wasn't my brain that was turning you on.' He stopped and turned to face her, risking life and limb to grab her again by the shoulders. 'Look, Liza, I like you. I like what I know about you, and I've been doing a little research since Jim dropped the bomb in Coraline's office. I'd like to get to know you better, and I'd like for us to start over and let bygones be bygones. I think we're gonna need to if we're gonna work together, don't you?' He lifted an eyebrow and cocked his head. 'What?

'You're starting to talk like her. I only caught about half of that.' She felt the tension drain from her shoulders. 'But I think it was the important part, the part I needed to hear. Shall we turn over a new leaf?' She extended her hand, which felt pretty stupid, considering the man had given her the best sex she'd ever had. Twice! And he still smelled like sex on wheels. But he took her hand in his, then instead of shaking it, his mouth curled into that edible smile and he brought it to his lips and laid a warm kiss on the back of her knuckles, and both of their scents spiked. But she forced herself not to notice.

Chapter Eight

The Skype tone ended abruptly, and Rita squinted at her laptop monitor. 'Mom? Are you all right?'

Coraline could tell she'd caught her daughter in her office at *Talkabout* magazine. She was always struck by how beautiful her Rita was, and how strong. She was proud of her. She told her that a lot these days. She wished she done it more when she was younger. 'I'm fine, darling, just fine. Do you have a few minutes?'

'Of course,' Rita said, lifting a cup in salute. 'Always time for a nice cuppa with me mum,' she put on her best British accent.

'I met Liza Calendar yesterday. It took me a while to remember how I knew her. She was your friend when you were in university, wasn't she?'

Rita offered the broad smile that had Martelli written all over it. 'Still is. I'm not ashamed to admit I pulled a few strings with Martelli to make sure her article didn't fall through the cracks.' There was that smile again. 'You're her hero, you know? Though I probably shouldn't tell you that. It'll go straight to your head.'

'Why did you never bring her home to meet me?' She hadn't intended to ask that question. The two of them pretty much left the past in the past now, and they were working hard to make up for lost time.

'Mom, you were never home, and –'

'And neither were you if you could help it. I know.

I'm sorry, darling. I didn't mean to bring that up. It's just that she's … well, she's a very interesting person.'

Rita leaned forward, clutching her cup between her palms. 'You know about her nose.'

'She came sniffing around the office yesterday, literally. I've never seen anyone like her. I could hardly contain myself. Has she always had such a sense of smell?'

'As long as I've known her, but she usually tries to hide it. What happened?'

Coraline lifted her own cup and sipped thoughtfully, wondering how much she should reveal. But then she was never known for her subtlety. 'She had sex with Paulo on the flight to Rome.'

Rita inhaled coffee, sputtered and then grabbed a couple of tissues to wipe the rain of caffeine off the monitor. 'She had sex with Paulo? Seriously?'

Coraline nodded. 'You seem surprised.'

'Why wouldn't I be? I mean obviously she liked the way Paulo smelled. It's just that it's so rare.'

'So rare what?' Coraline motioned Alessandro into her office, and he made a show of placing a fresh coffee and a pastry in front of her before he turned and left.

Once Rita was sure they were alone again, she leaned closer to the monitor. 'Well, most men have a hard time getting past Liza's nose.'

Coraline let that sink in with a rise of butterflies. This woman sounded better and better all the time. 'Then she doesn't …'

'No, Mom, she most definitely doesn't sleep around. In fact some guy in New York who was hot for her actually made her sneeze. I laughed when she told me, and then I felt bad about it. I mean can you imagine? Oh, and emotions. She smells emotions. Actually, she used to be great fun in bars. We'd go in and order a drink and she could sniff out who was hitting on whom, who'd been doing the nasty in the alley, who was jealous, who was horny. Liza's amazing.'

'Why did you never tell me about Liza's nose – me, a woman whose livelihood and that of her daughter at the time, depends on scent?'

Rita blew out a sharp breath. 'Mom, I never told you anything at the time. You were never home and when you were, we weren't talking.'

'Sorry. Again asking questions I know the answers to.' She nibbled at her croissant and dabbed the crumbs from her lips with a linen napkin. 'I want her, Rita. If she's anywhere nearly as good as you and Paulo seem to think, then I want her for Martelli.'

The smile disappeared from Rita's face, and she folded arms across her chest. 'Mom, is that all Paulo is interested in? Is that the only reason he fucked Liza, because if it is, I'll kill him, and you can tell him that for me. She's one of my best friends, and toying with her is beneath him, or it damned well better be.'

Coraline lifted her hands as though she could fend off the verbal attack. 'You'll have to talk to your brother about that, darling, but if it's any help, he seemed as dazed and confused by what happened as Ms Calendar was.'

'Oh I'll talk to him, alright, don't you worry, and I'll come over and personally kick his ass if he hurts her.'

Coraline couldn't hold back the smile. Though Paulo wasn't Rita's biological brother, they had always related to each other like older brother to kid sister, and when the time came that they were both of an age at which something less platonic might have developed, it never did. Though Coraline would have been all right with it if their relationship had gone in that direction, really, she had always secretly seen her daughter with Edward. Of course she'd never tell Rita that. Rita would have seen it as her meddling again. Which it was, but then what was a mother for if not to meddle – especially when she knew she was right.

'What are you smirking at?' Rita glared at her mother. A face that used to mean a fight now meant a friendly argument.

'You've always been a good friend, sweetheart, and you know your brother well enough to know he's not the kind who would deliberately hurt anyone. I'm sure he won't do wrong by Liza Calendar.'

Rita raised an eyebrow. 'And what about you, Mom? What are your plans for Liza Calendar?'

The smirk became a full-blown chuckle. 'Me? I simply want to see what the woman's nose can do before I make her an offer she can't refuse.'

Rita laughed at her mother's *Godfather* impression, and that was just fine. Rita could laugh, but Coraline was about to meddle again.

Augusto Paulo Delacour was easy to be with. In the sun-drenched ruins of the Forum under the blue Roman sky, their scents seemed to blend in a different way. He knew his city, and it was clear he loved it. And Liza loved watching his enthusiasm and sharing it. No one could live their whole life at a fever pitch. There had to be something more to admire about a person than the fact that he smelled amazing and he was a fabulous fuck. She couldn't keep from wondering if the scent of a person told more about them than just how sexually compatible they were or the present state of their emotions. She knew so much about Coraline Martelli and the business she had taken over from her father. The woman was her hero in so many ways. But she'd not paid much attention to the man who was the heir apparent to the Martelli empire, the man who was good enough to step in and take over for the daughter who wasn't interested. His nickname was Paulo, the Nose. How had she missed that? A quick internet search had informed her that he was the child of a Portuguese secretary who had worked for Coraline and an Italian father, who died of a heart attack when Paulo was eight. His mother died only a two years later. With no other relatives except an ancient great aunt in Lisbon, Coraline took the boy in, and the rest was history. Still, being all but adopted by Coraline Martelli didn't account for his talent and drive. The man couldn't do what he did if he didn't live through his nose, maybe not exactly like Liza did, but his livelihood depended on it nonetheless.

Her attention returned to the Forum and the intriguing man who stood next to her. It was one of those rare occasions when there was no one in the House of the Vestal Virgins except the two of them. The reflecting pools were deep azure under the midday sky, and most people had moved to shadier places, but she lingered. After the cool damp of Portland, where she now lived, the heat felt delicious against her skin, and Paulo seemed used to it. The place had that wonderful scent of ancient history writ large, then left to crumble and age in the sun.

'The Vestals had freedom no other women in Rome did,' Paulo said. 'I think in some ways Coraline is a modern example of a Vestal Virgin.' He laughed to himself. 'Minus the virgin part, of course.'

A part of Coraline Martelli's appeal to Liza had always been that the woman had gotten pregnant on purpose because she wanted a daughter. She never took the father's name for her child, never mentioned who he was. She rose above the scandal by doing what her father did, only better, by making his business twice the business it had been; by giving Rita the Martelli name and never once letting anyone look down on her for choosing to raise Rita as she had. Liza smiled at her image in the reflecting pool. 'No, definitely not a virgin.'

They walked together in silence admiring the statuary around the outer courtyard. 'So who has the right to do what in their kitchen?' Paulo asked.

When she gave him a questioning look, he said, 'You know, the text you accidentally sent me last night?'

'Oh. No one important.' She left it at that, and he didn't pry. After her embarrassing mistake, she'd deleted the message and decided to ignore Carl a while longer. But she could almost smell all the questions Paulo wanted to ask about the strange woman who had all but attacked him in the airport lounge.

'Do you always sniff out your men?' When he did finally ask a question, she bristled, then stopped and bent to smell one of the roses in bloom in the courtyard to calm herself before she spoke. 'As a matter of fact I do.'

'I see,' he said. 'And how has that worked out for you?'

Surely he wasn't jealous. But that sour citric smell was there. 'It sucks, actually.'

'How so?' He turned and nearly ran into her.

She looked up into his eyes and drew in a deep breath, which was a mistake because it brought with it the heat of his scent. 'Would you enjoy making love to me if I smelled like rotting vegetation or wet garbage? How about if all you could smell on me was deceit? How about if the smell of me made your nose itch or made you sneeze uncontrollably? Would you still want to make love with me? Would you even be able to?'

Before he could do more that gape at her in

surprise, she jerked her head toward a couple who had just passed them, hand in hand. 'Those two,' she whispered, 'they just had sex here somewhere close by in the Forum. She's still wet from him, even though he tried to clean them both. He probably has a handkerchief or something because his right-hand pocket, when he brushed past me, smells strong of them. He's smug, she's uncertain of how she feels about what they've done. They smell like too much garlic fried in burnt butter. That man over there?' She nodded to a man with a camera glaring into the reflecting pond. 'I don't know what he's angry about, but he smells like mustard and wet dog. How easy do you think it is for me to have a love life when I live with this every day?' She brushed the tip of her nose with her fingers.

Before she could recover from her outburst enough to apologize, he gathered her hand, brought her palm to his lips, and kissed it fervently. 'I'm sorry,' he whispered. 'Sorry for what I just said. Sorry I don't completely understand, but not sorry about how I smell to you. I'm so not sorry about that.'

'Liza, hi, it's me again. I'm … I'm just so, so sorry about what happened. It's … Well I missed you so much, with us living so far apart. I just got lonely, and it … it just happened. She meant nothing to me, darling. You have to know that. We need to talk, Liza. Please. We can work this out. I know we can.'

Carl Blain listened as Liza's voicemail played back his message. When he was certain it sounded acceptably contrite, he disconnected. The phone had rung over to Liza's voicemail ever since his first attempt to call her after she caught him fucking Connie on the kitchen counter … or was it Courtney? He wasn't so much sorry that he'd fucked Connie – she had one tight pussy – as he was sorry he'd gotten caught. In fact he really wasn't as sorry as he was pissed off. What the hell was Liza thinking, showing up at his flat unexpected? He'd given her his key, yes, but it had only meant that he planned to fuck her the next time he saw her, and he wasn't going to take no for an answer after all her putting him off.

He contemplated the situation for a few moments then he called Liza's business partner. He knew they were also good friends. It wouldn't hurt to have her in his corner, and he figured he could charm her. As she picked up, he plastered on his best I'm-your-friend's-sexy-lover smile and spoke. 'Good morning, Addie,' Carl forced his teeth into the smile to help him sound more cheerful even though he didn't feel it. 'Just wondering how things are going for Liza in Rome?'

'As far as I know, just fine.' He could hear the suspicion in her voice, like why the hell wouldn't Liza have contacted the man she was dating with at least a text.

'Well,' he chuckled, 'if I know our Liza, she's probably already so focused on Martelli Fragrance that she's forgotten all about both of us.'

On the other end of the phone, he heard the woman laugh softly. 'She does tend to get a bit tunnel-visioned. And she was particularly excited about meeting Coraline Martelli in person. I got an email saying she was safely at the flat, but I'm sure I'll get a full update when there's something to tell, and so will you, no doubt.'

So, Liza hadn't told her. That was both a relief and a surprise. He though the first thing women did when they were upset with their men was to commiserate with each other so they could discuss what bastards all men are.

'Liza's a law unto herself, Carl, and that's what

makes her so good at what she does.'

At least the woman had the good grace not to ask him how his night with Liza had gone. He wouldn't have to lie. No doubt she'd hear all about it soon enough, but at least for the moment, she was blissfully ignorant. Just then, his cell phone rang. The display on the screen made his shoulders tighten and the coffee in his stomach turn to acid. 'I've gotta go, Addie. I have another call. Have a lovely day, and give my love to Liza when you speak to her.' He hung up and ground his teeth, then answered his cell.

'What is it, Latimer?' He didn't try to hide his irritation. The PI knew not to call at his office.

'I thought you'd like to know that my people have caught up with the lady in question in Rome.'

'And how is that valuable to me? I knew she was going to Rome, and I knew what she was going to be doing there.' That's why Liza catching him banging Carrie or Kellie or whatever her name, was such a fiasco. He was counting on a little help from her while she was in Rome.

Latimer cleared his throat as though he was either embarrassed or he was about to impart the wisdom of the ages. 'It's not so much what she's doing in Rome as *who* she's doing in Rome, if you get me, Blain.'

'Who she's doing?' Carl barely felt the arrogance of the man calling him by his last name. 'What do you mean who she's doing?' He'd never met such a prude as Liza Calendar. How many times had he wined and dined her and she still hadn't put out? It certainly wasn't like he needed a piece. He could have it whenever he wanted, and he did. But Liza Calendar, well she was one of those women who wanted more than just a good fucking, and even that was OK considering what he wanted from her. In fact that had been perfect. And if she hadn't caught him with his cock crammed up Connie, or Carrie's cunt, he would have made their first time special for her and she would have had stars in her eyes and done exactly what he wanted. 'What the fuck are you talking about, Latimer? Get on with it.' He didn't need the goddamned pause for effect.

'Liza Calendar is doing A. P. Delacour.'

For a second, Carl could hear nothing over the loud ringing in his ears. Miss Sweet and Innocent was fucking Delacour? Seriously? He wondered how the man felt about her sneezing all over him.

'Blain?'

'You're sure,' Carl finally managed.

'Deke, one of the attendants of the flight she was on – which coincidentally happened to be the same flight Delacour was on – said Delacour followed her back to coach then the two were all over each other before they finally snuck into the restroom. Now I can't think of any other reason a man and a woman who were giving each other the grope would go into a toilet on an airplane together, can you?'

When Carl made no immediate response, Latimer continued. 'There's more. Two of my men did a little pick-pocket routine on her while she was out doing the touristy thing. Turned out to be a little rougher than they expected. The woman's feisty.'

'You didn't hurt her, did you?' Though at the moment a part of him didn't care if they'd beaten the shit out of the bitch, she'd be of no use to him in the hospital.

'No, no, of course not. But strangely enough, out of the blue, who should come to her rescue but Delacour himself. He took her back to his place, and then went about the business of giving her a personal tour or the Eternal City.'

Carl felt his stomach clench. It was unprofessional.

That had been the excuse Liza Calendar had used repeatedly to put him off. It wasn't until her article on Blain Holdings was finished that he could even get her to go out to dinner with him. He struggled to focus on what the man was saying.

'Anyway, it seems that her first afternoon in Rome she actually met with the big three themselves.'

'Seriously?' Carl sat up straight in his chair and the leather squeaked beneath his ass. How the hell had she managed that when she was a nobody? Goddamn it! Why'd she have to come to his place early! This should have been information gathering for him! She should have been his ace in the hole!

'Vera said the woman's ballsiness was all Jim Dryer could talk about afterward. She said he was laughing at how Ms Calendar showed up sniffing around. Seems security brought her upstairs and right on into the lioness's den. Apparently she not only came out in one piece, but she left the Queen Bitch smiling.'

Coraline Martelli smiling. That didn't happen very often, unless she had just ripped someone's throat out with her fangs. 'So let me get this straight, Liza Calendar, sneezing, sniffing, snuffling Liza Calendar, has elbowed her way right on into the Martelli inner circle and she's banging the man himself?'

'The evidence is certainly pointing in that direction. Vera's still trying to get in with either Dryer or Delacour, but it looks like Delacour is dipping his wick elsewhere now. She says Dryer'll take the bait and she'll be in in no time.'

Carl switched his phone to the other ear and flipped absently through the copy of *The Wall Street Journal* his secretary had delivered earlier. 'I want you to keep on her, Latimer, and have Vera keep on her toes. Do you know where Liza's staying?' he asked.

Latimer gave him an address, which he wrote down quickly. Then he hung up and buzzed his secretary. 'Sally, I need you to call the florist and have a very large, very expensive bouquet of flowers delivered to Number 14 Bernini Place in Rome.' He gave her the details then hung up and swiveled his chair to look out the window at Central Park far below. This was not at all how he'd planned things to work out between him and Liza Calendar, but he had to remind himself that most of the time plans didn't work right out of the block. There were always back-up plans, and even back-ups of back-ups. His father had forgotten that when he'd tried to take down the Martelli Empire. Well, he wasn't his father, and he wouldn't forget, and his instincts told him that Liza Calendar was still very much a key player in his plan. He couldn't for the life of him figure the sudden and very surprising sexual connection between her and Delacour. From what she'd told him, she didn't know Delacour. She practically worshiped Coraline Martelli, and Jim Dryer was her ticket to the story she wanted to write. In fact, he couldn't recall that she'd ever done more than brush his mentions of Delacour aside as though the man were of no importance at all. Perhaps she was a better player than he thought. Perhaps he needed to deliver more than a bouquet of flowers to Liza Calendar's door.

Chapter Nine

'Whoa! Testosterone in large doses. Not a big surprise with the chick ovulating.' Liza nodded discretely to three backpackers who had just brushed past them as they made their way along one of the narrow side streets off the Via Del Corso, heading toward Piazza Navona. The woman, who looked to be barely out of her teens, was sandwiched between the two guys who didn't look much older, but they were both obviously vying for her attention.

'You can smell testosterone?' Paulo asked, finding his own desire to pull her close and protect her from the hustle and bustle of the crowd difficult to control.

'The testosterone is obvious,' she said. 'I don't have to smell it. I smell her heat, like something primal, like she'd like to have them both, then have them again. I smell their response to her heat, like sharp citrus and black pepper.' They stopped on the street and watched the trio that had just brushed past them. One guy had his hand on the girl's cut-off-clad bottom. The other one had his arm draped around her neck, fingers dangling dangerously close to a well-displayed braless breast, nipples heavily peaked beneath a pale yellow tank top. 'I think she'll have them both,' Liza said, her eyes following the trio. 'I think they'll get drunk tonight, go back to wherever it is they're staying, and have a really filthy threesome, and –' she sniffed, then added '– I think we both like that thought just a little too much.'

He grunted. 'You got that right. Come on, the place I'm taking you for lunch is just around the corner and maybe the smell of great Italian cooking will take your mind off how we smell.' He held her gaze. 'I'm very hungry.' Both of their scents spiked, and he could smell the blending even on the busy, sweaty street. For a moment they walked along in silence, then he said, 'You can really smell all that, just in a passing moment on a busy street?'

'I can. Of course their smell got my attention, first of all because it's sex and jealousy and lust, and second of all because they bumped into us. What did you smell?'

'You,' he replied as he guided her into a small café and on through to a vine-shaded garden behind. 'It was hard for me to notice anything else but you.'

She offered him a wicked smile. 'Testosterone has tunnel-vision, or tunnel-smell, in this case,' she replied.

They were late to lunch. There was no one else in the secluded garden but the two of them and, he had to admit, that was exactly why he'd brought her there. In the cool shade of heavily hung grapevines and the scent of the herb garden along the wall he could smell the soft dew of her perspiration, the subtle scent of the soap the maid always furnished the flat with, and her lust. He smelled her lust. Now that it had been brought to his attention, he would always be aware of it and never be able to miss the seashore and honey-butter scent. Now there was a subtle undertone that was like freshly brewed tea. That wasn't lust, but something else, something that kept her focused on more than just his lust for her, which he had no doubt she smelled. God, how the hell was he ever going to be able to stay away from her?

The waiter was just taking their order when

Coraline Martelli marched through the door to the garden, sat down at their table, and ordered the carbonara from the surprised waiter. That done, she helped herself to a glass of wine from the carafe almost before she said, 'how are you.'

When the waiter finally left, Paulo spoke between gritted teeth. 'Coraline, we weren't expecting you.' No doubt Liza could smell the irritation rolling off him.

'Oh, I know, I know, but I just couldn't wait any longer. I had to talk to Liza, and I figured I'd find you two here.' She turned her attention to Liza. 'It's Paulo's favourite place, and he likes to eat late –' she patted Liza's hand and gave her a knowing smile '– for the privacy.' Christ, the woman could actually be subtle when she wanted to, but subtly didn't seem to be on today's menu.

As the waiter brought a first plate of Roman gnocchi, Coraline sipped daintily at her wine and studied Liza. 'I Skyped with Rita this morning.'

Liza toyed with her gnocchi. 'Oh? How is she?'

'Fine! Rita's fine. Unrepentant that she never introduced the two of us and that she never told me about your nose.'

Liza smiled down at her plate. 'Rita's always been pretty protective of me and my nose.'

'Mmm. And it seems she felt she needed to protect you from her own mother.'

Probably wise of Rita, Paulo observed.

'Why would I need protection from you?'

Oh God, he thought, that was not a question to ask.

'Paulo, have you shown her your proposal?' Coraline turned her attention to him. Just like her to answer a question with a question.

'What proposal?'

Before Paulo could respond, Coraline was off and running. 'I took the liberty of bringing a flash drive for you, darling …' She dug in her bag, being her usual evasive self, '… because I figured by now Paulo would have had time for a proper apology for his indiscretions, and I'm anxious to move forward.' She handed the drive to Liza with a broad smile. 'Liza, dear, I want your nose.'

'What?' Liza nearly dropped the drive in her gnocchi.

'I want your nose to help us develop our new line of fragrances.' Before Liza could respond she raised her hand to silence both her and Paulo. 'Oh I know you're an excellent journalist and businesswoman or *High Rising* wouldn't be doing so well. I'm perfectly happy to let you use your experience for your article, with a few exceptions that involve … shall we say … Martelli trade secrets. Your unique abilities –' she nodded to Liza's nose '– are an asset I'm willing to pay well for, and I think the opportunity I'm offering you at Martelli intrigues you very much, doesn't it?'

Paulo could see the thud, thud of Liza's pulse against the tender spot on her throat, but her face gave nothing away. They all sat quietly as the waiter brought their main courses and refilled everyone's wine glass. Once he was done fussing, Liza leaned across the table, eyes wide, pupils dilated with interest. 'What do I have to do?'

Coraline made a point of digging into her carbonara and oohing and aahing about the chef's magic before she wiped her mouth daintily and spoke. 'Read Paulo's proposal.' She nodded to the flash drive Liza still clenched in her hand. 'It's not complete, and you may have some suggestions. Then tonight, I'll send a car for you at 7.00.'

Paulo felt his heart somersault. Surely Coraline wasn't going to throw Liza in at the deep end, but the woman shot him a warning glance, followed by a quick smile that was the look he had seen on the faces of predators before they made a kill.

'For what?' Liza asked.

'Are you involving The Mount?' Paulo suddenly lost his appetite.

'Of course, Paulo,' Coraline batted her lashes at him. 'Just exactly like you planned.'

'Coraline,' He scooted closer to the table. No use trying to hide what they were saying in Italian, since Liza spoke better Italian the even Jim did, and he supposed his half-whisper, half-ventriloquist act was a dead giveaway that he didn't want to involve her in the conversation, but he did it anyway. 'Coraline, don't you think taking her to the villa is a bit premature?'

His boss barely glanced at him. 'Not at all. Once she's read your proposal the next step is to take her to The Mount's villa. Better sooner than later and best if she goes with no expectations, then we know her response will be unbiased. Don't you agree, Liza?'

'That makes sense,' Liza said. 'It all sounds so intriguing.'

She had no idea, Paulo thought. And this a woman who had been abstinent until the night before last. Was she in for a surprise.

Chapter Ten

It was actually a limo that picked Liza up in front of Bernini Place. She did get the odd limo service from time to time in her line of work, but it still felt like an unexpected luxury when it happened. She figured she'd be taken to the Martelli offices or the research facilities, which were outside Rome and not far from Ostia Antica. She remembered that because Ostia Antica was one of the tourist sites at the top of her must-see list before she left Rome. Instead, she was taken out toward Tivoli. In one of her earlier trips to the Eternal City, she had visited the Villa d'Este, built on the hills at the edge of the town. The weather and been close and hot, and she had relished the cool gardens with the myriad Renaissance fountains. As she strolled down memory lane, the limo climbed the winding road toward the town. She watched out the window allowing her mind to wander over Paulo's exciting proposal, over the fact that Ms Martelli had said whatever happened tonight was off the record and Paulo had clearly not been thrilled about her participation.

The limo turned off the main road into the countryside, still climbing until it was practically consumed by the hills. At last the driver approached elaborately crafted wrought-iron gates the height of a two-storey building. They opened automatically and the limo moved down a long road that twisted and turned and continued to ascend until the vista opened onto a villa built against the breast of the hill. It was flanked by sculptures that could have passed, in their detail, for Bernini's work except that these sculptures were beyond romantic, beyond the romp of fawns or even beyond satyrs showing off their packages. The sculptures were intentionally erotic, beautifully so. They were mostly based on stories from mythology, but no proverbial bedroom doors were closed and nothing was left to the imagination. As Liza was ushered out of the limo and into the villa by a man the size of a small Italian car, she noticed that the frieze above the door sported a much more graphic version of the stylized Martelli logo: Ares and Aphrodite in that magical moment just before penetration, his very substantial cock and her very exposed pussy poised at the ready. Liza smelled the spike of her own scent at the erotic views, but her escort seemed completely unaffected by them – no doubt jaded from seeing them every day. Inside, he led her up a long, curving staircase, which divided halfway with both staircases then continued upward curving in opposite directions. He took her to the left.

From the time she entered the villa, Liza could smell Paulo's lightning storm scent, and it grew stronger as she ascended the stairs in growing anticipation. At the top, in front of a closed door Coraline Martelli waited with a leather-bound notebook and a pen in her hand. She spoke quietly to Jim Dryer, who stood with his head slightly bowed, the look on his face deep concentration. Though Paulo's scent was strong, he wasn't with them.

'There you are, Liza,' Ms Martelli said. 'We're ready for you.' She nodded to Jim, who held three sealed zip-lock bags. 'These are the T-shirts from another experiment the lab's conducting. Our volunteers have slept in them for the past three nights.

Could you tell us what you smell?'

Jim handed Liza the first one, which was labeled A. She opened it cautiously and sniffed, then blinked to keep her eyes from watering. 'You also asked them not to bathe for those three days?' The two shot each other a quick look, and Jim nodded. 'Believe me, that wasn't necessary.' She took a shallow breath through her mouth for self-preservation. 'This belongs to a man and from the smell he's pretty aroused. Clearly he eats in bed, 'cause garlic! Wow! And anchovies.' She handed the bag back, holding it with her fingertips.

Without comment, Jim offered her another bag and this time she sniffed more cautiously. 'Another man, not quite as pungent, but also very aroused.' She noticed Coraline Martelli was scribbling in the leather notebook.

Jim handed her the final zip-lock.

'A woman, ovulating, also very horny. What's this all about?'

Another look passed between them then Jim spoke. 'We've been doing a lot of testing and experimenting with pheromones, as you will have read in Paulo's proposal. But to take our theories to the next level is … well, it's risky.'

'It's innovative,' Coraline corrected.

Liza felt butterflies take flight in her stomach. The smell of other people's arousal was something she had gotten used to and had learned to block out, especially when she could tell such a great deal about people's sex lives from their scent. When she'd had a flat mate, she always knew when she brought home her boyfriend. She knew, even with the substantial wall that separated her room from her flat mates, when the foreplay began, when orgasms happened for both of them, and she could tell when Ellen was faking it, which happened often and was part of the reason for their break-up. Liza could also smell the comedown and could tell when the two drifted off to sleep. Ellen was a good flat mate and the sex was always quiet, but Liza's nose never missed anything. It still embarrassed her to recall how many times she'd lain awake in her own bed, inhaling the scent of sex coming from next door, imagining where Dan was touching Ellen, sensing the moment of penetration; fantasizing about how he touched her, what position they were in; masturbating and secretly blending her own scent of arousal with theirs. Sadly, back then that had been as close to real sex as her nose would allow her.

'What exactly does this experiment involve?' she asked, as the acidic tang of her own nervousness spiked with a nettle sting.

'Oh, don't worry, darling,' Coraline said. 'Your job is simply to tell us what you smell and make observations. The room is equipped with a recording device so that you won't be distracted by having to write anything down. Paulo will be with you. Jim will be watching from the two-way mirror next door, and me, well I don't want to know until it's finished. That'll keep me unbiased as well.'

The idea of a two-way mirror ratcheted up the scent of nerves even higher. But it was knowing that Paulo would be with her that changed the game plan. Didn't they realise that his scent was the scent she smelled above all else? She supposed she should remind them of that, but she didn't.

Jim's BlackBerry buzzed a text. 'All right.' He stuffed it back into his pocket and smiled at Liza. 'Time to dance. Paulo's waiting.' He nodded to the door then turned and went into the room up the hall. Coraline watched her expectantly, as she turned the door handle with sweating fingers, took one deep breath, and stepped inside.

Liza found herself in a small entryway not unlike that of a hotel room. As always her sense of smell entered the room first; it was heavy with fragrant arousal. Immediately she recognized the scents of three other people present. But they paled to insignificance compared to Paulo's, and she wondered how she would ever be able to block the delicious smell of him enough that she could focus on the other three. Once the scents were sorted, she could hear the wind rush of heavy breathing along with the wet sounds of kissing. For a sharp instant her own scent peaked with jealousy. The thought of Paulo with someone else made her chest tight, which was ridiculous. She'd only been with him twice. She was nothing to him. Still the sting of finding a man in the arms of another woman was a repeat performance she wasn't keen on witnessing. She took a shaky breath to steady herself and, it was in that breath, she became aware that only three of the four scents were blending. Paulo's scent was not in the mix. It was somehow separate. That intriguing fact gave her the courage to move forward.

Though Paulo had been distractedly listening for Liza to enter the room, he kept an eye on what was happening in the bed. After all, this was exactly what he'd hoped for, exactly what he'd never dreamed Coraline would give her OK for until Liza Calendar and her magnificent nose came into the picture. Unfortunately there was baggage that came with her nose, and that was the fact that he wanted her in the worst way. Even if she didn't run away outraged at the first sight of the three on the bed and what they were doing, having her here with him observing what was about to happen wasn't likely to do anything to subdue his lust. It was her little gasp of surprise that got

Paulo's attention from where he leaned against the wall at the foot of a large bed on which the three people writhing and shifting had progressed to a partial state of undress. She inhaled deeply, breathing in the situation on the bed. Then she sniffed again, and her eyes locked on his, which was rather amazing considering that Pietro had his lips wrapped around one of Livinia's heavy gum-drop nipples, his tightly trimmed beard swishing against the pinkening pale skin of her ample breasts. David knelt beside her head, his white-blond hair falling over his face as he watched her nimble fingers working on his fly. And yet, Liza Calendar watched Paulo.

'I'm sorry she didn't warn you,' he blurted. 'I wanted to but she said it was better this way – Coraline.'

She sniffed again, and this time he knew as well as he knew his own name that it was his scent she took in. Then she turned her gaze back to the action on the bed. 'These were the certain types of "experiments" you were talking about,' she made quotation marks in the air with her fingers, speaking in a whisper as though she feared her voice might interrupt the *ménage* on the bed. This time it was Paulo's turn to sniff. It had never been difficult for him to recognize the smell of sex, nor the smell of obvious arousal, but with her focus on the action and her standing so close to him, it was her scent he wanted. And for a moment he wished like hell he could smell her the way she had just smelled him. Still it was there, the subtle heat of her. It was there like it had been on the plane. And for a second his stomach knotted and he resisted the urge to pull her into his arms and take her against the wall. He wanted her attention off what was happening on the bed and focused completely on him, and what he could do for her. His pulse beat a rapid tattoo against his throat, as she shot a raised-eyebrowed look over her shoulder at him. Had he been caught in the act? He wondered if she could smell his thoughts. But she turned her attention back to the action. 'It's a good idea,' she said, watching as Livinia freed David's cock, which bounced only once before she worried it into her mouth. Pietro had shoved up Livinia's short skirt and there was a sudden wave of seashore heat in the room that even Paulo could smell. He reminded himself that until Liza Calendar came along, his was the definitive nose at Martelli Fragrance. 'It's an excellent idea, in fact,' she continued. 'Exactly what I was thinking when I read your proposal, although I'm not sure I would have begun with this combination.'

Paulo felt the tension leave his shoulders so quickly that his knees nearly gave, and the accompanying sigh of relief, well, he hoped she would mistake that for his efforts to smell what she smelled. 'You're OK with this then?'

'Of course I'm OK with it.' To his surprise, she began pacing around the bed sniffing, then pausing and closing her eyes, then repeating the process. 'The scents of sex are the perfect building blocks for fragrances that will do what perfumes were intended to do from the beginning – enhance desirability. That's really just a euphemism for arousal if you look at it from a biological point of view. It's a mammal thing, isn't it?' She moved still closer to the bed, sniffing as she went, and he followed.

She leaned in until her nose was only centimeters away from where David's cock shoved in and out of Livinia's tight mouth. There she inhaled with her lips slightly parted. David's eyelids fluttered and he moaned and shoved his jeans down until his bare ass was exposed to Liza's view. Pietro, with his eyes locked on Liza, licked his way down Livinia's belly, sniffed her splayed pussy, then began to lap it with the flat of his tongue, but his focus was clearly on Liza.

'Can you smell that?' Liza asked, without turning to Paulo. She sniffed again. 'My presence makes a difference in the equation.'

'Of course,' David managed without losing his rhythm. 'It's at least as much of a turn-on to be sniffed as it is to be watched.' The other two, with their mouths full, nodded and mmphed their agreement.

She turned to Paulo. 'These three have done this before, haven't they?'

Paulo nodded. 'They have, yes.'

'What are they, porn stars?'

All three of them laughed, Livinia nearly chocking on David's cock.

'No,' Paulo said. 'They're not porn stars, and I'm not at liberty to say more at the moment.'

She backed to the foot of the bed and paced, watching the three in action. 'If it's a performance it'll smell like a performance, and it smells like a performance to me.'

'Jesus,' Paulo said, running his hand through his hair. 'What? Do you hang out on porn sets?'

'I don't have to hang out on porn sets to know when something is an act. The honesty, the edginess, the forbidden thrill of something is a scent unto itself. When the lion takes over the pride in the Serengeti and gets to fuck all the lionesses, the element of performance is that he gets to shag the ladies because he won the pride, and the way he won the pride is what makes him the one the ladies fuck.' She nodded to the bed, where the three had stopped what they were doing to listen to her. 'This is a strip club, this is a porn rerun,' she said, waving a hand at the bed. 'This is cheap cologne, not Martelli Fragrance. It just doesn't smell right, though I get what you're trying to do.'

‘What would you suggest?’ Paulo said, coming to her side and looking down at the three now sitting thoughtfully and half naked on the mattress.

Liza paced again, still sniffing and studying the three lovers. The she stopped and shoved her hands on her hips. ‘She’s not the main course in this scent fest.’ She pointed to Livinia. ‘She’s the intruder invited in to play.’

The three on the bed looked at each other, then back at her.

‘Were you going for a sandwich?’ she snapped her fingers as though trying to find a word. ‘Double penetration.’

They nodded.

‘That’s not how you picture it in your heads though, is it? It’s not what would really turn *you* on.’

Livinia spoke up. ‘It’s what we thought wouldn’t shock you too badly, and Paulo agreed.’

Paulo was surprised at Liza’s guttural laugh. ‘How about you don’t worry about shocking me? How about you concentrate on shocking each other?’

Paulo’s cock jerked in his trousers in a sudden surge of lust, and his respect for this woman skyrocketed as the light bulbs went on in the heads of the three on the bed. They shifted until they all three were lying down with Livinia in the middle. The two men began at the top of her head kissing and caressing, moving her hair away from her ears and stroking and licking down her sensitive nape in unison, almost as though one were the mirror image of the other. At her mouth, they both lingered, not taking turns, but jostling and shoving to try and take her at the same time. She reached out pulling them both to her and, as she did so, their hands snaked down her armpits and found their way to her anxious breasts in kneading, cupping strokes.

‘There,’ Liza breathed. Paulo could hear her pulse in her whisper. ‘Can you smell it? Can you smell the shift?’ He sniffed and sniffed again. He wasn’t sure that he could, but there was no denying something in the room had driven the lust up to sizzling. As he watched the two men pinch Livinia’s nipples to hard peaks, watched her grinding and shifting her ass into the mattress, he became aware of the heat of Liza’s body so close to his. The men kissed and licked down Livinia’s throat and collarbones and onto her breasts with such precision that is was almost like they’d read each other’s minds. Paulo felt that shift in the heaviness of his sac, made even heavier by the knowledge that, in the midst of it all, Liza smelled him too.

‘Can … Can I touch them?’ she asked.

‘Of course.’ If he could smell his own emotions, he wondered if there would be a tiny nip of jealousy in the air.

For a second, she stood at the side of the bed studying the situation and sniffing. Her eyes went from one man to the other, then she crawled onto the mattress. What happened next left Paulo breathless and fully, even painfully erect. With a sigh of frustration, she kicked off her pumps, hiked her pencil skirt up until she could spread her legs, and there was a collective gasp of surprise as she straddled Livinia. ‘Don’t stop what you’re doing,’ she ordered.

Paulo had never dreamed her to be the kind of person who would just hop right into the action, certainly not if all that he’d been told by her was true, so what the hell was going on?

As she wriggled her way up over Livi in an awkward knee walk, the men making room for her as she went, she paused just above her rib cage, and as the men laved sloppy kisses over her Livi’s breasts,

Liza laid an open palm on the bare shoulder of each man and began to deliberately knead and massage in circular motions up toward their necks. They both moaned and shivered beneath her touch, and it was the little intuitive gasp from Livi that telegraphed what was to come. Paulo's heart hammered, and his cock felt like it would shove its way through his trousers. Surely she wouldn't. Surely she wasn't bold enough. He held his breath as Liza's hands paused to stroke each man's hair, then snaked down and around to each man's throat beneath their chins, lifting and shifting and making it just uncomfortable enough until she had forced the first touch of nose to nose then breath to breath. Lust did the rest as both men fairly shot to their knees, their mouths locking on each other in a deep, probing tongue kiss with the luscious sound of heavy breathing and wet against wet. Both men sighed, and Livi whimpered. Then she reached to fist their cocks and stroked them in unison. Liza inhaled a heavy gasp.

'There, that's better, that smells like unbridled lust, that smells like the place where the rule-breaking happens and it all gets good.' Her last word ended in a sharp breath as the two kissing men enveloped her in arms that slid over her bottom and up under her skirt. Their mouths came to lave and lick each side of her neck as, in unison, their hands found her breasts. She managed a little yelp of surprise as one of Livi's hands worked its way between her spread legs.

It was than that Paulo catapulted into action. He wrapped an arm around Liza's waist and pulled her bodily off the bed and, though he hadn't intended to do it, he caught her mouth, an open O of surprise, as she turned her head over her shoulder at his sudden invasion. Then she swallowed his breath as her tongue darted in and out against his and her arms came up over her head and around his neck. Somewhere in the back of his mind, he was aware that the three on the bed had picked up where they left off, a little more frantically, a little more urgently. Or maybe it was his own urgency he felt. Eating at her mouth as though his life depended on it, the arm around her waist pulled her backward against his belly, and his splayed hand moved up to cup her breasts. She squirmed against him and gasped, and though her feet touched the floor, her legs didn't engage. Still holding her against him, he pulled her onto his lap and onto the overstuffed chair near the bed, and they both began speaking breathlessly into each other's mouth. 'We can't do this, we're being watched,' he managed just as she spoke.

'We need to be able to smell them.' She kissed him and pulled away, off his lap, shoving her skirt back in place. 'We need to be able to smell them,' she gasped again, and with an effort that felt like it ripped him open, she scrambled to the far side of the bed near the headboard. Her chest rose and fell as though she were about to hyperventilate. She closed her eyes and struggled for control, and fuck if he wasn't more than half tempted to go grab her and take her right there next to the bed – fuck the experiment, fuck it all. Christ, he wanted her!

A few deep breaths and she once more focused her attention on the trio in the bed. David had thrust up into Livi's pussy and Pietro knelt behind him, rubbing saliva over David's anus with one hand. He spat onto his other and stroked his cock until it glistened in the subdued lighting, then he thrust home, and even Paulo could sense the edginess, the shift in scent. As far as he knew, these two men had never had any encounters that weren't strictly hetero until now, but he was pretty sure Liza Calendar had just inadvertently opened a whole new vista of lust for them. His own cock ached under its heavy weight, and he struggled to concentrate.

'It's the edge,' Liza said, breathing heavily. 'It's crossing boundaries and playing it a little dangerously, that's the scent of sex Martelli needs to strive for. That's the driving force, the creative force, and, God, it's good. It's so good.'

It was a domino effect with Livi coming first, driving her heels into David's ribs, then David following suit, with Pietro pumping out his wad into David's ass. Paulo watched stunned as Liza's whole body quivered in sympathy. Dear God, she was coming! The scent alone was making her come. And Goddamnit, he wasn't going to come in his trousers again like some teenage boy, but hell he was close.

'That was amazing,' she said. 'Is there any paper to write on because there's something that happens with a *ménage* that makes for a base note that's not there when there are just two people, not that I've had that much experience, but it's something different and it's almost like someone is ... Paulo? Paulo what are you doing?'

He ploughed around the bed and grabbed her arm, then he dragged her into the bathroom and slammed the door. 'You know exactly what I'm doing. If you want me to think,' he said, shoving his hand up her skirt and tugging the crotch of her panties aside until he could finger the swell of her. 'Then you're gonna have to help me out a little bit, because I'm way past thinking at the moment.' He fumbled with the condom from his pocket and reintroduced his mouth to hers for the few prickly awkward seconds it took them to sheath him, then he lifted her against the wall, shifted his hips forward, and drove into her, both of them growling like wildcats. Her arms encircled his neck and her fist clenched at the back of his shirt until he could feel the gouge of her nails. The harder he thrust, the harder she took it and gave it right back, spurring her heals in his hips like he was a stallion she planned to ride and tame, and fuck if he didn't believe she could do exactly that. It was over way too soon, but the need was too great, and they did have a job to do. He convulsed his load into her until he thought his back would break while she clenched his cock in the strangle hold of another orgasm. Then she kissed him hard. 'Damn, you smell good,' she whispered against his neck.

'Damn, we smell good together,' he managed between gasps for breath.

She laughed a low, raunchy chuckle. 'You're learning, Mr Delacour. You're learning.'

Chapter Eleven

In spite of the late night past, Jim was in early. He'd just made himself coffee in the kitchen after yet another intimate session with his cock in the bathroom. And he hadn't slept much. He just couldn't get what he'd seen at The Mount's villa out of his head. He'd known coming in what to expect. Coraline had given him the heads-up and told him that if he didn't want to be a part of the very unconventional experiments for the new line, she would understand. But if he were actually going to earn his place at Martelli Fragrance and earn the respect of Coraline and Paulo, then he'd have to grow a pair. Coraline Martelli didn't get where she was by playing it safe and with the competition being so stiff in the perfume industry, and considering the difficult situation Martelli Fragrance was dealing with, innovation was essential for survival. Still, he'd never expected anything so bold and brash. Beyond that he'd never expected straight-shooting Liza Calendar to roll up her sleeves, jump right on in, and take control of the situation.

'She's a natural, Dom,' Coraline had said proudly when she'd viewed the video, with Jim sitting next to her blushing like a lobster and shifting from ass cheek to ass cheek hoping his boss wouldn't notice his hard-on. When Coraline reached the part where Paulo had pulled Liza Calendar off the bed, she brought her fingers to her lips with a little sigh. 'On the other hand, as well as she handles Paulo's dominant streak, it's more likely she's a good switch.' That had sent Jim scrambling to the internet later to find out what a switch was. Christ! Sometimes the world of The Mount scared the shit out of him, but most of the time it had him slapping the monkey until repetitive strain syndrome was a real concern. He'd been given an open invitation to check it out, but he hadn't managed to get up the courage. He wanted to. He really did, but he supposed his Midwest upbringing was just prudish enough that he struggled with the idea of sex on demand with different, even multiple partners. Was too much of a good thing really even better? And why wasn't he brave enough to find out? Jim resisted the urge to view the video again. He'd already watched it three times, and each time he'd ended up with his cock in his hand.

There was a soft knock on his door and Vera Bellini sauntered in. He tried not to notice how the round tops of her breasts played peekaboo from beneath the one-too-many open buttons of her siren-red blouse, but it was difficult when she laid a folder on his desk and leaned down until he could practically bury his face in her cleavage. She opened the folder. 'I need these signed.' She pointed an apple-coloured nail to where the document needed his signature, then offered a smile. 'I'm filling in for Alessandro today. His mother's having surgery – nothing life-threatening, but they're close and he wanted to be there.'

'Hope everything goes well,' Jim mumbled, as he scribbled his signature, glad that she couldn't see the swelling in the general area of his fly.

She leaned closer, her voice nearly an intimate whisper. 'I don't know what went on last night with Ms Martelli, but the woman's actually smiling. Ear to ear.' She batted her lashes at him and leaned a little closer. 'You don't see that very often. You have a meeting with her this morning, don't you? Any idea what's going on?'

'If I told you, I'd have to kill you.' He offered her his best James Bond smirk.

She responded with a wicked smile. 'Well it must have been very good for business to make her smile like that. I'd love to have been a fly on the wall.'

She had no idea, Jim thought.

As she turned to go, she stopped at the door and stepped back to face him. 'What does a girl have to do to get you to go out for coffee with her after work this evening?'

He blinked, and it took him half a second to realize he was staring at her with his mouth open. He quickly recovered and offered a lazy smile. 'All a girl has to do is ask.'

'Good,' she said. 'Consider yourself asked. I'll stop back by your office say a little after five?'

'I'll be here,' he said,' leaning back in his chair as though he were suddenly king of the universe. To be honest, seeing the way Paulo had dragged Liza into the bathroom after last night's session had left him a little discouraged. He'd been in Rome nine months now and hadn't actually dated anyone. Though in all fairness, his position with Martelli Fragrance had an extremely steep learning curve, and it had only been in the last few weeks that he started to feel he had a handle on things enough to breathe, enough to consider at least some semblance of life outside Martelli. He considered a date for coffee with the very well-endowed Vera Bellini a great beginning.

Liza had been up since five. Though some of it was probably jet lag, most of it was the buzzing high that last night had given her. She'd not actually gotten to bed until two. Her mind had been too busy with ideas, with notes and observations about the night. She had written them up and sent them off to Coraline, Paulo, and Jim, and then from those notes she put together some thoughts and observations for the story she would do for *High Rising*. All that before she'd gone to bed. She'd had no idea what to expect, and would have probably opted out gracefully if she had, even though it was exactly the kind of experiment she would have dreamed up for the best way to link sex and fragrance. She was amazed at how easy it was to follow her intuition and her nose. In spite of the arousal such an atmosphere generated, she had not been nearly as uncomfortable as she would have thought – at least not once she let her nose take control.

The very literal climax, of course, was Paulo taking her in the bathroom against the wall. She couldn't think about it without feeling the tension below her belly. God, the man smelled amazing, and he was right, they smelled amazing together. When she was unable to go back to sleep at five, she put on shorts and went out for a walk. She knew Paulo wouldn't approve, but she loved the feel of the city when it slept, or came as close to sleeping as it ever did. She hadn't showered when she got home last night. She couldn't bear washing the smell of Paulo off her body, and after the walk, it was with a sigh of resignation that she'd showered and gotten ready for the early morning meeting at Martelli. She straightened her skirt as the lift closed and she ascended to the Executive Suites of the Martelli Building. Her heart did a somersault. This was not at all what she had expected of her time with Martelli Fragrance, but she was pretty sure no one turned down Coraline Martelli. And in all honesty, as intriguing as the situation and working with Paulo Delacour was, she didn't want to.

'Good morning, Ms Calendar.' A woman who looked well turned out enough to be a movie star addressed Liza as she got off the elevator. 'I'm Vera, and I'm filling in for Alessandro, Ms Martelli's PA. If you'll –'

'I've got it, Vera. No worries. I'll escort Ms Calendar in.' The wave of lightning storm and forest floor scent arrived before Paulo as he immerged from the kitchen and motioned Liza inside. Even as the muscles in her stomach did their version of a happy dance, she didn't miss the tang of displeasure that suddenly rolled off Vera's perfect body, and there was definitely an undertone of acidic jealousy even though the woman offered both of them a cheerful smile.

'Very well then. Let me know if there's anything either of you need.' She gave them both a little nod of her perfectly coiffed dark hair and turned to go, her very expensive, very high heels click-clicking on the marble floor as she went.

Before Liza had time to dwell much on Vera, Paulo nodded her into the small kitchen. 'It was a short night. I need coffee,' he said, as the mocha maker began to bubble out the elixir of life. 'Want some?'

'No thanks. I've already had enough to make a bull moose twitch.'

'Then I would say you're good for at least another cup. Everyone knows moose don't handle their caffeine very well.' He raised an eyebrow and nodded to the pot.

'Well, OK, but only so you don't have to drink alone.'

For a moment he went about the business of making and pouring coffee and the air felt tight with the mineral scent of awkwardness. Then he handed her a cup and his gaze became serious. 'You all right?'

'Yes! Yes, I'm fine. Still amazed by last night's experience.'

He dropped his gaze to his coffee. 'I gathered as much from the email with attachments that you sent out this morning at, what was it? Two thirty?'

Her laugh came out nervous and high-pitched. 'And you were up at two thirty in the morning to receive it?'

'Believe me,' he said in a scuffed velvet voice that made him sound like he'd just gotten out of bed, 'after experiencing you in action last night, I had a lot of things on my mind but sleep wasn't one of them.' The look he raked over her body was so brief anyone observing would have missed it, but she felt it from the crown of her head to the crotch of her panties and all the way to the tips of her toes. And she felt the aftermath of the blush that climbed her throat, but before she could respond, he spoke again. 'I won't even pretend that it was just because the experiment was … stimulating. And don't you pretend you don't smell me right now, because I sure as hell smell you.' Like something predatory, he was in her personal space before she could do more than offer a soft gasp of surprise. Then he brushed a wisp of a coffee-scented kiss across her lips with just enough of an intimation of tongue that she'd have dropped her coffee cup if she'd not been close enough to the counter to set it down with an aromatic splash. His warm breath feathered across her throat and her neck until she could feel the heat of his lips against her ear as he whispered. 'Coraline tells me I can fuck you if I want, as long as I get your nose to work for Martelli.' Before she could protest, he ran fingertips along her bare arm leaving a trail of goose flesh. 'I've got news for Coraline, I would do whatever it takes to stay close to that delicious nose of yours …' his tongue flicked over the seashell hollow of her ear '… and the rest of the irresistible woman that goes with it.'

Oh for fuck sake, please say she didn't just whimper. He stepped back, offered her a lazy cat-got-the-cream smile and handed her back her cup. 'Best not keep Coraline waiting. She's as anxious to talk about what you sniffed out last night as I am.' He nodded toward the door.

On legs that were none too steady, she followed Paulo into a corner conference room with an incredible view of Bernini's angels gracefully flanking the Ponte Sant'Angelo that spanned the Tiber to Castle Sant'Angelo and Vatican City beyond. Paulo motioned her to sit across from Jim, who blushed and offered an overly enthusiastic good morning. Clearly last night was as much of an eye-opener for him as it had been for her, and he wasn't stupid: surely he knew exactly why Paulo had dragged her, more than willingly, off to the bathroom after their little experiment. Paulo sat down next to her just as the not-overly-happy-smelling Vera delivered coffee and the morning's selection of Italian pastries. She was just about to sit down next to Jim when Coraline blew into the room looking like she'd just been shopping on the Via del Corso.

'Vera, I need you to take care of a few items for me while I'm in this meeting. I emailed a list to your computer.' The dirty dishwater smell of malcontent bloomed so strong with the woman's own damp root scent that it nearly made Liza's eyes water. And beneath that there was something basic, something acidic hidden under buttercream. She was always amazed that no one else could smell such strong swings of emotions. The look on the woman's face didn't change. She offered Coraline an enthusiastic smile and nodded her good-bye to everyone at the table. Truly, no one had noticed but Liza.

Everyone waited in silence until Coraline had opened her laptop, sipped her coffee, and carefully chosen a sweet roll, all of which she did as though she were completely alone in the room and in absolutely no hurry. She straightened her jacket of sea green linen, offered an angelic smile, and then turned her full attention on Liza, who suddenly felt like a rabbit in the headlights.

'Liza Calendar, I know you're still jet-lagged, and I am very aware of what jet-lag can do to one's ability to focus and process information in a coherent way.'

Lisa felt heat rush to her face and her whole body tensed. Here it was, another person telling her that her olfactory sensitivity was really something she needed to see a shrink about because it was just a figment of her imagination. She tried not to clench her hands where they lay folded in front of her laptop. Beneath the table, Paulo move his thigh just enough to touch hers, an act that felt like the completion of a circuit, and the scent that peaked between them was electric. She held her breath as Coraline scrolled through her notes, shaking her head as she did so. In her mind's eye, Liza was already slinking back to the Martelli flat to pack for the next flight home to Portland.

'Yes, jet-lagged.' Coraline spoke as much to herself as to anyone at the table. Then her gaze locked on Liza and held. 'I can only imagine what brilliance you might have come up with if you'd been well-rested and if I hadn't played the bitch and dumped such a shocker in your lap so unexpectedly. Liza, darling, this is bloody brilliant.'

There was a collective sigh as Coraline's face broke into a broad smile and Liza nearly slid out of her chair from the sense of relief that rolled over her.

'You didn't waste any time, did you, Ms Calendar,' she said. 'And neither have we,' she nodded to the two men who sat po-faced at the table looking down at their own laptops and the copies of the presentation. 'I dare say we've had even less sleep than you last night, Liza. Scent excites us at Martelli, and what we observed with you last night excited us in the extreme.' She nodded to Paulo and offered a wicked quirk of a smile, 'Some of us more than others.'

Liza blushed, but Paulo only smiled to himself.

She continued. 'I had Vera put together a couple of slides for us this morning just so we could all look at the plan and brainstorm together. But before I did that I called human resources who are liaising with my lawyers, here and in the States, to put together a contract for you.' Before Liza could respond, Coraline raised a hand to stop her. 'I know you run your own business, and I also know that your partner is quite capable of taking care of things on US end until we're finished here. Also, as I've said before, I'm very happy for you to take a story away from your experience with Martelli, minus anything that involves The Mount, and Paulo will explain to you about The Mount later. Now ...' she ploughed forward without asking if Liza would accept Martelli's offer. '... here's the plan. Feel free to suggest any improvements.' She pulled up the first slide, and in typical Coraline Martelli fashion, steamrolled right on in to the main event.

'The business of scent is the business of attraction. I believe you said something to that effect last night, Liza, though a little bit more crudely. Attraction is the path to sex, and there has never been a point when the scents humans add to their own scent hasn't ultimately been for the purpose of attraction – and sex. Paulo has been saying all along that we need to approach the new line more from that basic premise, and watching you in my office and then at the villa last night has convinced me he's right.'

She flipped to the next slide. 'Based on your report and what we could observe, these are the scents we'll be looking to create for Martelli's new line. They'll either be unisex or we'll create scents for both sexes, depending on what your nose thinks is best.' The slide read:

1. Romantic vanilla
2. Dom
3. sub
4. Kink
5. Wild animal/al fresco

She gave Liza a chance to take them in then said, 'Of course we'll have better names for them, but these are the scents we're looking for, especially in the brave new world that's obsessed with BDSM and kink.' Once again she gave Liza no time to respond. 'You said last night, in your report and while you were in the room with the trio from The Mount that it was the edgy, kinky scent of sex that would attract people, like the practice of a woman dabbing a bit of her own scent on her pulse points when she spends time with a man with whom she hopes to have sex. By changing and rearranging our *ménage* as you did last night, especially in the way you did, you changed the scent. After you left, a team collected the clothing, the bedding, and the towels used to clean up after sex. Everything was then bagged and taken to our labs to analyze for corresponding scents. What I need to know from you, Ms Calendar, what we all need to know from you, is if you can help us set conditions and come up with the right sexual combinations to reproduce, in our research facility, the basic olfactory and pheromonal building blocks for the scents we've listed.'

When no one spoke, when all eyes were on her, Liza took a deep breath, smelling the mix of excitement and anticipation in the room with just a nip of doubt thrown in to keep her on her toes. 'You want me to sniff people having sex to help you create perfumes that will generate similar responses?'

Everyone nodded in unison.

There was a tightness in her chest at what was actually being expected of her, and her own scent smelled of fire freshly kindled. 'I can sniff out all of these things. I can walk down any street in any city and pick up intimations of all of what you're looking for in the new line and more besides, but I have no idea how to go about orchestrating a sexual encounter to offer the results you want, nor how to create fragrances that correspond.'

'We can orchestrate it.' This time it was Paulo who spoke. 'That won't be a problem. And of course we don't expect you to know how to create the corresponding fragrances. That's our job. What we need to know is if you can come up with ideas for who and how and under what circumstances we might elicit the desired effects. The rest we can teach you. You said it yourself that while last night was a good idea, it wasn't the way you would have set it up, and you changed it. All right, Ms Calendar, what we're asking is for you to plan it, for you to tell us what your nose tells you needs to happen in order for us to create a base for these five fragrances.'

Again all eyes were on her. 'You have Martelli's full resources behind you, Liza,' Coraline said. 'We're all very excited about this line, a line which would be nearly impossible to do without some serious innovation, a good deal of which will involve your nose and your intuition. Can you do it?'

Liza stared at the list of future fragrances still up on the slide and felt her pulse quicken as ideas flashed through her head. 'How much access will I have to … well to people I need to do stuff like what the *ménage* did last night?'

'Unlimited,' Coraline said. She nodded to the slide. 'Whatever you need. You'll have. Can you do it?' She asked again.

Liza's mind was racing. This was outrageous. This was insane, and yet she already had ideas flooding into her brain about how to elicit just the right scents that would drive each fragrance. She released a shaky breath. 'Yes. I can do it.'

There was a collective sigh of relief, and she felt Paulo's thigh press tighter against hers.

'Good,' Coraline said. 'Paulo can see that whatever resources you need are yours for the asking, and he'll take you back to The Mount's villa tonight, introduce you to the players, and help you understand what The Mount is all about. Oh, and there will be a non-disclosure you'll have to sign for the protection of The Mount, but it shouldn't interfere with your article. Of course, the Bernini flat is yours for the duration. And I trust you'll find the salary and the benefits more than adequate. You can talk to human resources about that when we're finished here. And –' she reached into her briefcase which sat on the chair next to her, and pulled out a Kindle in a blue leather cover. 'I don't know if you read erotica, Liza, but if you don't, now would be a good time to start. I've taken the liberty of downloading some classics, some of my favourites and some favourites of the people at The Mount. Anything else you want to add to your erotic research library, feel free to, at Martelli's expense, of course.' She handed the Kindle to Liza. Liza had her own and she did have quite a stash of erotica. With her lack of a love life due to her sensitive nose, erotica had been about as close as she got to hot sex before Paulo.

'Also, I've had a good collection of porn added to the entertainment library in the flat, though you probably won't have time to watch it, you might find it handy for inspiration.'

Liza struggled to get her head around the idea of being paid and housed in a luxury flat in Rome to watch porn, read erotica, and orchestrate … well orchestrate great-smelling sex. Surely she must still be asleep in her cramped coach seat on the plane dreaming about the delicious-smelling man from the lounge that she would never meet again. Surely her brain was just compensating for her total lack of a sex life and for the royal fuck-up that had been her almost-relationship with Carl. She would have pinched herself, but as the stroking and kneading of Paulo's hand against her thigh made her scent rise up and wrap around his like an intimate embrace, she decided if she were dreaming, she sure as hell didn't want to wake up any time soon.

'I'll leave you in Paulo's quite capable hands,' Coraline didn't even try to hide the knowledge that she knew exactly what that meant. 'He knows Martelli as well as I do, and he's on the High Council at The Mount, much to his chagrin.' She offered him a smile, and Liza warmed to the growl at the back of his throat. If she didn't get out of here soon, she was going to push back her chair and straddle the man, and surely that wasn't a very good way to influence the boss. But then again, the boss had turned her over to her dominatrix head of security and then taken her to witness a small orgy last night and asked her to sniff it out with running commentary. It was very quickly becoming evident that Martelli Fragrance did not follow the typical business model.

Chapter Twelve

Liza's office at Martelli was far nicer than the rented space above a law firm from which she and Addie ran *High Rising*. She worked for several hours brainstorming and putting together ideas for the sexy scents Martelli had in mind for its new line. Then Jim picked her up and took her for a tour of the research facilities, dropping her back at her flat a little before five. There was another message on her BlackBerry from Carl, whom she had nearly forgotten about between the excitement of what was happening at Martelli and the heat generating between her and Paulo. In the phone message, he'd had the balls to mention that since they hadn't been having sex, he wasn't sure if they even had a relationship – though he wanted one, he'd added quickly. She couldn't argue that there'd been little between them to begin with, and a relationship with the man was now the last thing she wanted. Cursing under her breath, she decided it was time to gut it up and take care of the situation for good. She returned his call and was surprised, but more than a little relieved, when she got only his voicemail.

'Hi Carl. Sorry I haven't returned your calls. I've been really busy, and I didn't want to talk to you. You're right, of course. There was no real commitment between us, and since I wasn't giving you what you needed, I can't blame you for seeking it elsewhere.' It was surprisingly easy to tell him politely to fuck off. She thought she sounded rather eloquent really. She continued. 'What happened the other night was just a wake-up call for me to realize that it was never going to work for us, and it was time to admit it. I wish you all the best, really, I do, and I have no hard feelings. Let's just let bygones be bygones and get on with our lives.' She broke the connection, relieved that she didn't actually have to talk to him, knowing that he would have argued, and she really didn't want an argument breaking her focus right now.

That done, she looked at her watch, then mentally figured the time difference between Rome and Portland and decided it was late enough to Skype Addie.

Her friend's image appeared on the monitor, short red hair spiked and wet from the shower. 'Hi sweetie,' she said with a bright smile. 'What's going on between you and Carl?'

Leave it to Addie to get right to the point. So she returned the favour. 'I broke it off. Found him banging some bimbo on the kitchen counter and realized at the end of the day, I really didn't care who he shagged as long as it wasn't me.'

Addie offered a sage nod. 'So it was him making you sneeze and not the vicious New York City pollen and leaf mould you'd been blaming. Garbage usually makes me sneeze too.' Her eyes sparkled with sympathetic anger. 'Follow your nose, hon. That's what you always told me. The bastard's been making it sound like everything is rosy when he's called me asking about you. I sort of felt like something was wrong.' She leaned into the monitor and studied Liza. 'You don't look any worse for the wear, sweetie. What's going on?'

Liza couldn't help it. She blushed. 'I met A.P. Delacour.'

'Yes, well I'm not surprised. I mean he is the heir apparent at Martelli.' Her bright blue eyes suddenly widened and her mouth became a round O of understanding. 'Oh. Oh! You mean you *met* A.P. Delacour.' She wiggled her eyebrows. Then swallowed back a 'Fuuuuck!' when Liza only nodded slightly.

'Paulo,' Liza said. 'He goes by Paulo.'

'And how does he smell?'

Only a good friend would ask such a question. Liza rolled her eyes and sighed. 'Heaven couldn't possibly smell better than he does.'

'Details, girl! I want details.' Addie was practically vibrating in her chair.

'I don't have time for details right now. I have to get ready. He's picking me up. But …' she leaned closer to the monitor, and her face nearly hurt from the huge smile '… it appears I'm going to be working for Martelli in quite a different capacity than the interview I'd expected. Martelli Fragrance wants to hire my nose.' With that she filled in her friend as much as she could without too much detail, understanding as she did, the edginess of what they were about to do. Addie assured her that she could take care of *High Rising* until Liza's consulting with Martelli was finished. Before she said goodbye, she made her promise a long Skype sesh with details about the very heavenly smelling Paulo Delacour. Still smiling as she closed her laptop, Liza headed in to take advantage of the swimming pool-sized Jacuzzi bath before she got ready to meet Paulo for their outing to The Mount's villa.

Instead of meeting Vera in his office, Jim met her at the café around the corner from the Martelli Building. He was late getting back from the research facility due to traffic. Clearly she'd had time to go home and change. She wore a pale yellow sundress that hugged her dangerous curves and contrasted beautifully with her golden skin, of which it showed plenty

'I'm very upset with you,' she said with a full-lipped pout that begged to be kissed. 'You took Liza Calendar to visit the research facility and you didn't take me.' She took his hand and pulled him through the back of the coffee shop to a postage stamp sized courtyard where a small fountain tinkled cheerfully amid a tiny garden of cyclamen in varying shades of red. They had barely settled when the waiter delivered two lattes. 'I hope you don't mind,' she said, 'but I took the liberty of ordering for us. Since I'm substituting for Alessandro. I know what everyone drinks.' She settled in at a tiny table and he sat down across from her

'I didn't know you wanted to see the research facility,' he said, focusing on the packets of sugar and his coffee rather than the mounds of her breasts, which rose and fell with each breath above the thin fabric of her dress, completely unrepentant of the brazen press of erect nipples.

'Of course I want to see the facility,' she said, offering him a flirty smile. 'But even more importantly, I want *you* to show it to me.' She leaned across the table, her eyes locked on his, though surely she had to know that it was taking all of his self-control to keep his gaze off her exposed frontage. Then she laughed almost shyly and sat back in her chair. 'What does a girl have to do to get you to pay attention to her, Jim? I thought about a striptease on the top of your desk after mail delivery, but I like my job, and I don't want to get fired.'

If Jim's cock wasn't already paying full attention, it certainly was now. He settled his cup onto the table and shifted in his seat. 'Well either you were very subtle or I am extremely obtuse.' He shrugged. 'Granted that's a real possibility, because if I'd had any idea you were interested I'd have made sure you had my full attention.' His last word ended in a little grunt as she settled a bare foot into his lap and wriggled her toes, offering him an open-mouthed what-do-you-think-of-that sort of look.

Then she giggles wickedly. 'I see I have your full attention now, Jim Dryer.'

'I'd say so, yes.' The yes sounded like a snake hissing as she ran her toes up and down the length of his cock in kneading little grabs that were amazingly agile for a foot.

As if she'd read his thought she whispered. 'Unzip your trousers, Jim. Let me show you just how talented my feet really are.'

He didn't even think twice. With one hand he unzipped and worried his distended penis free from the breach while the other stroked her gripping foot.

'You're big,' she breathed. 'I knew you were. I could tell by the way your trousers ride against your package.' The warm bare skin of her feet moved up and down his shaft. The smile she offered him was almost shy. 'I've made more than a few trips to the ladies room to take care of myself while thinking about that hefty package of yours.' She bit her lip and gasped, and for a minute her stroking of his cock became awkward. He could tell she was shifting to get a hand up under her dress. When she made contact, her eyelids fluttered and she whimpered, 'Mmm, I can't tell you how wet you make me, Jim. Shall I show you my tits? I know you're dying to look at them, but you're always the polite one, aren't you? Always all business and focus.' Without waiting for the response he wasn't sure he had the brains left to give, she pushed down the straps of her dress and let her breasts tumble into plain view. Her nipples were dark and heavy against the puckered rise of her areolae and, even though he couldn't imagine it possible, when she pinched and tweaked them between her thumb and forefinger, they got still bigger.

'I'm going to do better than treat you to coffee, Jim,' she said, sucking her bottom lip and offering a little moan. She rode her fingers with a jerk and grind that shivered up through her breasts. 'I'm going to give you dessert too. And then –' she stood up straight to give him just a glimpse of her fingers darting in and out of her pantyless crotch '– I'll take you back to my place for the main course.' She slipped under the table and in less than a heartbeat, his cock that had responded so deliciously to her long, agile toes was being deep throated in a grip that had him squirming and clenching all over the seat. If she'd left him any brain cells that weren't focused on what she was doing under the table, he might have been worried about the waiter finding them in a compromising position, but she hadn't planned to linger, and it didn't take long before he reared back in the chair and unloaded into her hard-working mouth with her swallowing and sucking for all she was worth.

When she finally came up for air, she wiped her mouth on the back of her hand and offered a wicked smile. 'Now, how about we head over to my place, Jim, and you can tell me all about the research facility … or maybe we'll just do a little research of our own.' She plopped several euro down on the table and reached for his hand, with him still tucking and smoothing as they walked back through the café.

Chapter Thirteen

Paulo had told Liza it would be a formal gathering in the gardens of the villa. She hadn't packed anything formal, but somehow, as if by magic, she had returned to Bernini Place to find a red gown that shimmered like sun-kissed cherries. It displayed the tops of her breasts like soft, round fruit cupped by a tight bodice, which accentuated her waist and caressed the flair of her hips and bottom. It was slit deliciously high up her right thigh. Whoever had done the personal shopping for her not only got her size spot-on, but made sure that all the accessories were included in the ensemble. Ms Martelli had even sent her own personal hairdresser. Though Liza seldom wore her hair up in anything more elaborate than a ponytail, she had to admit, the simple chignon showcased her cheekbones and her long neck. She thought she'd cleaned up rather nicely. The look Paulo gave her when he arrived at the flat, along with the spicy surge in his scent told her he heartily agreed. He picked her up in a midnight blue Porsche, but she barely noticed the car when the man driving it was positively edible in a tux that looked like it had been made for him, which no doubt it has been.

He drove the Porsche like it was an extension of his own body, as once again they headed out of Rome and onto the winding road leading to Tivoli. His running commentary on Roman history and the quarrying of travertine in the area said less about his own nervousness than the citrus note that now capped his scent. That he was nervous did little to calm the citric spike of her own nerves. 'Not everyone will be there tonight,' he said. 'But you'll meet some of the people who'll be participating in our little experiments, and you'll meet the people in charge.'

'Coraline mentioned that you were a member of The Mount's High Council.'

He offered her a quick flash of a smile that seemed to take some effort, and the flint and steel spark of irritability shot through his scent.

'Fidelia's now the head of the High Council,' he said. 'That role changes every four years so that too much power isn't concentrated in the hands of one person. Fidelia's good in the position.' He gave her a quick glance as he downshifted onto the road leading to the villa.

'And you?'

'I'm only on the council because I couldn't get out of it.'

'I take it you're not pleased with the position.'

'I don't consider myself very well suited for it, that's all.'

She slid sideways in her seat and studied him as the Porsche hugged the curves of the mountain road. 'You're a natural leader, Paulo, or you wouldn't be the heir apparent to Martelli Fragrance.'

'I'm the heir apparent because I have a good nose and I have a good sense for the business. The Mount, well that's a completely different animal. You'll understand once you've been introduced.' It almost sounded like she would be having an audience with the pope.

This time the front of the villa was lit with fairy lights, and expensive cars were being driven away by liveried valets after they disgorged the beautiful people from their posh interiors. Liza's stomach knotted, and she was glad that Paulo couldn't smell *her* nerves. She certainly could. As they approached the entrance, he rested a warm hand on her thigh and offered a reassuring smile. 'Don't worry, Liza, you're fabulous, and everyone will know that the second they see you.' Perhaps the man's nose was better than she thought. But then again, it probably didn't take an ace sense of smell to figure out that she was nervous. Paulo shooed the valet away from Liza's door and opened it himself, offering her his hand as she struggled out of the low seat less gracefully than she would have liked. Thanks to Paulo, no one saw her awkwardness around the mantling of his body.

A man who could have passed for a model in his coat and tails and air-brush-perfect black hair handed each of them a flute of prosecco and led them through a long tiled corridor out into a Renaissance garden that surely rivaled the Villa d'Este. Fountains like tumbling streams banistered the wide travertine steps that descended into the terraced garden below. At the end of each terrace, the water spilled down into the next around sculptures of lovers in a whole Kama Sutra of positions, but with that same Bernini attention to detail. Though the statuary seemed to have no effect on Paulo's scent, surely he must be able to tell that it was heating hers up nicely. At the bottom of the steps, he led her into a topiary maze that made her pulse race as it twisted and curved back on itself until she could never find her way back through without his help. And just when she was about to ask him if he was certain he knew where they were going, the maze opened through an arch of shrubbery. There in the middle of a richly mosaicked patio surrounded by the same type of banister fountains that flanked the travertine steps, was a stone dining table, long and slender. At one end, dressed in rich black silk that caressed her full breasts like a second skin, sat Fidelia.

'Ah, our guest has arrived,' she said, offering a smile that was warm enough, but not without the wicked edge Liza had experienced in the basement at Martelli Fragrance.

Paulo cupped Liza's elbow and guided her to stand in front of the table on which a rich array of antipasti had been served up. 'Fidelia and David, you know,' Paulo said. She noticed the man who had been in the *ménage* last night sat opposite her dressed in a black tux not unlike the one Paulo wore. 'And you know Alessandro.' Liza was surprised to find Coraline Martelli's PA smiling broadly at her in an immaculate grey tux with tails. 'Lucia.' He introduced a delicate-boned woman in flounces of pastel taffeta and lace, who looked like she might have just returned from the Land of Fairy, but the scent of her was slightly metallic and charcoal sharp, and Liza knew immediately that the tiny woman was the most dangerous of all to play with. It was clear from her scent that she really wanted to play with the fresh meat Paulo had brought. 'Coraline, of course you know. She's not here at the moment and I don't know where Angelo is.'

'Last I saw he was playing in the dungeon,' the fairy queen said without taking her hungry gaze off Liza.

'No surprise there, Luci,' David said, adding his own raking gaze across Liza. The scent of metal and heat that rose around the table felt predatory, even in its blending of cinnamon and nutmeg curiosity and the coriander smell of skepticism.

'Tell me, how do I smell?' The fairy queen asked, leaning over until her small breasts were visible all the way to large cherry-licorice nipples.

'You smell like you'd like to catch me and eat me in the corner of the garden, bones and all.'

The whole table went silent. Christ, when was she going to learn to keep her mouth shut?

Then David broke into a raucous laugh and everyone else at the table followed suit, including the fairy queen. 'She's got your scent all right, Luci,' he said.

Luci pushed back her chair and moved around the table in a swish, swish of taffeta to stand in front of Liza. 'Tell me, Ms Nose, if I could smell you as well as you can smell me, would I smell nerves?' She brought her nose to rest against the pulse point of Liza's neck, an effort which had her standing on the tippy-toes of her bare feet with one hand resting on Liza's shoulder for balance. Then she inhaled with a sigh. 'Or perhaps I'd smell fear. Or maybe something a little sweeter?' Her hand slipped off Liza's shoulder to cup her breast, which she kneaded before giving Liza's straining nipple a hard pinch.

'You'd probably smell a good mix of all three,' Liza managed with a hiss of breath between her teeth.

'And you can smell us all, Ms Calendar?' The woman asked, walking behind her trailing fingers around and down until they rested low on Liza's belly. Her hot breath smelled of fennel and seaweed against Liza's neck. Next to her, Paulo's scent thickened with protective iron and heat.

'Would you like me to go around the table and sniff everyone for you?' Liza sounded much calmer than she felt. And she certainly wouldn't have to sniff everyone to get their scents. They were all that obvious. But she didn't tell the fairy queen that. Besides, getting past the jitters was less of a challenge with so many intriguing smells.

'Maybe later,' the woman said in a breathy voice.

'For now, sit down and eat, and let us get to know you.' She led Liza back around the table and pulled out a chair between her and David, forcing Paulo to sit across from her. Liza could tell by his scent he wasn't happy about that. Without asking her what she wanted, the fairy queen began filling the plate in front of her with succulent treats. Then, with her fingers she picked up a ripe, juicy olive and shoved it between Liza's lips. 'There, darling, isn't that nice,' she said. 'David and Fidelia have both told us about their experiences with your magnificent nose. And, of course, Paulo's experiences, as much as we know of them, have been whispered amongst us in hushed tones, so I think we can safely assume we know more about you than you do about us.'

'So what is The Mount then, some sort of fetish sex club?' Liza managed before Paulo growled at her response, and the fairy queen stuffed a piece of basil and tomato bruschetta into her mouth. Liza bit and gnawed and chewed like mad struggling to maintain good table manners. There was a titter of laughter around the table.

'So Paulo really has kept his mouth shut about us?'

Liza nodded and covered her overly-full mouth.

'No one knows anything about The Mount unless they're members, or have special dispensation, and you fall into the latter category, darling,' Fidelia said, her eyes locked on Liza's mouth as though she found the mastication fascinating.

'I suppose you could say we're a fetish club, but a sex cult would be more accurate, though probably no less offensive to the ears of the uninitiated, or to Paulo,' the fairy queen said. Paulo growled again. Then she held a glass of wine up to Liza's lips and slapped her hands away when she attempted to take it for herself. As Liza gave up the battle and leaned forward to take the drink, the fairy queen tipped it just a little too much, sending a cascade of primitivo sluicing down into Liza's cleavage. 'Oh dear. How clumsy of me,' she said, making a groping effort to wipe up the spill with a thick linen napkin.

If looks could kill, the look Paulo sent the woman would have been fatal, but he said nothing, only turned to Liza and offered an apologetic grimace. 'Come on, I'll show you where the ladies room is so you can clean up.'

'Not necessary, Paulo.' Fidelia raised a hand. 'Sylvia can show her. There's business we need to sort, and we don't want to bore poor Liza.' She nodded to a tiny woman in a miniscule French maid's uniform with masses of dark hair tucked up under a lacy cap. She offered Liza a bright smile and motioned her to follow. Paulo nodded reassuringly.

It hadn't taken Liza long to clean herself. Very little of the wine had actually gotten on the gown. Most had splashed across her neck and cleavage. She had immediately dismissed the maid, promising that she could find her own way back to the table. In truth, she wasn't in any real hurry to do so. She figured Paulo would be discussing with them The Mount's willingness to help with his little experiment and, apparently those at the table, minus Coraline Martelli and this Angelo person, made up the High Council – whatever the hell that meant.

She took her time freshening up, and decided that with Fidelia dismissing her so the council could talk business, and with the glorious full moon, it was a perfect night to explore the villa's exquisite renaissance garden. Of course there was a grotto. Every renaissance garden had a grotto, but as she approached it, the watery smell of the fountain that cascaded over its secret depths and the smell of the lush greenery all around were subsumed in the scent of sex. Though Liza could hear only the sound of running water, which drowned out the sounds of pleasure, the scent was unmistakable, so she turned away, not wanting to interrupt the fun. She felt her own heat kindle inside the lacy red thong as she recalled the fairy queen's declaration that The Mount was a sex cult. Did she really think that would somehow appall Liza? Liza could think of no place better to study the scents of attraction and arousal, nor could she think of any place where Paulo might better recruit the help they would need to generate just the right scents for the five new perfumes Martelli was planning.

She had not been led back through the maze when Sylvia had shown her to the ladies room, so it would be no hardship to find her way back to Paulo and the council when the time came and, since she wasn't anxious to be scrutinized further, she continued her explorations. The place was a pornographic version of the Villa d'Este, with each sculpture and each fountain a little naughtier than the one before. There were fountains with broad-chested, muscular-assed men with their faces buried in water gushing pussies of full-breasted, round-hipped women. There were threesomes in every combination imaginable doing every thing imaginable. There were scenes of seduction from Greek mythology, complete with pornographic detail lacking in all other artistic representations Liza had ever seen. As she wound her way amid the fountains and the foliage, the scent of sex blended into the rising night in nooks and crannies and hidey-holes that she was sure were designed especially for such encounters. Overhead an owl trilled and the grunt of an orgasm filtered from behind a flowering shrub. Even the heady scent of its blossoms couldn't block out the moment of release. To avoid having to walk around a couple in mid-fuck on the edge of one of the stone benches, she turned behind a sculpture of a very well-endowed satyr who was about to bury his cock in the exposed pussy of a startled young woman. It was then that she realized not only had she come to the stone wall that surely must delineate the edge of the garden, but she was also lost. She looked around for the travertine steps, hoping that she could see them from a distance and somehow make her way around the outer edge of the maze, but the foliage was too high and the corner of the garden in which she now found herself was too dark. Retracing her steps to where she thought she had left the couple mid-fuck, she had hoped her nose would lead her back to the centre of the garden where the council was meeting. She didn't want Paulo to worry.

Somehow she ended up by a fountain of Psyche and Eros in a far more erotic embrace than any she had ever seen depicted. Opposite the fountain was a stone archway with a heavy wooden door standing open. There was a light shining from inside. As she drew nearer, she could see that the door led down a set of worn travertine steps. Clearly the wall, the door and the steps were older than the rest of the villa, but then everything had its roots in antiquity in Italy. The light from the depths was an orange glow that danced like firelight. The steps were steep and the maw beneath the wall looked anything but inviting. Liza would have turned and tried another path if not for the scent of sex emanating from the depths. But it was more than just the scent of sex. It was the scent of lots of sex. It was almost like the history of sex written in stone. Trying to sip little gulps of the olfactory feast, as though she feared she might disturb any occupants, she tiptoed closer. The scent of deep earth permeated the air, the scent at the boundary where soil and growth give way to bedrock and cavern. From below she was almost certain she heard a moan. It was followed by the sharp scents of flint and steel and sulphur, of that first spark of fire against dry twigs. It was sex as she had never smelled it, and though she knew she shouldn't, though she knew she should find her way back to the council meeting, her feet moved forward almost as though they had a mind of their own, and slowly, carefully, she made her way down the worn steps, bracing her hand against the dry cool stone of the wall.

She descended one flight and the steps curved back under themselves, going deeper. She could hear the sound of dripping water, more irregular than the tinkling of the fountains. She reckoned the steps had turned back into the grounds beneath the villa. There were sconces along the wall that flickered with gas lighting. It wasn't difficult to see her path, but it wasn't easy either. She had just begun the second flight of steps when there was a sharp crack of sound and someone cried out. She covered her own mouth to hold back a yelp, but the covering of her mouth meant that her nose took the scent deep into her sinuses, and the scent was marshy thick, mineral water sharp, laced with the tide pool of female heat. There was another crack, another moan and the deep rumble of a man's voice, too muffled for her to understand, but by the tone of his voice and by the sharp metal scent of his arousal, there was no missing the fact that he was in charge.

As she descended the second flight of steps, she could smell old leather, heavy perspiration, and other wet smells that made her heart pound in her chest, that made her own wet smell sharp-edged and anise seeded with just a touch of wet metal fear, and enough cinnamon and cloves of curiosity to push her forward. She knew where she was, as sure as she knew her own name. This was the dungeon. It had to be. As the stairs gave way to uneven stone floor, the room opened into a cavernous space, the smell of which was so overwhelming that Liza's knees gave from under her and she dropped onto the last of the steps, both hands tight across her mouth to hold back the gasp.

Chapter Fourteen

In the centre of the room was a bed that was more like a wooden rack. On it lay a woman cuffed spread-eagle and silenced by the ball gag in her mouth. She wore only black stockings and a black corset that forced her breasts up high and tight. Her hips had been elevated by something that didn't look soft enough to be a pillow, but it ensured that her pussy was exposed and open at the perfect angle for penetration. From the scent, she was more than ready for the man kneeling between her legs, leather trousers pulled down to expose his red-welted ass and his very heavy erection. From a wooden table next to the bed, he took a string of hefty anal beads from a selection of dildos and butt plugs arranged on black velvet, then he leaned forward and eased the beads one at a time into her well-lubricated anus.

It was only when Liza found the strength to get to her feet and tiptoe into the room that she got the whole picture. The flint and steel male heat, the driving force of the olfactory story unfolding before her nose was not the man kneeling between the woman's legs, but another man, a man sitting in a ladder-back chair, turned front to back so that his long jean-clad legs were splayed on either side. His feet were bare and he was naked from the waist up. His face was silhouetted and lost in shadow. His tattooed, muscular arms were draped over the back of the chair as he surveyed the couple on the bed. 'Hold your wad, Vittorio,' he called out. 'You'll come when I say you can come, when I say Chiara can come. Maybe I'll let her come and make you hold it. I wonder just how full your sac will get, just how hard your cock will get if I make you watch me fuck her. Hmmm?'

Crack! The end of the bullwhip that Liza hadn't noticed in the man's hand snapped out so quickly and so perfectly controlled across Vittorio's bare ass that Liza didn't have time to force back her cry.

'Stop!' The man said as she turned to run. And in spite of the hair raising along the back of her bare neck, in spite of the fear tightening her belly in a cold metal clench, she obeyed.

'Ask Vittorio how the whip across his bare ass feels before you consider running.' He said all of that without looking at her, but Vittorio's eyes and the wide mascara-darkened eyes of Chiara were on her.

She stood unmoving. It was not the scent of fear rising from her pores that made her knees weak. It was the forest fire inferno of lust rolling off the man in the chair in waves that were nearly physical.

'Come here,' he said, still not looking at her.

Did lust always overcome fear? She didn't know, but it certainly seemed to be doing just that for her as she moved in steps she was hardly aware of toward the man with the whip, sniffing as she went.

'In this dungeon, I'm the audience, woman. I don't need any help with that task.' He still hadn't looked at her. His grip on the handle of the whip tightened, but the cinnamon scent of his curiosity curled itself around the inferno of lust, and she knew he wouldn't hit her, at least not just yet. 'Liza Calendar, I presume,' he said, still toying with the handle of the bullwhip.

'Yes.' Her voice came out rough and throaty as though she had forgotten how to use it.

He threw back his head and laughed, having no

trouble finding the resonant fullness of his own voice. In the flickering light of the wall sconces his hair looked like burnt copper, curled around his ears and low on his neck in the dampness of his own dark wood-scented perspiration. 'At last I meet the one everyone is speaking of in hushed tones, the Nose.' Before she could respond, his arm darted out and snaked around her, pulling her down on his knee into the heat of his body. 'So tell me, Nose, what do you smell?' Before she could say anything, his hand fisted in her hair, and he pulled her to his mouth, nipping at her lips until they opened, until his tongue could battle its way in and steal her breath. When he pulled away, breathing hard enough for both of them, he said again. 'What do you smell?'

'I smell burnt sugar and the spark just before a flame, and smoke on dark wood. I smell dry summer earth and cloves and sunbaked grass. I smell –'

He kissed her again, and lifted her in one arm while he shifted the chair around with the other, making a loud scrape of wooden legs against stone before he shoved up her skirt and settled her astraddle the heavy press of his hard-on through his jeans. 'My nose may not be as sophisticated as yours, but I smell your pussy,' he said, rocking and raking himself up against the crotch of panties she knew were wet. He dropped his face into her cleavage and bit. 'And I smell your lust.' Then as if she weighed nothing he shifted her around so that she still sat on his lap but she could see the couple on the bed in front of them.

'Chiara, Vittorio, this is Liza Calendar, Martelli Fragrance's new nose, and I think it would be really welcoming of us if we let her smell you two fucking, don't you?'

They both nodded, wide-eyed.

'Leave the beads in her little asshole, Vittorio. You

know our Chiara likes to have all of her holes filled.' Liza watched as the man grabbed Chiara by her hips and shoved home. She uttered a stifled cry into the ball gag and Liza could see tears making mascara-blackened tracks out the corner of her eyes and down her face. As the two began to fuck, the man beneath Liza shifted and rocked against the damp crotch of her panties until she could feel the shape of his hard-on rubbing a wet trough between her labia. She had hardly been aware of her own shifting and rocking until his heavy hand moved up under her the slit of her gown and began stroke and tweak her clit.

'Don't. Please don't,' she whispered. 'I'm here with someone.'

'From what I could see, that didn't matter much when you were with Fidelia. Oh yes, I was watching the action, lovely Liza. That's what the cameras are for. Maybe you'd prefer that I turn you over my knee and spank you. Hmm? You did come into my dungeon uninvited after all.'

'If Ms Calendar is going to get spanked, it'll be me doing the spanking.' Paulo's scent cut through the coriander and sulphur of confusion that had engulfed her. Breathing in the lightning storm and desert of him gave her courage to shove her way off the man's lap. She stumbled backward and would have fallen on her ass if Paulo hadn't caught her.

'She's a guest here at The Mount and doesn't have clearance to play. You know that, Angelo.' He slid a protective arm around her and she breathed in great gulps of his scent, now mixed liberally with the metal and heat of anger.

The sounds and scents of orgasm erupted from the couple on the bed who were just too far gone to hold off any longer no matter if the roof fell in around them. And in all honesty no one was paying attention anymore. Angelo stretched his long lean body out in the chair and folded arms tattooed with multi-coloured dragons across his chest. 'She doesn't have clearance to invade my dungeon either, does she?' He raked Liza with a wicked gaze followed by the heavy scent of lust that took her breath away. Her own scent spiked in response. 'You know the rules. She has to be punished.'

'What happened, Liza?' Paulo asked, still holding her protectively.

'It was the smell.' It pissed her off that her voice came out shaky and forced. But she held this Angelo's gaze. 'I was walking in the garden and I smelled it, this place, the lust, the pain, the pain that somehow felt good, smelled good.'

For the tiniest of moments, the arousal rolling off Angelo peaked with the bramble scent of intrigue before the heavy heat smell of need took over again. He pushed himself to his feet and with the gate of a predator came to pace in front of them, his eyes locked on Liza. 'Paulo, you need to teach this woman something of dungeon etiquette unless you want me to stretch her out on that bed and play with her.' With a nod of his head, the man on the bed, who had been kneeling silently waiting for Angelo's permission, began to undo the bonds around the woman's ankles and wrists and rub the circulation back into them. 'You've both been good tonight,' Angelo said without looking at them. 'I'll reward you by letting you watch how a Dom punishes his misbehaving sub.'

'I'm not his sub –'

Before she could finish, Angelo raised a shushing finger to his lips and held her gaze. 'Best you keep your mouth shut, Ms Calendar or you'll get yourself into more trouble.' Before anyone could do or say anything else, there was a wave of scent, lust, concern, curiosity, and the sound of multiple feet on the steps as the entire High Council, minus Coraline Martelli, stepped into the dungeon. Fidelia held up a hand to silence everyone.

Angelo's eyes were nearly black in the flicker of gas light, but he held Liza in a gaze that made her want to bury her face in Paulo's chest. 'Well, Paulo? You said if anyone was going to spank her it would be you.'

'Angelo, she's our guest and you know she's already been spanked,' Fidelia said. 'You can use one of us as a whipping boy.'

'No!' Liza was surprised at how strong her voice was this time as she stepped out of Paulo's protective embrace. The inhale of her breath sounded like a sob, but it was a sniff, a chance to take in all of the scents that she wished she could bottle. 'No, Angelo is right. I wasn't invited. I'll take my punishment.'

There was a murmur from the High Council and a raised eyebrow from Angelo and, for a second, the room was dominated by the alum scent of surprise that settled quickly to cinnamon and cloves laced through with the smell of excited pussies and cocks. Liza closed her eyes to better take it all in, realizing that her own scent was far more metallic than usual and Paulo's scent was more like hot ash. Is this what it smelled like to be exposed, to be uncomfortable, to know that she was about to get more uncomfortable? When Paulo laid a questioning hand on her shoulder, she opened her eyes and her gaze locked on his – dark and dangerous, pupils dilated. She smelled the rainwater scent of understanding. The nod he gave her was barely perceptible.

'Once you're mine, you'll do exactly as I say, Liza Calendar. You won't speak unless I ask you to. If you do you'll make your punishment harder.'

'She needs a safe word,' Alessandro said. 'I doubt that she's ever played in a dungeon before.'

'Does she even know what a safe word is?' the fairy queen asked.

'I know what a safe word is,' Liza said. Her eyes were opened just a slit as she took in the smells around her. Losing herself in the orgy of scent seemed to sharpen her other senses too. She noticed a nod pass between Paulo and David, and David disappeared back up the steps. Then Paulo turned his attention to her.

'I don't need a safe word.' She curled her fingers in his hair and pulled him down to where his nose rested on the pulse point of her throat. 'My scent will tell you if I need you to stop.'

'With your lack of experience, you have to have one, or you can't play in my dungeon,' Angelo said.

For a second she said nothing, then she whispered into Paulo's ear, 'bouquet then. If we must, then let it be bouquet.'

There was a louder murmur among the audience, and there was the scent of several other people joining the gawkers, including Coraline Martelli. Feeling somehow outside herself, Liza turned her attention to Angelo and spoke with lowered eyes. 'I'm sorry that I trespassed in your dungeon. I humbly accept my punishment.' She was surprised that her action sharpened the hot rock, heat-lightning scent of his arousal. But she had little time to think about it before she found herself enveloped in Paulo's lush thickening scent as he slid out of his jacket and handed it to Alessandro, then placed his arm around her and led her away from the chair, undoing his tie as he went. 'This is going to get really intimate really fast, let me know now if you want to back out.'

She sucked in a deep breath and shook her head just enough that only he saw. His own breath came out harsh and tight, and he spoke between barely parted lips. 'Helluva a way to research the new line.' He was still speaking when he looped his tie over a pipe that ran the length of the room. Then he caught her wrists in one large hand and bound them. She offered a gasp of surprise as he secured, hoisted, and tightened until she stood with her arms stretched over her head, not on her toes, but without her heels she would be. Her heart raced and, for a second, she fought back a surge of burnt-coffee anger, forcing herself to remember that she had given him permission for this.

With both hands, he grabbed the bodice of her dress where it covered her breasts, and with a swift, efficient move, ripped it all the way down until it hung like an open bathrobe, exposing the red lace thong. Her pulse raced in a wave of cold, metal fear that accompanied the hiss of tearing silk and the collective catch of breath by the audience that now filled the dungeon. She wore no bra. She felt a wave of shame wash over her like stagnant water. Her face burned, and she closed her eyes, but only long enough to take in the smorgasbord of scent. Then she opened them again and focused on Paulo.

For a long moment he stood inspecting her, his gaze moving over her body in a caress that made her skin goose-flesh, then warm, as though it were heated just below the surface. He turned her slightly so that her audience could view the red welts on her bottom, almost as though he were demonstrating why he chose the method of punishment he had. From the implements hanging on the wall, he selected a crop not unlike the one Fidelia had used. Then with the flat of his hand he slid her legs apart as far as he could and still allow her to keep her balance. He ran the pliant tip of the crop around each of her nipples until they jutted like pebbles in front of her. His gaze on her was neutral, distant, as though she were an experiment that interested him. An experiment that interested both of them, she thought. But his scent gave him away. He was smoldering ash and summer storm agitated. He was cinnamon and aniseed, he was dark, rich earth, deep, dangerous and wanting … wanting her. She moaned involuntarily as he brought the tip of the crop up between her legs, up the valley between her labia, circling it around the nudge of her clit, teasing her through the thong, and her own scent was a riptide lapping at his. How the hell could no one else smell what was going on?

With a move that startled her in its swiftness, he brought the crop up with a tap that was more of a shock that pain against her clit. She tensed, her belly goose-fleshed, and her pussy gripped at its own juices. Holding her gaze, he moved forward and slid the flat of his hand into the front of her thong and down until his middle and index fingers could scissor into the wet trough of her and his thumb could press against her clit. He gave her a knowing smile when her eyelids fluttered and she bit her lip. Heat flashed up over her breasts and climbed her neck.

Then without warning he dropped his mouth to her nipples, suckling first one and then the other to hard tips that chilled in the dry air from the saliva he'd left on each. And when they were hard and tight and so sensitive that it was all she could do not to whimper each time he suckled, he pulled back and brought the force of the crop down with a sharp snap against first one engorged nipple and then another. She bit her tongue and held her breath to keep from crying out, but the tears that forced their way out of the corner of her eyes she could do nothing about. Then he cupped each breast in turn and brought the crop snap-snap-snapping up against the underside of each while he tweaked her nipples between thumb and forefingers.

'That's my girl.' His breath was hot against her sternum, 'That's my girl. Take your punishment just like you deserve, then afterwards I'll make you feel better.'

She was wet with thoughts of him making her better, and his eyes widened and his nostrils flared. She knew he smelled it, her desire, her need for him, the strange pleasure she felt in the pain he dished out to her so lovingly. Once again he slipped fingers into her thong and felt her, all swollen and wet. A murmur from the audience suddenly made her aware of the fact that they had something to do with what she was feeling. Their presence made the experience and the scent different, more intense somehow. But there was little time to dwell on her audience. Paulo hooked his fingers in the sides of her thong and hauled them down her legs, squatting in front of her as he did so, moving so that his breath brushed her tightly trimmed pubic curls before he slid the thong off one foot and then the other, steadying her with one hand on her hip. For a moment he knelt there, breathing her in. Then he cupped her ass cheeks gently enough not to hurt, but firmly enough to remind her that she had been punished before. He drew her to his face and placed a kiss against her mons, then moved low enough that his tongue flicked over the hard node of her clit, and this time she moaned out loud. Before he stood, he ran his tongue down the inside of her left leg and lifted it until he cupped the heel of her shoe, which he then slipped off and tossed aside. For a long, delicious moment, he bathed her foot with his tongue and his lips, pausing to suckle her toes until she writhed against her bonds. Then he repeated his efforts with her other foot, if anything, lingering even longer. It was only when he settled her weight back onto her feet that she realized what he had done. He had forced her onto the balls of her feet by taking away her heels. The acrid smell of her discomfort filled her sinuses.

Again he took up the crop and whisked it back and forth between her thighs to make sure her legs were as far apart as they could be. And just when she had regained balance and had convinced herself not to think about the burn she could already feel in her calves and in her arms bound over her head, he ran a splayed hand along her throat, over her sternum and down her belly to curl his fingers against her mons. His mouth clamped on hers in a possessive kiss. Just when he pulled away leaving her breathless, he brought the crop down with a sharp snap against the upper front of her right thigh and she swallowed back a curse, breathing hard through her nose at the harsh sting of it. Before she could breathe through the pain, he brought the crop down on the other thigh and the room around her blurred out of focus in front of her watering eyes. One hand snaked up the back of her neck and pulled pins from her hair with a calm efficiency she could scarcely believe, as he took her mouth again and ran the threat of the crop up the backs of her thighs. The kiss was deep and leisurely, with his tongue trailing like velvet against hers, against her hard palate, against the backs of her teeth. Once her hair was free, he ran his hand through it, loosening it, fluffing it, spreading it over her shoulders. Then the crop came down again hard and fast against the fronts of her thighs until there was the beginning of a lattice of red marks. Then without warning, he repeated his efforts against just the tips of her nipples until they stung and, once again, he took them into his mouth and suckled until she felt the effects down deep in her core. 'You won't disturb Angelo in his dungeon again, will you, Ms Calendar?' His voice was harsh, his words cut through with his efforts to breath.

'No, Mr Delacour. I won't,' she replied, her own voice nearly as breathless. A half a dozen more stinging smacks across her thighs and he dropped the crop to the floor. Then with a single slip of a knot, he loosened the tie until her arms fell free, and he guided the dead weight of them around his neck before she could stumble. Holding her gaze, he undid his fly, then lifted her into his arms. 'I'm going to fuck you now, Ms Calendar, because you've made me horny.' Somewhere a long way off Liza could hear the murmurs of the council and she could smell the intense wave of arousal rolling off all of them. But when Paulo lifted her onto him with a single thrust and wrapped her legs around him, her focus was completely and totally on the man in her arms. It didn't take long for either of them to come, and then what happened afterward seemed vague to her. She remembered Paulo giving instructions to David – something about zip-lock bags, then he slipped his jacket around her, lifted her into his arms, and carried her up the stairs and out into the silky-rich Italian night. He carried her through the maze and up the travertine steps flanked by the roll and tumble of fountains. The valet had his car ready, and Paulo eased her into the passenger seat of the midnight blue Porch, shutting out the star-studded night sky. He leaned in and kissed her before he closed the door and settled in next to her.

Neither of them spoke on the ride home. Somehow it seemed wrong to. Somehow it seemed like what had happened was something that shouldn't be spoken about, something that needed to be held close inside, to be reflected on for a long time before thoughts of it were shared in the light of day. The scent between them, the scent of them together was warm honey and strong tea, and cool water flowing in a stream. There had been a million questions she wanted to ask before what happened in the dungeon, but at the moment she could find voice for none of them.

At Bernini Place, he still refused to let her walk, but carried her into the flat, eased her out of the torn clothes, and into a warm bath. While she half dozed, he brought her cold water to drink and fed her fresh melon and prosciutto. Then he bathed her as though she were precious, wrapped her in a thick terry towel, and carried her to the bed. By the time he had pulled back the covers and tucked her in she could barely hold her eyes open. He smoothed the hair away from her face and spoke gently. 'Just so you know, you don't need a condom with me. Being clean and safe is a requirement for members of The Mount. And I'm pretty sure from what you told me, I don't have to worry with you either.'

'I'm on the pill,' she said softly. In spite of the exhaustion that threatening to smother her in a blanket of soft warm sleep, her stomach did a tight little somersault. He was planning to have sex with her again. Good. She liked that idea. She was just about to invite him under the covers to try out their newfound freedom but she never got the chance. She dropped off into a deep, dreamless sleep before she could even say goodnight.

Chapter Fifteen

'I've convinced Jim Dryer to show me around the research facility,' Vera said.

'How'd you manage that?' Carl admired her from where she stood in front of the hotel room window, the late morning sunlight all but making her summer sheath transparent. He'd checked into the room especially for their meeting. Better not to run any risks of getting caught with his pants down this time.

'I blew him,' she replied. 'Then I took him back to my place and fucked him. Twice.'

Carl chuckled, as he undid his tie and tossed it over the back of the chair. 'You always did have a silver tongue,' he said. 'And what you can do with the rest of your body is even better. So what did you find out?'

'Only that Coraline Martelli is extremely unhappy with the progress on the new line and she's pulled the stops on the work her team was doing, in spite of the shitload of money they'd already invested in it. But you already knew that. If they're worried about your threat of a takeover, they're keeping their cards close to their chest.'

'Wouldn't expect them to do otherwise. But trust me, Vera, they're worried all right.'

She turned to face him. 'What's really strange is how Martelli, Delacour, and Dryer are all three treating Liza Calendar like she's made of gold. Isn't she just here to do a story on Martelli Fragrance for her little magazine?'

‘That’s what you’re supposed to be finding out for me, Vera.’

‘Well, you might find this interesting.’ She dug through the handbag she’d dropped on the chair and handed him a flash drive. ‘Coraline Martelli had me make up a couple of slides for her the other day while her little PA was away.’ She followed him back to the desk where his computer was already up and running and watched as he shoved the drive into the port. ‘Sadly I wasn’t at the meeting she had me make it for but she, Delacour, and Dryer were all there, and little Ms Calendar was invited right on in with the inner circle.’

‘What?’ Carl looked up at her. ‘That doesn’t make any sense. The woman’s a good journalist, granted, but all she knows of the perfume industry is what she’s done to research her story, and it’s certainly not likely that the entire big three would meet with her for that story, nor would they discuss me with her. What the hell?’ He pulled up the slide, and she looked over his shoulder.

1. Romantic vanilla
2. Dom
3. sub
4. Kink
5. Animal heat/al fresco

‘What the fuck is this?’ He asked looking up at her.

‘Apparently that’s the revamped new line,’ she replied. ‘Or will be as soon as they come up with fragrances to go along with the names.’

‘Seriously? They’re no farther than simply the raw ideas? That means another huge outlay of money. I love it! I might as well hire someone to redecorate Coraline’s office for me.’

Vera opened the bottle of wine chilling on the table by the window and poured them both a glass. 'Actually, I think they're starting over completely from scratch. That's sure what it looks like, which means they have, indeed, lost a tonne of money on their first attempts. Still, Carl, I've never seen three people more excited, and Delacour escorted Liza Calendar into the meeting like she was their top secret weapon.' She handed him the glass. 'And when she came out, she looked pretty damned excited. In fact, they all did. Does she know you're in Rome?'

Carl pulled her down on his lap, nearly spilling her wine. 'She will soon enough, honey, I promise you that. I'll let her know when it works best to my advantage.' He gave Vera's tits a little squeeze and her tongue snaked out over her upper lip all porn-star like. 'So –' he tried not to grind his teeth '– Liza Calendar's more than just Delacour's bimbo then, is she? That's very interesting. Very interesting indeed.' He toyed with the hem of her skirt, which had slipped up to reveal a good bit of firm thigh. 'And what did you find out from Dryer?'

'Well –' She sat her wine glass on the desk then reached behind her back to unzip her dress. Wriggling it off her shoulders and down over her hips, she offered him a cheap little stripper's pout '– he says she has the most incredible sense of smell of anyone he or anyone at Martelli has ever met. He says you wouldn't believe what she can smell.' She undid her push-up bra and let it slide off onto the floor on top of her dress, and his cock stretched lazily in his trousers. The woman had nice tits.

'And they're going to use her sense of smell for this new line of theirs? I don't see how.'

She looked down at him from the height of her Louboutins and offered him a heavy-lipped pout that made him think of what she'd done to Dryer to get information. 'Oh, and apparently she's not as much of a prude as you thought. Dryer said she had a hot date with Delacour and she was dressed to the nines when they drove off in his Porsche. He said they've definitely been doing the nasty. In fact, he says they joined the Mile High Club on their flight to Rome.' She shrugged. 'Didn't really figure Delacour for a kiss and tell sort of guy, but then you never know, do you?' She squatted in front of him and began to tease open his fly, raking over the fabric with long fingernails. 'As for Dryer, well, it's amazing what a man'll tell you when he's about to get his cock sucked.'

'Isn't it just,' Carl said, as he shifted in his chair and let his erection bounce from his open fly right into her waiting mouth. It pissed him off that Liza Calendar wouldn't fuck him but she didn't even make it to Rome before she was spreading her legs for Delacour. Well at the end of the day they'd see who got fucked, wouldn't they?

'She's already over at the labs.' Coraline spoke around a mouthful of pastry as Paulo stepped into her office and closed the door behind him. God there were times when he wished the woman couldn't read him quite so well.

'I –'

'You stopped by her flat, yes, I suspected as much. She had Jim take her over.'

He couldn't help but feel a bit hurt that she'd called Jim and not him, but then Jim was right next door. 'I'm amazed that she was up so early after …'

She wiped her mouth daintily and tossed back the last of her coffee. 'Did *you* sleep?'

He shook his head. 'But she was out cold when I left her.'

'I figured as much or you wouldn't have left her.' Christ, was he really that transparent? 'I have no doubt she was exhausted after what you did to her last night.' There was no accusation in Coraline's voice, so why did he feel so damned defensive, like he'd done something wrong.

'Angelo left me no choice.'

She smiled lazily. 'Yes, Angelo. Your constant pain in the ass.'

'He's that alright,' Paulo agreed.

'The problem is that the two of you are too much alike, Paulo.'

His shoulders tightened, and he growled. 'I'm not like him. He's irresponsible and he's out of control.'

'And you're hyper-responsible and extremely in control,' Coraline nodded. 'Opposite sides of the same coin.' Then she changed the subject. 'They've never seen you like that, Paulo, like you were last night. No one at The Mount has ever seen you that way. They were all stunned.'

Paulo shifted uncomfortably from foot to foot. He wasn't sure he liked that everyone had seen him so vulnerable. Of course they didn't know how vulnerable he was, though he wondered how the hell they could have missed it. No doubt Angelo hadn't.

'I don't think that dungeon, in all of its years of use, has ever seen such a powerful display of dominance and submission,' Coraline was saying. 'Lots of attempts at it. Lots of wannabes, but what you two did, well, it was stunning. Oh, I know she's not a sub. Nothing about her is submissive, except that her instincts are the best I've ever seen. Personally …' she rose and came to stand in front of him, straightening his tie that was already flawlessly straight, '… I think she plays off your scent. She responds to the smell of arousal, and she responds in kind – sort of olfactory empathy, if I may be allowed to coin my own term.' She smiled up at him. 'And frankly, Paulo, I don't know about you, but on a professional level, that excites the hell out of me. And on the psychosexual level, the implications are astounding. Don't you think?'

Paulo reached for the chair behind him and dropped into it, suddenly unable to catch his breath. He hadn't thought about any of those things when he was with Liza last night. He had been so caught up in the moment, so caught up in what the woman did to him, so determined to protect her from a situation that she clearly didn't need protecting from, that he hadn't really thought about what it all meant to Martelli Fragrance. He hadn't really thought about what it all meant to The Mount – not just The Mount in Rome, but to The Mount International. Here was a woman who knew scent and experienced it like no one else on the planet, and she had a way of expressing it, understanding it that would change the face of fragrance, and very possibly of human sexuality. It scared him more than anything that he had missed the implications. Of course he'd had the presence of mind to have David bring bags and zip-lock underwear and cleanup towels for the labs, but beyond that he was totally and completely focused on the woman, who so willing gave herself over to him in what, for most people would have been a frightening, even disturbing situation. And Liza had made him aware of the scent of them together, which rendered the whole experience far more textured and full-bodied than any dungeon play he'd ever been involved in before.

'Paulo?' He jerked his attention back to Coraline, who now sat in the chair next to his, her hand on his forearm. She smiled at him. 'Sometimes it's OK to lose control.'

His laugh sounded more like a groan. 'I like dungeon play because I'm always in control there. I guess I wasn't as in control last night as I thought I was.'

He could feel her sharp gaze as she studied him. 'Control is relative, Paulo – far more so than most people think. You've not been a member of The Mount long enough to know that, and you've certainly never encountered anyone like Liza Calendar before. Paulo, it's the first time you've ever made love in front of anyone at The Mount. There were a lot of stunned people in that dungeon, myself included. You don't very often let anyone in. I know that better than most, and you certainly have never let a whole roomful of people in before.'

Interesting that she had used the words 'made love' rather than had sex, or fucked. 'I didn't,' he replied. 'I only let Liza in. Everyone else just happened to be there.' Paulo liked the role of Dom in the dungeon because he was in control, and he chose, for the most part, to orchestrate situations between submissives while he watched. Then he took his lust home with him and dealt with it there. It wasn't that he was a prude. It wasn't even so much that he cared if people saw him fucking, or at least he certainly hadn't last night. But in truth, he had wanted everyone in the dungeon to know that Liza Calendar was with him, that he could possess her and she would allow it. She would allow it. Her power gave him power, and he felt it as he'd never felt it before, no matter how many scenarios he'd orchestrated in the dungeon.

Both of their BlackBerries buzzed simultaneously, and Coraline patted his arm and returned to her desk. 'I'm betting that's from the research facility.'

It was from Liza. His fingers tightened around the device. The email read:

I have a basic plan in mind for the experiments we'll need to run. Most of what we need to do, we can do at TM, though I may need some time to explore the city a little more for some scents I feel will be essential if we're to make this work. Also we'll need to have volunteers to 'zip-lock' their at-home sexual experiences for us to be certain our presence doesn't interfere with the scents we want. Below is a rough outline for the first experiment.

There was an attachment.

'She's excited,' Coraline said. 'Her enthusiasm is contagious, but then with her sense of smell, I'm inclined to be enthusiastic myself.'

'I'm going to her,' Paulo said. 'I'll have to make arrangements for her to come and go at The Mount as she pleases ...' He liked that she had been discreet enough not to refer to The Mount by name, understanding just how seriously the secrecy of the organization was taken '... and I'm happy to escort her on whatever jaunts about the city she feels she needs.'

'Great! Then I'm making her your responsibility, Paulo.' Coraline began to doodle on her desk blotter. 'The two of you have a certain rapport, and she trusts you. Though if I were you, I'd speak to Angelo. You didn't stick around long enough to see, and you were too occupied to notice, but he was pretty taken aback by all that happened last night, and I think he was pretty taken by our Ms Calendar.' She waved a hand. 'That's for you and him to work out, but I'd do it soon if I were you, or Liza may be caught in the crossfire.'

So what are we planning first?

The text from Paulo sped up the beat of her heart, and she nearly dropped her BlackBerry in her effort respond.

I'm voting for al fresco. We're so close to Ostia Antica, I'm having Jim take me out there for a peek. Hoping we can get permission to do it there. Or not. How do you feel about trespassing? It would add another dimension to the scent.

Keep it simple. Keep it businesslike, Liza told herself. She needed time to process what happened last night, and she needed it away from the man who she was pretty sure she'd throw herself at the minute she saw him if she didn't give herself a moment – or in this case, a couple of hours.

Always up for trespassing if it's with you. Lose Jim & I'll be right there.

Her fingers trembled on the keys as she replied.

Are you kidding? If you were here I wouldn't be thinking about Martelli Fragrance. Besides we're already at Ostia.

There was a short pause and then he replied.

Have just texted the lucky bastard & told him to get the job done, keep his hands to himself, and get you back here ASAP.

She couldn't keep from giggling when she noticed Jim getting a text, then glancing at her with a raised eyebrow. She was poised to text back when her phone rang. She was just about to answer it, thinking it might be Paulo, when Carl's name flashed on the caller ID. At the very same moment, her toe caught on the uneven cobbles and sent the device flying from her hand. She would have gone flying too if Jim hadn't caught her.

'Whoa, whoa, whoa! Paulo and Coraline will both skin me alive if I bring you home injured.' He settled her onto her feet. 'Besides I don't want to have to carry you piggy back to the Temple of Hercules if you sprain an ankle.' He chased down her device, which had rung over to voicemail, gave her a stern look, and nodded down the Decumano Massimo. They'd only gone a little way when he asked, 'Were you going to answer that? Was it Paulo?'

'No, not Paulo. I'll take care of it later.' She stuffed the device into her pocket as they past the Tabernae of the Fishmongers and turned down the Via della Foce. Christ, she was hoping that Carl would just let it go when he got her message. In fact, she figured he would. It seemed like the face-saving thing for him to do. And really, he didn't owe her an explanation. She pushed thoughts of him out of her mind, and it was surprisingly easy to do with the challenges Martelli Fragrance had set before her, and with another incoming text from Paulo.

So tell me, what do you think of Hercules's butt? And don't tell me you didn't notice.

She was about to reply she didn't know what he was talking about when Jim led her off the path to the Temple of the Republic and up close and personal to a weathered marble sculpture that was missing an arm and a head, but all the parts that defined him as male were very well in tact.

Not his butt I'm looking at, she fired back.

Behave! Both of you. We're trying to work here! came the text from Jim, who only smiled at her and waved as she examined the anatomy of the statue thought to have been Hercules, and as she looked at the temple surrounds and the nearby Domus of Amor and Psyche, an idea began to form in her head.

Chapter Sixteen

He should have been excited and, in truth he was, but it was hard not to be just a little grumpy when Paulo had actually hoped he would have Liza all to himself this evening. Instead – and he suspected Coraline was in on this – someone had thrown their weight around in just the right way and in just the right places to get the permission they needed for Liza's experiment, and he found himself at the ruined the Roman city of Ostia Antica after hours. He hadn't even been able to drive Liza there this time. The set-up had been quick and simple. Liza had insisted that it was better that way, and since she and Jim were already there, they'd had pizza somewhere close by and were waiting for him at the car park when he arrived. He could tell by the slight flare of her nostrils that she had scented him. Her lovely full lips curled upward in an energetic smile he was dying to kiss right off her face. 'You made it,' she said, fingers dancing over the screen of her iPad, eyes drawn in a sexy librarian squint as she tried to make out whatever it was she was looking at in lighting that wasn't ideal.

'I can't believe it's all happening so fast,' she said, as he moved as close to her as he could without making his need to be near her too obvious. Vera had let it slip to one of the secretaries who had let it slip to Alessandro, which meant it was now all over the Martelli offices that she and Jim had entertained each other quite well last night at her place, so Paulo was pretty sure Jim wasn't competition for Liza's affection. But, fuck, the man had had her to himself all day long, and Paulo couldn't believe that Liza didn't feel the need to talk about last night and their time in the dungeon at least as much as he did. Or maybe she was avoiding him. She didn't seem to be avoiding him. If he could smell her as well as she could smell him then he'd know if she were avoiding him or not. Unconsciously he sniffed, and she looked up at him and smiled. All he knew for sure was that she smelled really good and she knew he was sniffing her.

David was already there with everything they'd need in order to bag and label necessary items of clothing. He worked in the research department of Martelli Fragrance and when Liza walked over to him, he held up the rucksack full of essentials. 'You know how Ms Martelli is,' he said. 'Now that there's a plan, the woman wants it done yesterday.'

'So who's going to have sex with you tonight?' Liza asked. Paulo couldn't help be a little proud that she said it without the slightest blush of embarrassment. But then he figured she was in research mode, and if their encounter with the *ménage* at the villa was any indication, where scent was concerned, she lost any inhibitions she might have and was totally and completely focused. She sniffed in David's direction. 'You didn't shower before you came over, did you?'

'Oh, I'm not having sex tonight,' he said, then he offered her a wicked smile, 'At least I'm not the one you'll be sniffing. Doesn't mean I won't be enjoying my work.' He made a rude gesture over his groin as though he were jerking off.

'I believe I have the honour tonight,' Angelo's resonant voice couldn't have caused more of a shudder for Paulo if it had been fingernails on a chalkboard. He didn't need Angelo's antics complicating the evening, and Angelo would be sure to figure some way to cause problems. The fucker looked at Liza like he wanted to eat her for dinner, and this time she did blush. Paulo ground his teeth.

'I see,' Liza said. To her credit, she still sounded all businesslike. 'And who will you be fucking?'

Paulo bit his lip and Jim tried unsuccessfully to swallow a snigger. The woman had guts, Paulo had to admit.

'Sadly not you, it would appear.'

'I'm not in your dungeon tonight, Angelo. You're in my domain now, and it's my job to sniff,' she said coolly. 'And who else will I be sniffing?'

'That would be me.' Lucia stepped out of a sporty red Audi, showing plenty of leg from beneath a black flip mini skirt as she did so. 'And frankly, I don't mind sharing Angelo if you care to join us, Ms Calendar. In fact, I think Angelo would have no problem doing us both.' She shot Paulo a heavy pout. 'Paulo kept you all to himself last night. The man can be so selfish.'

Fuck! Was this Coraline's idea of a joke? She couldn't have gotten a harder couple to work with if she had made a special effort.

'We volunteered,' Angelo said, smiling at Paulo as though he'd read his thoughts. 'Besides it was a bit of a short notice to be too picky, wasn't it? Trust me, Ms Calendar ...' he gave Luci's braless breasts a good grope, but his eyes never left Liza's '... we'll give you plenty to sniff.'

As they headed in through the gate and along the Decumano Massimo, past the necropolis and then the ruins of the theatre, Paulo slid a possessive arm around Liza's waist. 'Is it just the six of us then?'

'I guess so,' Liza said. 'I don't know who made the arrangements. I only know that Coraline wants it done as fast as we can realistically manage it, and we were already here. I like the way Angelo and Lucia smell together. Or maybe I should say I like both of their scents, but if they're not willing to play nice, the results won't be the same. '

He leaned close to her ear so no one else would hear. 'I would think after last night you would see that sometimes not playing nice results in something very nice indeed.' He sniffed and thought he could smell her scent spike. But so often it was difficult to tell if he could really smell the subtleties she spoke of to him or if he only hoped that he could.

'Believe me,' her voice sounded thicker, rougher, and she made no effort to hide her deep inhalation of his scent. 'I'm very well aware of the delicious results of not playing nice. And I've got the welts and sore muscles to prove it. Plus I've spent a good chunk of the day analyzing the data you had the presence of mind to get David to collect for us. I've been trying to pull corresponding scents from the perfume organ, and I've got some really great ideas for the Dom and sub scents. I thought we'd use Angelo for those. I didn't figure him to be a sex al fresco sort of guy.' She shrugged, her gaze locked on Angelo, who walked ahead of them. 'Though I could easily figure him for a bit of an animal.'

Paulo bristled in spite of himself. He didn't like Liza thinking about Angelo at all. But this was business, he reminded himself. 'Do you wonder what might have happened if I hadn't shown up last night when I did?' Fuck! Why the hell had he said that? And worse, he knew full well that she could smell his jealousy.

Her lips tipped upward into a Mona Lisa smile. 'It smells to me like you've spent way more time wondering about that than I have.'

For a long moment they walked in silence while he struggled to regroup 'That's unfair advantage, you know? Using your nose like that.'

She nodded. 'It's unfair of you to assume that things turned out any way other than the way I wanted them to turn out last night. Except, of course, I would have stayed awake a little longer and wore you out a little better.' She sniffed. 'You like that idea, don't you?'

'Maybe we can shoot for another nice outcome tonight when we're finished here?'

'Maybe.'

The conversation ended abruptly when Lucia approached the statue of headless Hercules with a little yelp of delight. The short flip skirt she was wearing barely covered her bright pink thong, which was clearly visible as she clambered up the remains of the ancient steps and began caressing the statue's cock, at rest against his balls, all of which rested, both discretely and exposed at the same time, against one thigh, raised on a plinth, a draping of cloth sculpted over it.

'What do you want us to do?' Angelo asked, trotting up the steps after Lucia.

'Whatever you want to do,' Liza said, 'as long as it leads to sex al fresco.'

The figure of Hercules was only slightly larger than life-size, and in part that was due to the sculpture's raised position. But Lucia wasn't shy, as she began to stroke and caress marble genitalia. Then, as though she were completely alone, she lifted her light summer sweater and cupped her breasts awkwardly around the statue's unresponsive package. Angelo leaned against the raised thigh of the statue and undid his fly. As he eased his already expanding cock out of his boxers, he observed from lowered eyelids as Lucia's large pink nipples rubbed and pressed and danced against the pale marble.

Paulo watched the two of them as his own cock tightened inside his trousers. Liza slipped away from him and moved slowly, cautiously up the steps, pausing with her eyes closed to breathe in the thickening scent of lust that only she could smell. Suddenly he had no interest in what Luci and Angelo were doing. He couldn't take his gaze off Liza in her blue sundress, nowhere nearly as sexy as what Luci was wearing, and yet Liza was by far the most captivating woman there, lost in her exploration of scent. He knew it and everyone else there knew it, he was certain. Though he doubted that Liza was aware of it. She would be wet and slippery by now, taking in the scent of sex like she was. He knew her heart would be racing with excitement. He knew that for her what was going on between Lucia and Angelo was an exciting olfactory story unfolding before her nose, and knowing what she was experiencing made his own heart race, made him wish desperately that he could smell it with her.

It was as she moved slowly up beside Luci, just far enough away not to disturb her that he noticed Angelo was not watching Luci at all. His eyes were locked on Liza, following her every move like a predator waiting to pounce. Paulo's fists clenched at his side until his knuckles popped, and he was halfway up the stairs behind Liza before he realized he'd even moved.

With his eyes still locked on Liza, Angelo moved in behind Lucia and shoved the tiny flip skirt up over her hips to expose her buttocks, separated by a thin strip of the pink thong. He tugged at the back of it until it rubbed up tight against her crotch. She gave a little grunt and slid one foot along the rubble by the plinth to open her legs. Then with his gaze still on Liza,

Angelo shoved the thong aside and thrust two fingers up into Lucia's pussy. She wriggled her hips against his probing until he pulled free and sniffed her juices. 'Mmmm! I can smell Lucia's sopping cunt too, Liza Calendar.' He gave himself a stroke. 'And in a minute I'm gonna fuck her until she comes all over my cock. Oh, would you look at that?' He thumbed the pre-cum off the tip of his erection. 'Can you smell me too, Ms Nose, can you smell my heat? Does it make your little pussy wet, sniffing us like you do?'

Paulo was ready to knock Angelo on his ass, but his crudeness didn't seem to bother Liza. 'Yes, it does.' She spoke to him almost as a teacher would who was trying to explain something important to a schoolboy. 'Of course it does, and I can smell that you're both as turned on by taunting me as you are by each other.'

'Oh I'm not turned on by taunting you, Liza Calendar, but by watching you sniff us. That makes me want to ram my cock up your wet little pussy.'

Paulo couldn't help it, he moved to lay a hand on Liza's shoulder and heard her gasp in the scent of him. Then she turned to him and found his mouth, her tongue probing deep between his parted lips, her body pressing against his. Angelo growled and mumbled something rude Paulo only half caught before Liza rose on her toes and spoke into his ear. 'I can only smell you when you're this close to me, and then I smell me wanting you. Please, go stand by Jim so I can concentrate.'

He curled his fingers in her hair and drew her nearer until she grunted out a heavy breath. 'I don't like him taunting you.'

'Let him. He smells good that way. And it gives me another idea.' He barely heard her words against his ear, but the reassuring squeeze of her hand and the spiking of her scent against his had him stepping back toward Jim.

As he did so, Angelo offered a throaty laugh. 'Sorry, Paulo. She's here to smell me tonight.' He kneed open Lucia's legs just a little further, eased his jeans and boxers down until his whole ass was exposed, then pushed into her pussy with a hard thrust that all but forced Lucia up into Hercules's naked lap. 'Tell me, what do you smell, love?' He fucked Lucia with all the indifference of a porn star, one hand curled into her skirt as though he were a cowboy and she were his horse, while the other rested on his hip.

It was only because Paulo was so attuned to Liza's voice, and only because he could do a little bit of lip-reading that Paulo caught what happened next. Jim and David were too busy watching the action to pay any attention to what was really going on. But Paulo was good at catching subtleties. That was why he was so good at his job. Liza moved closer to the rutting couple, much closer. With one hand resting on Hercules' marble torso, she leaned in and sniffed. Then she spoke quietly to Angelo. 'I smell your dominance like hot iron and your arrogance like chlorine in a swimming pool, Angelo. Shall I tell you what your arrogance is doing to Lucia's scent, or would you prefer not to know?'

Angelo jerked as though he'd been slapped. His back stiffened, his body eased to a stop with his cock still buried inside Lucia. For a tense moment, his gaze flashed white-hot, locked on Liza. Paulo's gut knotted with the tension that passed between the two of them. Then, slowly, very slowly, Angelo slid a large hand up to rest low on Lucia's back, then around her waist where he wriggled it into her thong to stroke her clit, and she gave a throaty grunt. Then he fisted his hand in her hair and leaned in to kiss and nibble her neck.

She gave a quiver of surprise as his tongue laved up her pulse point and over her ear. With his cock still buried to the hilt, he stood to his full height and shed his shirt. In the dying light, Paulo was surprised to see that his fingers trembled on the buttons. He gave one last thrust, much gentler than before, and pulled out, his cock shining with Lucia's heat. She offered a little growl of protest, which died in her throat as he dropped into a squat and, holding the thong aside with one hand, he buried his face in her pussy. With the other hand, he awkwardly, but effectively spread his shirt at Hercules's feet. Again he pulled away, and as Lucia's knees gave, he caught her and lowered her onto his shirt. A murmur passed between Jim and David and Liza's inhaled gasp told Paulo that something major had shifted in the olfactory stew. Though Paulo couldn't actually smell it, the tremor low in his belly and the speeding up of his pulse told him something had definitely changed between the couple. There was a shifting of power, a loosening of control, even a sense of yielding that didn't have to be smelled to be sensed.

Angelo knelt between Lucia's legs and then with slow deliberateness of which Paulo would have thought the man incapable, he nipped and sucked and licked his way up the inside of Lucia's left thigh. Her arms flailed and she groaned out loud, curling one fist into a tuft of grass that had grown up between the travertine stones and fisting the other in Angelo's hair as though she could drag him up her body faster, but he took his time.

'Angelo, please. Please! Angelo, Angelo, Angelo!' By the time he had rested her bare feet on his shoulders and settled into the feast she offered between her thighs, Lucia called out his name like a mantra, and Paulo was convinced that a person would have to have no sense of smell at all not to smell the heat. His cock was hard inside his trousers as much from watching Liza's response to Angelo's shift in game plan as to what Angelo and Lucia were actually doing.

'That's better, oh God, that's better, so much better,' Liza said between gasps for breath.

'What do you smell?' Lucia managed with a little yelp as Angelo nibbled her clit. 'Tell us what you smell.'

'I smell arid summer and pine, I smell honey and lime and seashore. I smell hot metal and wet forest floor, I smell … I smell your orgasm like a sea storm.'

And before she finished the sentence Lucia bucked her hips and grasped Angelo tightly between her thighs as her cries echoed off the ancient walls of the ruins.

'I want you in my mouth! I want you in my mouth, I want you in my mouth,' Lucia babbled incoherently. To Paulo's surprise, Angelo wasn't the Dom tonight. He obeyed, shifting until his body arched over her, shoving and kicking until his trousers and boxers were off in a heap at his side. Then he lowered his cock into her mouth, positioning himself carefully so that she could take him into her throat, her head back, her mouth wide and begging like a baby bird, moaning pleasure as he lowered himself into a classic 69 position. Then with the flat of his hand, he opened her thighs, planted a lazy tongue kiss in her navel, then battled the front of the beleaguered thong to bury his face back in her slit. Almost immediately she whimpered against his cock and her hips bucked. Lucia could come all night long. Everyone at The Mount knew that about her.

But it was what Liza was doing that had Paulo on the edge of coming. The way she sniffed, the way her eyelids fluttered then closed, the way she encouraged the lovers, the way she talked to herself of the scent of sea and earth and heavy thunderstorms. Oh God, he wanted to march right over to her, push up her skirt, and bury his cock in her soft wet folds, and he knew she would be so wet, so slick. He knew she would be ready and yielding and that she would take him to the hilt and he would be in ecstasy with her butter and honey scent curling around his lightning storm heat. He stood very still, breathing deeply – deeply enough to smell sex, deeply enough to feel it in his cells, but as Angelo wiped his face on his arm and repositioned himself to thrust into Lucia's pussy again, and as she wrapped her legs around him and howled another orgasm, it wasn't either of them that was making him desperate for some relief of his own. It was Liza, Liza reveling in an orgy of scent, Liza like a goddess in her element.

And when Angelo ejaculated with a roar, like a lion before Hercules, when his whole body convulsed like it would break apart, Paulo knew without a shadow of a doubt the man was feeling something he had never felt before. He was experiencing another dimension to sex, and he was a man who was jaded by experience.

But Liza knew that too. He could see it as she dropped to her knees gasping for breath, eyes closed, trembling all over. And Paulo could hold back no more, he rushed to her side and pulled her possessively into his arms. She uttered a startled yelp, then she looked up at him as though she wasn't sure how he'd gotten there, as though she had been somewhere far away. Then she flung her arms around his neck and kissed him long and hard.

Liza couldn't breathe. It wasn't that she couldn't breathe, it was just that she couldn't breathe in enough of Paulo's scent as he pulled her into his arms and kissed her, tongue writhing and sliding over and around hers, teeth nibbling, lips suckling at hers until she felt as though he would pull all of her into his mouth and devour her whole, and God she was totally willing. Then Paulo's phone rang, and he cursed under his breath just as Jim stepped up next to them.

'Hey guys, if we have to wait, you have to wait,' Jim said. 'How about you save it for later, and help us finish up here so we can all get some relief?'

'Vera waiting for you?' David said, loud enough that his voice echoed off the brick, and Liza could smell Jim's herby, woody, good-natured embarrassment at being caught out. David laughed. 'No secrets at Martelli, and Vera isn't keeping any either.' He slapped several plastic bags in Paulo's hands and snapped his fingers at Lucia and Angelo. 'Get 'em off and clean up your bits, Martelli wants to smell you.'

'Don't brush it off,' Liza said, when Angelo picked up his shirt off the ground. 'The scent of a place as powerful and full of human memory as this has to be a part of what Martelli is trying to get.'

Angelo obeyed her without batting an eye, dropping his shirt into the zip-lock bag she was now holding for him, along with his trousers and underwear. Then with his eyes locked on her, he stood naked next to the statue of Hercules, wiping his cock on the towel David had handed him. The similarities weren't lost on her, neither was the hot metal and spice scent of his lust, so different from the lust he'd spent on Lucia, but even while he had been inside the woman, even when he had seemed to be totally focused on the sex, she could smell his dark earth-scented press for her attention.

Without taking his eyes off her, he stroked and

wiped at his wet penis, which was once again expanding in his hand. 'I'm usually the voyeur, not the exhibitionist,' he said. 'But to be sniffed by you, Liza Calendar, I'm happy to expose myself.' Then he dropped the used towel into the bag, and it was all she could do not to inhale his scent, especially when his cock pointed invitingly at her.

Paulo had stepped away and was busy talking on the phone to Coraline. Lucia was shamelessly flirting with Jim and David, and no one noticed when Angelo scooped Liza into his arms, pressing a hand into the small of her back and pulling her up tight against his heavy penis and his sex-fevered chest. 'This is for you, Liza Calendar. Just for you.' The kiss was both savage and fast, gunmetal and flint, sparks catching in dry grass and drowning summer rain all at once, and her knees buckled, but he held her just long enough to settle her onto her feet. He caught the bag as it slipped from her hand, and still holding her gaze, pulled the edge of the towel from it and she watched, the sound of her own breath drowning out all else as he stroked his cock twice, then three times, then with a grunt, spilled his semen into the towel.

'For you, Liza Calendar, and when Paulo stops arsing around at the Mount and figures out it's OK to share, there's lots more where that came from.' Then he turned his back on her and began to dress in the clothes he'd brought in his rucksack.

She felt like she'd been gut punched. She felt like she'd been fucked. She felt like she'd been ensnared in some sort of bizarre magic. What the hell was he talking about, when Paulo figures out it's OK to share? What the fuck was that supposed to mean?

'What did he do? What did he do?'

It took her a second to realize that Paulo had asked her twice as he slipped his arm around her, and the cold steel smell of anger cut through his scent like a knife. ‘What the fuck did Angelo do?’

‘Tell me about The Mount,’ she said, instead of answering the question. ‘I think you need to tell me *all* about The Mount.’ She looked up into his eyes. ‘This time no interruptions and nothing left out.’

Chapter Seventeen

It wasn't what Paulo wanted, wasn't his plan. Liza wouldn't even ride back into Rome with him. She told him it was safer at the moment for her to be with Jim. Fuck Jim! Fuck Angelo! Fuck them all! Coraline had called to say, at Liza's request, she'd had Jim deliver her to the villa and for him to meet them there. When he arrived, the footman escorted him to The Suite. The Suite was the heart of the Roman Mount. Whoever was the head of the High Council at the time had access to what was actually a huge apartment within the villa. The council's head could reside there full-time until tenure was up, but no one ever did. The only one who ever actually stayed there was Coraline. Most everyone simply thought of it as her suite anyway.

The apartment, however, was not the reason why The Suite was the heart of the Roman Mount. The real reason was why they should have shown it to Liza last night before things got out of hand in the dungeon. Coraline met him at the door.

'This was a bit of a muck-up.' She didn't give him a chance to reply. 'Not yours. All of ours. Oh I don't mean tonight. That went really well. I think we'll have everything we need for the animal/al fresco scent, and Liza is pleased. But tell me, what were we thinking, letting her get away from the villa last night without making sure she knew exactly what The Mount was and what it was all about?' Coraline's rapid-fire monologue told Paulo that she was upset. 'We can't afford for Liza to be unhappy. We don't want to keep secrets from her. We let last night pass without making sure our main, and really our only purpose was achieved. I don't know if Angelo is aware of what he did, but I have every intention of flaying him properly for the mess he's made. The man never seems to know when to keep his mouth shut and stay out of things.'

Paulo shivered at the thought of being flayed by Coraline Martelli. Even Angelo was a lightweight in the dungeon compared to Coraline. But then again, as far as he was concerned, Angelo deserved what he got.

'Is she all right? Where is she?' he asked, having no other real response to give Coraline.

'She's in the shower. Jim says she didn't say a word all the way back from Ostia Antica.'

'Did she tell you what Angelo said to her that upset her so?' he asked.

She shook her head. 'She said relatively little since she got here, other than she needed a shower.'

'Well whatever it was, the bastard really upset her.' Paulo said. 'I couldn't hear it. I turned around just in time to see the fucker ...' Christ! He couldn't even say what he'd seen.

'Coming in front of me.' With a start, they both turned to see Liza standing by the door in a soft, floral summer dress, wet hair hanging loose around her shoulders. 'You turned around just to see Angelo shooting his wad in front of me.' Without a hint of a blush, without so much as a flinch, she looked from one of them to the other. 'He told me that when Paulo stops arsing around at The Mount and figures out it's OK to share, there was lots more where that came from. That's what he told me.' Before either of them could respond to Angelo's bad behavior, she said, 'I need to know what The Mount really is, and what it has to do with Martelli Fragrance. And what the hell does it have with Paulo and Angelo thinking they should share me?'

'It has nothing to do with Martelli Fragrance,' Coraline said. 'It's connected only in that I'm a member of The Mount, as my father was before me and both Martelli Fragrance and The Mount have been mutually beneficial to each other while at the same time being mutually exclusive. Martellis have been members of The Mount for a long, long time. Rita's a member of The Mount in London.' She paused for a moment to let that sink in. Coraline had told Paulo that Rita and Liza were good friends. She continued. 'Quite coincidental there are several members of The Mount who work for Martelli, including David.'

'It was my idea to use members of The Mount in the research for our new line,' Paulo said. 'And that idea only became something concrete, something I could actually put a plan with, when I met you, Liza.'

'I've already been told that The Mount is a sex cult. Fidelia said that. I'm OK with that. I figured it was something like that when I was brought here to observe the threesome. I know for the kind of experiments we're talking about, we aren't going to be hiring people off the streets to help us. I understand that. I'm OK with that. What I'm not OK with is being broadsided with aspects of The Mount I know nothing about, aspects that clearly Angelo thinks should somehow have an effect on me.'

Paulo wished like hell he could smell her now. He needed to know what she felt, what was going on with her. He needed to know the two of them were all right. She could no doubt smell his discomfort, and it pissed him off that he had no way of hiding himself from her. He wasn't used to being this vulnerable.

'Paulo will show you the vaults,' Coraline said, 'and answer any of your questions.' Though she knew

The Mount and its history much better than he did, Paulo was relieved that Coraline was willing to let him handle it. He'd had a sneaking suspicion that she shared Angelo's opinion. He was pretty sure everyone else at The Mount did. He should be OK with that. He knew that he should. 'Paulo?' Coraline interrupted his thoughts.

He motioned for Liza to follow him. As she fell in close behind him, he thought he heard her sniff, and he couldn't keep from tensing, even as he knew that she would smell that too.

He led her to a central hallway in the huge flat, a hallway that had no windows and, at this time of night, no natural light. At the end of the hall, he pushed aside a thick velvet curtain to reveal a heavy wooden door, which opened inward onto a narrow stairway lit by evenly spaced wall sconces. Behind him, Liza caught her breath at the sight.

Liza could just make out the steep dimly lit stairway beyond Paulo's broad shoulders. The scent of stone and age and dry dust filled her nose, for a second superseding Paulo's tart citrus scent of nerves and the bite of irritation. 'Another dungeon?' she asked, though it didn't smell at all like the dungeon she was in last night.

'No dungeon. This is the heart of The Mount. If we had a holy of holies, I suppose this would be it.'

'Then you really are some kind of cult?'

His chuckle sounded brittle. 'I suppose some would see it that way, but no. This is a place where we keep our archives.' He descended the steps. 'The Mount has been around for a long time, and the Roman Mount is the oldest of all the covens.'

'Covens? You're witches? You practise magic?'

'Not witches, no. But I doubt you'd find anyone in

The Mount who would deny that there's magic involved in good sex.'

At the bottom of the steps the scent changed, and she could smell parchment and old books. Above the arched doorway they passed through she looked up to see a simplified version of Venus and Mars embracing. Beneath the bas-relief written in Latin were the words, "*The depths of our animal nature and the highest mount of our divinity*". Interesting that though Coraline Martelli claimed that there was no connection between Martelli Fragrance and The Mount that the same simple image of Venus and Mars embracing and the same motto graced the Martelli letterhead.

The vaulted room Paulo led her into reminded her of a wine cellar, but it was spotlessly clean, and the ceiling to floor shelves along either side housed books instead of wine. She leaned close and squinted at the volumes nearest the entrance. The gold gothic lettering was in Latin. It read, *The Laws and Statutes of the Covens of The Mount*.

'There are lots of books of coven law,' Paulo said. 'And they're not all in Latin. They're near the door because they're most often referred to, much more so than the older histories, though we consider the older histories far more valuable.' Those books, she noticed, as she looked down the long row of shelves, were protected behind glass.

'Someday Alessandro hopes to get everything on computer, but I think he's only dreaming. Some of the histories are so old, so fragile that they're not even kept in this room. There's a temperature-controlled vault in the next chamber. The oldest and the most fragile manuscripts of Mount History are kept there.'

She grabbed at the wall to steady herself. 'Let me get this straight. The Mount is a sex cult.'

Paulo nodded.

'And it's how old?'

'No one knows for sure. We expect some of the earlier manuscripts were lost when Nero burned Rome.'

The room suddenly spun around her in a wave of vertigo. Paulo moved to steady her. 'It's a lot to take in, I know. You have to understand that there's been very little time in Western history in which human sexuality hasn't been controlled and regulated by either religion or government. The reasons for that control were most often property and inheritance, though both could be easily wrapped up in religious dogma. There have always been people who didn't like someone else telling them how they should behave as sexual beings, who they should have sex with and under what circumstances. There have always been people who have felt that rational human beings, when given the right information, when given the freedom to enjoy what is clearly a natural part of their biology, would regulate their own desires with wisdom and self-control.'

'So it's not about wild orgies and sex parties then? I mean when I had a wander about last night, there was sex going on all over the gardens.'

'It's about celebrating our sexuality as consenting adults, Liza. That's what it's about.'

She pulled away from him and paced in front of the glassed in shelves, her eyes locked on row after row of books to avoid his gaze. 'Then Angelo is right. About you sharing, I mean.'

'You're not a member of The Mount.'

'Then what happened to me when I got caught sniffing in your office that first afternoon? What … what Fidelia and I did?'

'What Fidelia and you did shouldn't have happened. It was really reckless of Coraline to order it, though I don't think she thought Fidelia would go that far. I don't think *she* thought you'd let Fidelia go that far.'

Liza ran her fingers along the cool, wood frame of the bookcase. 'Would she have given me a choice?'

'Would you have wanted one?'

'I don't know,' she said quietly, suddenly, strangely close to tears. 'If you'd asked me that a few days before I met you in the lounge at JFK, I'm sure I'd have been horrified at the thought. Now,' she looked up at him. 'Now it just … excites me.'

He moved to her and took her in his arms, and she didn't protest as he rested his chin on the top of her head. His relief and his concern for her blended into a herby, watery, sweet scent mixing with his own that she could never get enough of. She could also scent the question that was like hot pepper flakes on the tip of his tongue.

'And you want to know how I feel about you sharing me with Angelo.' His arms tensed around her and his scent became more metallic.

'Well the truth is, it excites me.' She laid a hand against his chest and pushed away just enough that she could look into his eyes. 'Not that I want to be alone with him. But the idea of the two of you. The idea of the two of you sharing me, it excites me.' She sniffed. 'And you can't say that it doesn't excite you too, because I can smell that it does.'

He groaned and pulled her back to him, so tight that she huffed out a breath, then inhaled the woody, lightning storm scent of him aroused 'God, Liza Calendar, you don't play fair, you know that?'

She raised her mouth to his. 'Do you want me to play fair, Paulo Delacour?'

At first his kiss was fleeting, as though he were afraid she'd run, but as she lifted her arms around his neck, the kiss deepened and warmed and was just beginning to heat up to the possibility of a good fuck against the bookshelves when there was a clearing of a throat, and they pulled a part to find Coraline standing at the foot of the stairs.

'Sex is what distracted the two of you last night, and though The Mount is most definitely the place for sexual distraction, Liza's not a member, Paulo. And she needs to see everything and understand everything before we run the risk of another nasty surprise from Angelo.' She nodded to Liza. 'Darling, why don't you come with me, and I'll show you around. Paulo, you go talk to Angelo. He's in the dungeon.'

The angry scent of cold metal overrode the scent of Paulo aroused, but Coraline glared at him. 'Do it.'

He stepped away from Liza, squared his shoulders, and nodded. But before he headed back up the stairs, he pulled her into a brutal kiss that had her heart racing and her knees turning to jelly. 'We have unfinished business,' he spoke against her mouth. Then he nipped her bottom lip, pulled away, and growled at Coraline before he headed up the stairs.

Chapter Eighteen

What Paulo had not expected was to find Angelo alone in the dungeon. The man was seldom alone when he was at The Mount, and he didn't have to be. He was the most sought after sexual partner there, though everyone knew that if they wanted a chance at sex with Angelo, they had to meet him in the dungeon. There were plenty of people who were fine with that, but there were others who just had to settle for fantasies because they weren't brave enough to meet Angelo on his home turf. And even Paulo knew that to meet Angelo anywhere else was to miss out on the full experience of the man's sexuality. Though in all honesty, he'd never seen Angelo like he was tonight at Ostia, and he'd never imagined the man would join the party above ground. That made him only more aware of just how taken Angelo was with Liza.

He lay sprawled across the hard wood of the bondage bed in nothing but jeans. They were partially undone. His left arm was thrown over his face as though he were attempting to block out too much light, and his right hand stroked his cock absently from the breach. 'Did Mum order you to come and make up?' he asked without looking at Paulo.

'Pretty much.' Paulo moved into the room and leaned against one of the bed's four posts.

'Did you bring her?'

'Jim did. Liza's with Coraline at the moment.'

Angelo's lips curled into a half smile, but he still

didn't move his hand or stop stroking his cock. 'Giving her the grand tour, is she?'

'Wants to make sure everything is above board so you can't pull any more surprises out of your ass.'

Angelo chuckled wickedly. 'Oh I have plenty of surprises still, and I don't need to pull them out my ass, though I certainly could if our lovely Liza is into that sort of thing.'

'Why don't you just admit, she got to you tonight?' Paulo said, then he immediately wished he'd kept his mouth shut.

'I'd say she got to both of us, bro, and you unwilling to share your toys. Therein lies the problem. Didn't your mother teach you better?'

Paulo bristled. 'Liza's not my toy.

'Did you ask her?' This time, Anglo moved his hand and pulled himself into a sitting position with his back against the headboard. 'Did you ask her if she wanted to be our toy? I don't think she would say no, Paulo, and I think that's what really bothers you.'

Paulo sat down onto the bed next to him and shoved back against the headboard. 'Oh I don't think she wants to be a toy for either of us.' He nodded down to Angelo's cock. 'I think the truth is, our Liza, as you so affectionately refer to her, would prefer for both of us to be *her* toys.'

Angelo raised an eyebrow and stopped stroking. For a long moment he sat in silence, then he shrugged. 'I suppose I could live with that. Though I would enjoy tying her up and giving her some proper discipline. You certainly seemed to enjoy it last night.'

For a moment the two men sat in silence. The only sounds in the dungeon were their breathing and the skin on skin stroke of Angelo's hand once again sliding up and down the length of his cock. Paulo was startled to realize that he recognized Angelo's scent.

Even in a darkened room, he would have recognized Angelo's scent. He took a deep breath and held it, taking in the smell of the man he had known for a good deal of his life. Clearly he hadn't bathed since he finished the experiment at Ostia Antica. In spite of his come-on to Liza, Paulo was sure that the experience had shaken him and that, rather than going to his flat, he had come here to think. Angelo spent more time at The Mount's villa than any of the other members. There was a small suite set aside for him upstairs, as there was for all of the High Council members, but most of the time, if one of the dungeons was free, that's where he ended up. Paulo sniffed again. Angelo smelled of sex and the kind of male perspiration that was clean, if a bit threatening. Paulo wondered if he sniffed a little harder he could still find Liza's scent on him.

Angelo huffed a throaty laugh and lifted his arm so that Paulo could see the soft auburn fluff beneath, dampened and curling slightly. 'Is our Liza giving you sniffing lessons?' Then the smile on his face slipped and his eyes darkened. 'You're wondering if you can smell her on me.' It wasn't a question.

'She likes the way you smell,' Paulo said.

Angelo sniffed his armpit, his hand still working his cock. Then he leaned over and sniffed Paulo. 'She tell you that, did she?'

Paulo didn't answer.

'That what set you off about me? Not that it usually takes much.'

Again Paulo didn't answer. Where Angelo was concerned, the history ran deep and thick between them, and it was definitely a mixed bag.

There was more silence. Paulo watched Angelo work his cock, breathed in the scent of the man who could have anyone he wanted pretty much any time –

in The Mount and out. He doubted anyone smelled more sexual than Angelo, and that intrigued him. He found himself wanting to know what Liza had smelled. She said he smelled good when he taunted her. He couldn't help wonder if on some unconscious level that it was pheromones that made Angelo so universally attractive. Was there a universal pheromone like there was a universal donor blood type? He'd ask Liza. But even he had to admit, Angelo was a good choice for their experiments, even if he was a pain in the ass. Paulo shifted on the bed, suddenly aware that his own cock was responding to Angelo's efforts, to Angelo's scent, and, with a start, he noticed Angelo was looking at his fly.

'You gonna let that thing out or you gonna force it to bust free on its own?' the man asked with a hint of a crooked smile.

'Fuck off,' Paulo mumbled, but even as he said it, his hand was already working on his fly. He could still feel Angelo's gaze locked on him, even though he'd closed his eyes with a sigh, and leaned back against the headboard, focusing on the smells of the dungeon, the smells of two alpha males with testosterone to burn and each with enough emotional baggage to fill the cargo hold of a 747. His own he was only too well aware of, but Angelo's; no one knew Angelo's baggage except for Coraline. Coraline could gossip better than anyone he knew. She knew everything about everyone, but to Coraline a secret was sacred, and the woman bore both of their secrets as though she knew neither of them. It was only in her treatment of them, in the way she moved and worked in their lives that either of them was ever aware of what she so carefully held for them.

'So tell me,' Angelo shifted slightly, and Paulo felt his bunched thigh muscles rub against his own, jean against jean, and the rustle of clothing told him he was probably freeing his balls. The shifting of shoulders let him know that the man had now engaged both hands in his efforts. 'Tell me what you smell. I can hear you sniffing, Paulo. You're not very subtle.'

'Testosterone amped up by pheromones and a good hand job smells like a desert lightning storm with just a hint of diesel.'

They both opened their eyes with a start that made the solid wood beneath them groan. Liza stood at the foot of the stairs, nostrils flared, eyes bright, mouth slightly open like a cat taking in the scent of prey. 'Don't stop,' she said. 'Please. I'm in heaven.'

There was a mutual groan, and Paulo was sure that the thought of their scent being heaven to Liza Calendar made both men hot enough to self-combust.

'What do you smell?' Angelo asked. Paulo could hear the ache in his voice, and it surprised him.

'I smell the hot metal of anger, but it's anger cooling, the acidic bite of jealousy has nearly worn itself out. I smell evergreen and dry grass in the summer sun. I smell hot, damp earth.' She stepped closer on tiptoes as though her footfalls might disturb her sense of smell. 'I smell that yeasty scent of new-made bread. That's such a masculine smell, a cock smell, a warm, damp, tetchy smell.' When at last she stood with her thighs resting against the bed frame, she caught her breath. 'And then I smell me. I smell the nutmeg of my intrigue at finding the two of you masturbating in the dungeon, I smell the honey butter of my arousal, the strong tea scent of impatience, of satisfaction denied.'

'Fuck,' Angelo whispered, and somehow it sounded like a plea for help.

She looked around the room and found the ladder-back chair Angelo had been sitting in when she was there last night. She pulled it next to the bed and sat down. 'Please don't stop,' she said again. Her voice was breathless as she pulled their scent into her. At first Paulo thought he was imagining her shifting and rocking against the chair, it was so subtle. But he certainly wasn't imagining the bullet points of her nipples straining against the deep scoop of her dress, and he was sure he could smell her. He sniffed and Angelo sniffed. They all sniffed.

Angelo shifted again and shoved his trousers down until his ass was bare against the thin leather padding of the bed.

'We need this,' she said, as Paulo did the same. 'Martelli needs this. The smell of two men – the testosterone, the phenomenal jolt will drive women, and men, crazy. There's a reason why women like reading male/male erotica,' she said. 'Imagine if they could smell it? Imagine if they could wear that scent, or have their lovers wear that scent? Man squared.'

'Or if they could pick up someone in a bar wearing that scent,' Angelo added. His laugh sounded raw, like it was raked through with sandpaper. 'Come on, Liza Calendar. It's hardly fair for you to sit there and watch us have a wank and not return the favour.' Before Paulo could decide if he liked the idea of Liza masturbating in front of Angelo, the man addressed him. 'What do you think, Paulo? Wouldn't you like to watch our lovely Ms Calendar get her rocks off? Wouldn't you like to see how she plays with herself while she sniffs a little male/male?'

For a second, Paulo had forgotten how to speak, so he nodded, then babbled that yes, he would like that, and he realized he really would, and he really didn't mind that Angelo Serafini was watching. In fact the whole idea was pretty fucking hot.

A lovely pink blush started just between Liza's

breasts and rose over their rounded tops like the ripening of fruit in the sun as it climbed her neck and caressed her cheeks.

At first she cupped hard at her left breast, as though it suddenly pained her, as though it caused her discomfort, as though it didn't sit quite right in the lacy bra he could imagine her wearing underneath. Angelo sucked breath between his teeth as she lifted her bottom from the seat of the chair and, with her eyes locked on them, she reached up under the skirt of her dress and wriggled out of her panties, then toed them off over her shoes, demurely keeping her knees together.

'Fuck,' Angelo whispered again. Paulo suspected that his vocabulary had become just as reduced by the riptide presence of Liza Calendar as his own had.

After that, she avoided their gaze, not in a shy or embarrassed way so much as a way that said she was having a private moment whether the two men on the bed were watching her or not and, Christ, that made it so much hotter than if she'd played the porn star and acted like she was flirting with the camera, like she was flirting with them. Instead, Liza focused wholly on the olfactory experience of the two of them on the bed and what it was causing to happen between her legs, at that delicious juncture hidden above her thighs. She squirmed, and then frowned as though she couldn't quite get comfortable on the seat. The hand kneading her breast had worried the nipple to an obscene press against the fabric as she wriggled and sniffed and wriggled and sniffed some more. When her other hand began to ease its way up under the hem of the dress, Paulo had to thumb the end of his cock to keep control. In his peripheral vision, he could see Angelo doing the same.

Liza made no attempt to hide the fact that she was

sniffing them, testing their scent, learning it, using it to heighten her arousal. All the while she shoved and scrunched at the dress until there was just a tight wad of fabric crushed in her palm up close and personal against her bare mons, obstructing the view of what Paulo and Angelo were both aching to see. The palm pressed, scrunched and relaxed, pressed, scrunched and relaxed in a motion that had to feel oh so good and yet not good enough. She sucked in a heavy breath and released it in a little whimper, then shifted until she could pull the fabric out from under her bottom. And when all that obstructed their view was her hand and the scrunched wad of fabric beneath it, she looked up at them, as though she'd only just realized they watched, as though begging their permission to indulge. Of course she had it. She shoved the fabric aside and looked down at her tightly trimmed curls as though this were the view she had also been waiting for. There was a collective moan from all three of them as she shifted again and opened her legs wide. With her eyes still locked on her mons, she slid her index and middle fingers down either side the heavy folds of her labia and pulled herself open.

Angelo released a strangled groan and Paulo went into shallow breathing mode to keep from coming as she began to thumb the garnet red press of her clit while slipping the two fingers up into her wetness, dipping and thrusting and rubbing until they glistened with her juices, and the smell of female heat joined the male-dominated scent in the dungeon. She bit her lip and wriggled her hips so that their view between her splayed legs was all the way back nearly to her anus. Then she uttered a little sigh. 'Can you smell us all together, the three of us? My God, I want this scent! I want to wear this scent all over my body. And I want more, and …' She looked up at them and caught her breath in a little sob '… I want it all blended together.' Her eyes locked on Paulo, and this time he understood. He understood that she was asking permission to play. Next to him, Angelo had stopped moving, stopped breathing, almost as though he had turned into the same marble from which the statue of Hercules in Ostia Antica had been sculpted. To his credit, he said nothing. There were no rude comments, no egging on. Paulo took one breath, then another, and with each he took in her tidal pool and honey scent and the dark scent of male rubbing up against male, and he yielded.

He reached out his hand to her and her moan came out a little gasp as she closed her fingers around his and let him pull her onto the bed, her dress still bunched up around her waist, her breasts still threatening to heave themselves over the scoop of the bodice.

Angelo's groan sounded nearly painful as he reached for her, impatient, and yet careful, as though he were afraid she still might run. The wallow of her on top of the two of them threatened the safety of cocks and balls before both men realized she was making space for herself in between, but not to sit as they did, rather to kneel. At first her mouth found Paulo's with a devastating kiss that nipped and pushed and shoved its way into his mouth. And while she kissed him, she guided Angelo's hand to her breast. He leaned forward to kiss and lick her collar bone, one hand fumbling for the zipper up the back of her dress, and once it was open, he tugged at it and the front hook of her bra until her breasts tumbled free into his hands, but not before she turned her attention to his mouth with the same devastation. Paulo had no time to feel the loss, as she guided his hand up into the velvety wet splay of her pussy, and he found himself once again battling for control.

'Can you smell us? Can you smell us? Oh God, can you smell us?' she whispered against Angelo's mouth, and both men nodded dumbly, as their hands went exploring and she seesawed between them, her tongue first in Paulo's mouth, then in Angelo's, her fingers curled in their hair, pulling them to her mouth, darting back and forth as though she were testing two of her favourite dishes. 'Can you smell us?' With each kiss, she drew them both closer to her. 'Oh God, can you smell us?' And with each kiss the mingling of their breath in that place in the middle was a maelstrom of moist heat and hunger. Their heads were all but touching, shoulders were pressed to pectoral muscles, stomach muscles fought each other for space in their effort to pump oxygen, in their effort to get closer to any delicious part of Liza Calendar. 'Can you smell it?' she breathed the words half into Paulo's mouth, half into Angelo's. 'Can you smell what I want? Surely you both have to smell it.' With a wet slide of a kiss that crossed boundaries and glided over both their mouths and settled in between, her fingers curled to tight fists in their hair and with a whimper of need, she pulled back just enough that Paulo's lips brushed Angelo's, just enough that Angelo's tongue glided across Paulo's lower lip.

There was a harsh sucking of breath and the woman between them shivered. 'Oh God yes! Oh fuck! You have to be able to smell that. It takes up all the breathing space. It's like downing in lust.' For a frozen moment, Angelo pulled away from Paulo just enough that the two men were nose to nose in their out-of-focus effort to search each other's face for permission. Then Liza's fists tightened in their hair, and the none-too-gentle pressure of her hands all but forced their mouths together again. The snake and glide of Paulo's tongue in between Angelo's lips, the yielding and opening of Angelo's mouth combined with the slip of the man's large hand to cradle the back of Paulo's neck and pull him deeper into the kiss might as well have been a gigantic 'permission granted' sign.

Liza sniffed and breathed and nipped at jawbones and ears, resting a hand on each man's outer shoulder in a three-way embrace. 'I'm in heaven,' she repeated. 'I'm in absolute paradise.'

'Fuck,' Angelo whispered into Paulo's mouth. 'Oh fuck.'

It was quite possible that Liza was the only one with even half her brain engaged at the moment, as she shifted and shoved to move her way down their bodies while they explored each other's mouths. Christ, it had been a long time since Paulo and Angelo had done anything even close to having sex with each other. Paulo was just thinking how good it felt when Liza simultaneously gave both of their sacs a cupping then fisted a cock in each hand and both men nearly skyrocketed off the bed. For a heartbeat, she held both of them, and Paulo was pretty sure he had totally forgotten how to breathe. Then she released their cocks and, did they both actually growl? But they needn't have felt bereft. It took her a second to shrug the rest of the way out of her bra and dress, the latter she used as a towel, wiping it up over both their bellies in turn and then down under their balls and over the length of their erections. Then she pulled the dress to her face and inhaled and moaned and inhaled again.

They were a captive audience, completely hypnotized by Liza Calendar's orgy of scent, her seeming worship of their bodies through that scent. She shoved the dress to the side, but not so far that it wasn't touching flesh, and then she got down to business. And fuck what a business it was! First, she took Paulo's cock into her mouth deeper than he would have thought possible, and she sucked and licked, all the while pumping Angelo with her fist. And then she switched and sucked Angelo's cock.

'Woman …' Angelo gulped breath between his teeth '… you keep that up there's gonna be a quick finish, and I don't know about you, but I like to make my fun last. Besides …' he curled his fingers in her hair and grunted as she sucked particularly hard '… I want to know if that lovely cunt of yours tastes anywhere near as luscious as it smells.'

There was a quick wordless exchange between Paulo and Angelo, and all the years fell away. Both men moved in unison, grabbing Liza beneath the armpit and hauling her up the bed in between them. There was another flurry of three-way kisses and then Paulo reached beneath the bed and pulled out a hank of soft rope. Angelo did the same on the other side. Liza let out a little yelp of surprise, then inhaled that surprise quickly as though she wanted to see how the appearance of the rope, how the mix of surprise with a tiny bit of fear would set with her nose. Both men took the mmmm that sounded almost like a cat purr to mean that the scent was to her liking. It was as though they shared the same thoughts as they worked wordlessly to bind her spread-eagle to the bedposts. From somewhere Anglo produced a leather rolled pillow and slid it under her hips, lingering to pinch her clit. And chuckle his satisfaction at her hiss of a response.

'We're not going to gag you, Liza, darling,' Angelo's voice was velvet smooth, 'but you'll need to keep quiet unless we ask you what you smell, or unless it's too much for you, then use your safeword. If you break that simple rule, well, there'll be punishment.'

She batted her eyes and nodded that she understood, all the while sniffing and snuffling like a wild animal who had been the predator but had suddenly become prey.

'Paulo, why don't you take first taste of that wet little pussy, and I think I'll enjoy her lovely tits until it's my turn.' The sudden and rare emergence of the American accent was thick, almost a southern drawl as Angelo caressed and kneaded Liza's breasts. Paulo didn't wait for a second invite. He lowered his head for a look at the engorged, shimmery-slick landscape pouting and begging before him. And the scent, dear God, the scent of Liza Calendar was ecstasy. He shivered two fingers up from her perineum to open her heavy folds so that he could see the slippery path to pleasure in between. For a second, he stroked two fingers into her wet hole and watched in fascination as her grip tightened around them, and all but sucked them into her. Then he leaned in and nipped her clit between his front teeth. She growled, bucked hard against him, and Angelo chuckled. 'Sonofabitch, bro, I think you made her come already. Where's the delayed gratification? Where's the making her wait?'

'I'm not a patient man, Angelo,' he breathed against Liza's trembling swell. 'And besides, this is only just a warm-up. You should know that.' He stroked and caressed her hips and bottom until the tremors in her slit eased and then he dove in tongue first, and Liza went wild.

'Hold still,' Angelo commanded, 'or we'll have to punish you. Hold still and let Paulo eat. In fact, you look pretty hungry yourself. Maybe you'd like to eat.' From somewhere Paulo hadn't seen, Angelo produced another pillow and placed it under Liza's head. Then he straddled her ribcage, cupped a breast in each hand and pushed them together until they formed a tight valley into which Angelo inserted his cock with a grunt. And Liza didn't need any coaching. She knew exactly what he wanted. With each thrust, as his cock slid up through her cleavage, she lapped at the head of it as though it were ice cream on a summer day, and that tongue of hers seemed to have a mind of its own.

Paulo would have loved to closed his eyes and concentrated on the delicious seashore taste of Liza's arousal and the smell that now coated his face, but he didn't want to miss what Angelo was doing either, though he only got the occasional glimpse from beyond the tightening thrust and press of the man's muscular ass cheeks and the grip and release, grip and release of his anus as he thrust.

'What do you smell?' Paulo said, pulling away and wiping his face on the inside of her thigh. And again it was as though the two men were working her in unison. Angelo found Paulo's shed shirt on the bed and wiped her mouth, his cock, and the valley between her breasts, then tossed it to Paulo who wiped the scent from between her legs and then rubbed it all over his chest while both she and Angelo watched. 'What do you smell?' he asked again, circling her clit with an index finger, then giving it a tweak that made her suck air.

'I smell cinnamon and burnt sugar lust.' Angelo rose over her on his hands and knees, one hand pumping his cock fast and furious, the other fingering her pussy in time. She grunted and squirmed and spoke faster as though she feared she wouldn't be able to finish. 'I smell earth and flit and steel and the first spark in dried summer grass just before it bursts into flame.' She threw her head back and arched against her bonds as Angelo buried his face between her legs and laved with his tongue her like she was dinner.

'What else?' Paulo urged, stroking his own cock for all it was worth. 'What else do you smell?'

'I smell the sea and honey and cream and lightning and rain in the desert. I smell citrus and hot metal. I smell hot pepper urgency and dark damp ground waiting to be cultivated.' Just then her body stiffened as though her back would break and she came hard into Angelo's mouth, but the man grasped her buttocks with both hands and held her still, eating at her mercilessly until she cried out in raw-throated sobs and convulsed against her bonds. And when she collapsed back against the bed, Angelo pulled away from her wet-faced and came to his knees between her legs, furiously pumping his cock. 'Take her, Paulo.' His voice was little more than a low growl. 'Take her now.' He bit back the last word with a harsh hiss as he came, his semen arching up over her belly and her breasts, the very act of which made her come again and Paulo felt his own balls tighten as he moved down between her legs and thrust into her warm slick depths feeling like he'd found his way home.

Angelo untied Liza's arms almost as though he intuited what the woman would do next, and then he watched while she rubbed his cum against her skin as though it were expensive lotion.

'You like that, don't you, Liza Calendar. You like the feel of my jizz as much as you do the scent.'

She nodded and grunted, too breathless to form words.

'Paulo's going to fuck you now.' He spoke first against her lips and then her throat. 'He's going to fuck you for both of us.'

Then he moved to untie the bonds from her ankles and she lifted her legs high around Paulo's hips. For a second, Angelo remained at the foot of the bed watching, then one hand came to rest on Paulo's shoulder. Paulo stilled, and Liza's nostrils flared.

'Oh God! Oh God! Oh my God,' she whispered, her eyes darting from Paulo to Angelo and back again. She sniffed hard. Paulo knew she smelled the change in scent. He wished he could smell it. He wish he knew what it must be like for her. He could feel the vibrations of the tug, tug, tug of Angelo's hand on his cock, which Paulo was certain was hard again. Then Angelo's hand slid from Paulo's shoulder down his back to rest for a second low on his hip, then his middle finger slid up into Paulo's anus.

Liza's sniff and moan became a low keening, as she clawed and clung and thrust against Paulo. 'Smells like wet earth, smells like hot bread, smells like hot iron and cloves.' Paulo scooped Liza close and rose up on his knees to give Angelo better access.

'He's going to fuck you.' Her voice was a breathless gasp of incredulity.

'I am, indeed,' Angelo said. Then he spat on his hand, slathered Paulo's anus and his own cock and shoved home in a thrust that nearly flattened Paulo onto Liza until they all caught their rhythm. 'It's been a while, Paulo,' he whispered against his nape, 'but you still take me with real gusto.'

Paulo made no response. He was too caught up in the moment, too caught up in Liza's wonder. He could see it in her eyes, feel it in her body. One of her arms was curled tightly around his neck and the other had reached beyond to caress Angelo, whose response to her touch was damn near a purr, and Angelo did not purr!

'Do it, lovely Liza,' Angelo gasped, nipping at Paulo's ear, then kissing her caressing hand. 'We're all ready. Finish it, so we can come together.'

She arched up, tightening her milking grip on Paulo just as Angelo thrust up hard in a follow-through and sure enough, they all came together. Liza's cry was deep and guttural as her nails scored Paulo's shoulder and both men roared their orgasms in unison as Liza whimpered with the last remains of her voice, 'smells so good, smells so good, smells so good.'

Together the men cleaned Liza and each other and, at her insistence, they bagged their clothing in zip-locks to be taken back to the Martelli research facility. From a closet at the far end of the dungeon, Angelo produced generic grey sweat bottoms and T-shirts. 'The Mount is well equipped with extra clothing,' Paulo told her as she slipped into the over-sized T-shirt. 'Clothing tends to get … damaged from time to time.'

Angelo had been strangely silent since their lovemaking and, really, Paulo could call it nothing else. Liza Calendar had gotten to him, he was pretty sure. And for some reason he no longer minded. For some reason, he wanted to slap the man on the back and tell him that he completely understood. He half felt guilty because he had every intention of driving the woman home and taking her again before the night was over. Though he found he had enjoyed their threesome far more than he would have thought possible, there was still a part of him that wanted her all to himself.

'Is Jim still here?' she asked as Paulo sealed up the last bag. 'Will he take bags to the facility?'

'We won't wait until morning,' Paulo said. 'Coraline has a driver waiting to deliver them.' He had called upstairs to find his boss was still in the Suite and not at all surprised that the three of them would be supplying new samples for the experiments. He knew her well enough to figure that was her plan when she sent Liza down to the dungeon.

'I'm trying not to let my feelings get hurt because you wanted me just for my smell, darlin'' Angelo said, then he gave them both a wicked smile. 'On the other hand, for what we just did,' he nodded toward the bondage bed they had just romped all over, 'you can sniff me any time.' He gave her a long, lingering kiss then, as an afterthought, he did the same to Paulo. While they both caught their breath, he settled back on the bed, looking a bit like the cat who ate the cream.

'Sweet dreams,' Paulo managed. Then slipped an arm around Liza's shoulder. 'Come on. I'll take you home.'

They turned to find Jim and Coraline standing at the foot of the stairs.

'Afraid you'll have to let one of my drivers have that honour, Paulo,' Coraline said, offering Liza an apologetic smile. 'I need to see both you and Jim in the Suite.'

'Your timing sucks,' Paulo said. Then he pulled Liza into his arms and made no attempt to hide the kiss that turned into a full-frontal rub-up. 'That's a down-payment with a promise of what's to come when I finally do manage to get you alone.' He wasn't sure if what he'd done was for Liza's benefit or for Angelo's. He didn't mind sharing her with the man when they were together, but he wasn't sure he liked the idea of leaving her alone with him. As they all turned to head back upstairs, Anglo flopped down on the bondage bed as though it were a primo mattress in a five-star hotel and stretched out with his arms folded behind his head as though they were already gone.

Chapter Nineteen

'What the hell is so important that it couldn't wait until morning?' Paulo asked the minute the door closed behind the three of them in the Suite.

'Sit down, Paulo,' Coraline said.

'Is it really going to take that long?'

'I don't know how long it's going to take, now sit down.' Her voice was soft as it always was, but there was no mistaken the sharp metal edge just beneath the velvet surface, the one no one with any sense of self-preservation would argue with. He found himself wondering what that edge would smell like to Liza.

As soon as he was seated on the burgundy leather sofa, she nodded to Jim.

The man cleared his throat and tugged at the tie Paulo was surprised to see he was still wearing.

'What's going on?' Paulo asked, feeling the muscles in his shoulders tense.

'Did you know that Liza Calendar has a relationship with Carl Blain?' Jim asked.

'What?' Paulo nearly came off the sofa. 'What the hell are you talking about?'

'She took a tumble at Ostia. Oh, nothing serious,' he shook an open hand as though he were erasing a chalkboard. 'Her BlackBerry rang; she went to answer it and tripped on the uneven cobbles. I caught her before she fell, but not before the device went sailing into the verge. When I picked it up to hand it back, I saw that the caller was Carl Blain.' He shot an apologetic look at Paulo. 'Oh, I know she's a journalist, and I discovered after the fact that her magazine did an article on the Blain Holdings what was it, six months ago? But it was the look on her face when she saw who it was that got my attention. I don't know if she was unhappy about the call or if she was unhappy about the timing. She certainly didn't realize that I saw who the call was from, but when I asked her if she needed to take it, she shoved the device into her bag and said no. It wasn't important.'

Paulo ran a palm over his face, suddenly realizing just how tired he was. 'Well maybe she said that because it wasn't important. You just told me her magazine had done an article. I don't think it's all that unusual for someone who's been interviewed by a magazine to get back in touch.'

Coraline nodded thoughtfully, and Jim shifted uncomfortably on the edge of an enormous wing-backed chair. 'They were dating.'

Paulo's heart stopped, then juddered forward. 'Dating?'

'Well it was obviously a long-distance sort of relationship with her living on the West Coast, but certain gossip columns were speculating about her possibly being the future Mrs Carl Blain, you know, sort of a Cinderella story.'

'And?' Paulo barely heard his own voice over the loud buzzing in his ears.

'Well, she was seen going into his apartment building the night before she flew to Rome.'

Paulo gripped the arm of the sofa until his knuckles were white. Fuck! She had been with Blain the night before she was with him on the flight to Rome? Surely he couldn't have misjudged her that badly, not Liza Calendar, not the woman he knew?

'My point is,' Jim continued, 'it seems like quite a

coincidence that Liza Calendar is with Carl Blain the night before her flight, then gets your attention on the flight in such a spectacular way.'

'I came on to her. In the plane, I mean.' Paulo struggled not to sound defensive. 'And there was no place else for me to sit in the lounge but next to her. She couldn't have planned that.'

'Never mind the flight and the lounge,' Coraline said. 'It's quite possible that was all just icing on the cake, an unexpected bonus.'

'And don't forget, security caught her sneaking into your office,' Jim said.

'But her story makes sense,' Paulo argued. 'She would have caught my scent and she would have been able to follow me there. You both know what she's capable of.'

'We know what she's capable of,' Coraline said, 'but without the Martelli facilities, her capabilities are irrelevant, aren't they?'

Paulo felt as though he were falling through the floor. 'You think she's working for Blain?'

'Think about it,' Jim said. 'Think of all the coincidences, and us with the new line, the very expensive new line that's already cost Martelli a fortune, all depending on her nose. It seems to me like the ideal set-up for Blain to use her to get to us and then force his hostile takeover – which he knows he doesn't have a snowball's chance in hell of pulling off otherwise.'

'Yes, the takeover.' For an instant Coraline seemed miles away. Then she added, 'Carl Blain is his father's son'.

'No.' Paulo shook his head wildly. 'Blain may be his father's son, of that I have no doubt, but Liza wouldn't do that. Liza would never betray us.'

'Look,' Coraline said, laying a hand on his knee.

'We're not saying that she would. We're just saying that it's a risk, and you need to be aware that there may be an enemy in the camp, and she may be someone we all thought we could trust.'

'Does Rita trust her?' Paulo asked.

Coraline blinked and straightened in her chair.

'You said she was Rita's friend. You said Rita helped arranged the Martelli connections Liza would need for the article she wanted to write.'

'Lots of people take advantage of their wealthy connections,' Jim said.

'I can't believe the two of you,' Paulo stood and began to pace. 'Rita trusts her. She's helping Martelli in ways we never could have thought possible, and we pulled her into this. Don't forget that, we pulled her in. If Rita trusts her that's good enough for me.'

'Rita's loyal,' Coraline said softly.

'Look, Paulo,' Jim stood to pace next to him, 'all I'm saying is there are a helluva lot of coincidences here, and the more research I do, the more I'm inclined to doubt Liza Calendar's motives.' He raised a hand before Paulo could speak. 'All I'm saying is be aware and keep an eye on her. You know the saying; "keep your friends close and your enemies closer." Well you're doing a good job of keeping her close, just keep it up.'

Paulo clenched his fists and held them tight to his sides resisting the sudden urge to punch Jim in the face. 'She's not the enemy.'

'And you're sure of that?' Jim asked.

'Are we finished here?' Paulo turned his attention to Coraline. 'Because I'm really tired and I need some rest. I have a busy day in the lab tomorrow.'

'We're finished,' Coraline said.

He didn't say good-bye; he just turned on his heels and headed toward the door.

‘Paulo,’ Coraline called. ‘All I’m asking is that you be aware of the possibility.’

He didn’t reply, but jerked the door open and did his best to slam it as he left. He was halfway down the hall toward the entrance to the villa, when he changed his mind, turned back through the house, and out through the gardens, all but running through the maze and past the fountains until he came to the entrance of the dungeon. He let himself in and took the stairs two at a time.

‘Back so soon?’ Angelo asked without looking up. He was still sprawled on the bondage bed as he had been when Paulo and Liza left. ‘Did you decide since you couldn’t get Liza alone, you’d settle for me? I’m flattered, but …’ as he rose to one elbow and looked up at Paulo, his words died in his throat. ‘What is it, bro? What’s wrong?’

‘I need a favour.’ Paulo sat down on the bed next to him.

‘Tell me.’ Angelo pulled himself up and sat with his legs crossed while Paulo told him what had happened upstairs.

‘That’s bullshit.’ He said when Paulo finished. ‘I don’t know Jim. But I know Coraline. She’s usually more intuitive than that.’

Paulo released a heavy breath. ‘There’s a lot at stake, like she says.’

‘And you want me to do a little snooping?’

Paulo held his gaze. ‘You know I wouldn’t ask –’

‘If we both didn’t have a warm spot for our lovely Liza? Yes, I know. And you don’t have to ask where she’s concerned. But in the meantime, there’s something you need to do that’ll give you peace of mind, hell, give us both peace of mind really.’

Paulo raised an eyebrow.

‘Ask her.’ Angelo swung his legs over the edge of

the bed to sit next to him. 'Ask Liza about Carl. Ask her to tell you what happened.' He held Paulo's gaze. 'Often a helluva lot of trouble and energy could have been saved if people would just ask.' His lips curled into a tight smile. 'In the meantime I'll do some research of my own. Jim's a paper-pusher and a Martelli cheerleader. He's not an expert when it comes to finding the dirt. If he were, I'm pretty sure he'd find the dirt at Carl Blain's door and not Liza's.' He gave Paulo a sharp slap on the back. 'Go home and get some sleep, bro. You look like hell, and I know it's not because you were poorly slept with. Get some shut-eye, calm down, and then tomorrow, take the woman out for lunch, or even breakfast, and ask her.' Angelo stood long enough for a good, hard stretch, raising muscular arms toward the ceiling, then he dropped them with a shake and sprawled back onto the bed. 'Turn out the light when you leave,' he said as Paulo stood to go. 'A man needs his beauty sleep, you know.'

At the steps, Paulo reached for the light switch and turned back to thank Angelo. But he had rolled onto his side with his back to Paulo, and though he looked to be already asleep, Paulo knew he was ruminating on what he'd just heard.

'Thanks, bro,' Paulo said softly, then he turned off the light and climbed the travertine steps into the moonlight.

Chapter Twenty

'You're going to need a boost midday to keep you going after the night you've had.' Vera's smile was wicked as she met Jim's gaze through the mirror in front of which she stood worrying a tiny purple thong up over her exquisite ass. Jim met her eyes briefly, but he couldn't keep his gaze off the brazen points of her nipples that crowned the stippled pinch of generous areolae on bare and way more than adequate breasts. Watching her reflection in the mirror, as he was, he'd been enjoying the shimmy and dance of her spectacular frontage as she put on her make-up. While he ogled her delicious front through the mirror, he also got a great view of the pillow-puffed heart shape of her bottom, with the occasional glimpse of her pink pussy when she bent forward toward the mirror to finesse her make-up. Had it been just twenty, maybe thirty minutes since he'd had his cock buried in the lovely little slit with her sitting on top of him whimpering and mewling and tugging at her bouncing tits? And that was just the last time. She was waiting in his flat when he got back from The Mount last night. He'd given her a key. After all, everyone knew that they were doing the nasty. He was amazed at how easily he'd been able to pump out another load this morning after the way she had ridden him and sucked him, and now here he was with his cock at a half-mast pressing against his Armani again.

'Afraid I'll have to settle for coffee and lots of it,' he said.

'I was thinking a nice blow job, you know, with me under your desk sucking and cupping.' Her giggle was throaty and thick. 'Who would know?'

He grunted. 'Liza Calendar would know. That's who.'

'So what? You get a lunch break. It's none of her business what you do on it.'

'I just don't like the idea that she can smell when I've had sex. It creeps me out. I mean it's amazing, don't get me wrong, but some things you just don't want the employees to know, even if they are on special dispensation.'

She glanced over her shoulder, then she went back to work on her mascara. 'Is she really that good?'

'She's that good and then some. At first I thought she was a fake, you know? I mean how can anyone have that good a sense of smell? But she's the real deal.' He moved to Vera's side and fumbled with his tie. 'I just wish I trusted her a little more.'

'Oh?' Her mouth was shaped like a lion about to roar as she did her bottom lashes.

'It's nothing. It's just, well some of her associations are a bit questionable, that's all.' And he'd already said too much. Christ, what was it about Vera that made him so talkative? He was usually very tight-lipped.

'Associates, like who?' She said, going back to her make-up.

For a second he watched the dance and sway of her breasts. She must have sensed him watching, but maybe it was just her way. She put the mascara back in her bag and stood admiring her efforts, absently cupping the breast closest to him and stroking the nipple with her thumb. 'Anyone I know?'

'Do you know Carl Blain?' Fuck, how had that slipped out?

She'd gone to pinching and tugging while still staring in the mirror at her reflection. 'I've heard of him, yes. Some big businessman in the States, right?'

'Apparently she's dating him.'

She raised an eyebrow. 'The woman gets around.' Now both hands were cupping and tugging and she looked into the mirror as though her thoughts were on something else entirely. She was horny again. He doubted she'd heard a word he said, and his cock was responding nicely to her caresses in spite of the hard workout she'd already given it. He moved closer, slapped one hand away, and went to work on the nearest breast with his lips. His cock was now in full press-up position, urging him on.

She moaned and slipped her hand, which now had nothing else to do, into the front of her thong and the jerk and shift of her wrist and forearm muscles told him she had found the sweet spot. 'So, are you going to take me to the research facility today? I really do want to see where it all happens. I mean I have a degree in chemistry, you know. I would love to see the process in action.'

'Yeah, why not?' He unzipped his fly and moved in behind her. She pulled the back of her thong out of the way and pressed her bottom toward him, opening her legs, as he parted her slippery pussy lips with his fingers and slid in with a tight grunt. 'I'm going there anyway this afternoon. How about I give you a tour? There's a really,' he thrust hard, 'really nice broom closet on the second floor that no one uses.'

'Mmmm. For me, the broom closet is always the highlight of a tour, Mr Dryer. It sounds perfect.'

And, he thought, as he slid a hand over her mons to tweak her clit, it was far enough away from where Liza Calendar would be working that she wouldn't smell them. He'd take Vera there after they saw the actual facility. God, he just hoped Paulo took their little conversation at The Mount's villa to heart. He knew he was fucking the woman, but there was way too much at stake for him to think with his cock, or even worse with his heart. And the evidence didn't look good at all. Thinking that Liza might be working for Carl Blain nearly caused him to lose his erection, but then Vera's pussy clamped down on his cock and focused his attention very firmly on the business at hand.

Honestly, Liza. I just can't end it this way. I owe you so much, not the least of which is an apology for my stupidity, for my total moronic stupidity! But a message on my voicemail is just not something I can settle for. Please call me back. At least meet me and let's talk this out like two adults. Please.

Liza ground her teeth at yet another fucking message from Carl. Why the hell was he to think he had the right to feel wounded by her? It was what it was, and frankly she didn't give a damn who he porked. She just wanted him to leave her alone, especially now when things were just getting truly interesting. Damn it, she supposed she would just have to bite the bullet and have a messy conversation with him to get it all over with. She'd really thought the phone call she made would have finished it.

'Morning,' Paulo said, sliding onto the stool next to her. Fuck, he looked good in the white research coat, and his scent, dear God, his scent was heavenly.

'Morning,' she replied with a little sniff. 'You're not going to believe all the lovely scents we got last night. Plus we've got several zip-locks from private erotic sessions some of The Mount's members sent in. It'll be good to compare how sex smells when no one's observing. I'd also like to get out in the city tonight and pick up on some scents in a group situation. I think if we've got … Paulo? What's wrong?'

'You all right?' he asked. She could see his pulse beating against his throat.

She smiled up at him from her notes, suddenly feeling a different kind of nerves, but she ploughed ahead. 'Never better. A little sore, but I had fun getting that way. You?'

When he didn't answer, she laid her pen down and found herself drowning deliciously in his creamy coffee gaze. 'What? What's going on?'

'You're all right with The Mount then, and what goes on there?' A blush flashed over his cheekbones. 'I mean I guess you must be after, you know, with Angelo and me and all.'

'Paulo,' she laid a hand, gloved in latex, on the sleeve of his coat, 'are you all right with what happened last night, because I wouldn't have … I wouldn't have done what I did if I'd thought you weren't.'

He nodded briskly, all businesslike again, and pulled her notepad to him for a peek. 'I'm all right with it. Really I am. Angelo's a pain in the ass but he's also a good friend.' The blush was back. 'More than a friend at one time, but I guess you could probably tell that,' he said, avoiding her gaze.

She picked up the pen and worried it between her fingers. 'Thought that might be the case, yes. That doesn't bother me either, if that's what you're worried about.'

'It's not that, I mean I don't mind that you know Angelo and I have a history. It's just, well, I'm amazed by the whole experience, actually. I mean things haven't been good between Angelo and me for a while, and Angelo, well Angelo's a law unto himself. He's unpredictable at the best of times, but I've never seen him like he was with you. Me, he figured he could have, and I'd be OK with it. But then, I hadn't expected how he … the way he actually …'

'The way he deferred to you when it came to having sex with me. I know. I got that, and it surprised me, I have to admit. So what's the problem then?'

'I'm just …'

'You're just what?'

'Well, I'm sorry I didn't get to go home with you. Seems like we never quite manage any serious alone time.'

'Paulo, I can smell you, remember? And you smell like swamp mud.' She shook her head. 'I don't mean you smell like swamp mud, but the fact that something's bothering you smells like swamp mud. Are you angry at me for what happened? Did I do something wrong? What's eating you? I can't sit here and work next to you with you smelling like that and me not knowing why.'

His laugh was self-conscious, like he'd been caught masturbating in the men's room. 'God, a conversation with you has interesting twists and turns, Liza Calendar.'

'Talk to me and I won't have to tie you to the post and sniff you up.'

He laughed again and shifted to face her, raising his eyes almost shyly. 'That's a proposition I could be totally tempted by. If you're threatening, you're going to have to do better than that.'

'Then tell me before I get nasty.'

'Are you sleeping with Carl Blain?' he blurted out, and she dropped the pen on the floor with a clatter that sounded like a car crash in the silence.

She smelled the adrenaline surge of her anger like

burnt coffee. 'No, I'm not sleeping with Carl Blain. If I were sleeping with Carl Blain I wouldn't be sleeping with you. I've never slept with Carl Blain. I had a couple of dates with him. Oh, I know what a few of the gossip columns said, but I don't know where they got their ideas, and really, it was something that just could have never worked.'

'Why?' His gaze was now locked on her like a pit bull, and though he didn't seem angry, it was clear she wasn't going to get away without full disclosure. 'Why would it have not worked?'

'He makes me sneeze.'

The burst of laughter made his eyes sparkle and then water. 'He makes you sneeze?'

'I know, right? I mean I tried taking allergy pills, and they suppressed my sense of smell so I could date him, but he wanted more, and well, in the end I had to trust my nose, I mean who wants to have sex with someone who makes them sneeze, and who wants to have sex with someone who sneezes all over them?'

He wiped tears of laughter from the corners of his eyes. 'You're amazing, Liza Calendar. The man makes you sneeze.' He was suddenly serious again, and he swallowed hard. 'But you were with him the night before you flew to Rome.'

She felt heat rush to her face. 'Not that it's any of your business, but I went to his apartment, yes. And yes, I knew that he wanted sex. I was early.' She hmphed out a laugh. 'Looking back, I guess I just wanted to get it over with. When I got there he was … already occupied, and from the smell of his flat, he was frequently occupied with a variety of partners.'

'Bastard,' Paulo hissed.

She smiled. 'Doesn't matter. Frankly it was like a get out of jail free card. I was just going to sneak away and send him a text saying so long. But then I started sneezing. He and the chick he was porking saw me. I sneezed all the way out the door and halfway to the Airport Hilton, where I spent my very exciting last night in New York City reading a romance novel I downloaded on my Kindle. So no. I'm not seeing Carl Blain and no, I've never fucked the man, and how the hell did you know about Blain?' But before he could reply she remembered. 'It was Jim, wasn't it? Carl was calling when I tripped and dropped my BlackBerry at Ostia. Jim must have seen the caller ID. I thought he acted strange afterward.'

Paulo bristled again and the air smelled of hot metal. 'Why was he calling?'

'For the life of me, I don't know. I left a message saying no harm no foul. I mean I can't blame the man for fucking someone else when I kept putting him off. I'll probably have to bite the bullet and talk to him to finally get it all behind me, but I'm not thinking about that now, so can we get back to work? We have so many lovely scents here to work with and, in my head, I can already picture most of these fragrances and what'll set them apart and make them send the message we want.'

He raised an eyebrow. 'Did you sleep at all last night or did you just come right on over here?'

'When you couldn't go home with me to distract me with your lovely scent, I arranged to ride with the driver Coraline was sending over to the facility with the bagged clothing.' She shrugged. 'I worked until I got too muzzy-headed, then I caught a couple of winks on the sofa in the lounge. After that I made coffee and raided the vending machine and voila! We're so close, Paulo, and it's all so exciting to have such an olfactory orgy. I'm getting way more from my Roman holiday than I expected.'

Chapter Twenty-one

Carl's laughter was hot on Vera's neck. 'Seriously?' He pulled her up tight against him until she could feel the hard press of his erection through her linen skirt. Then he slid a hand inside her panties. 'It's her sense of smell they're after? The woman was on allergy meds the whole time I knew her.'

Vera elbowed him away. 'Look I know it sounds ridiculous, but after all the money Martelli has already spent on research, Coraline wouldn't be handing the new line over to Liza Calendar all tied up with a pretty red bow if she didn't think the woman could perform.' She elbowed him again as he grabbed her breast. 'I'm on my way to the research facility, Carl, and if I smell like you, she may know.'

'That's the most ridiculous thing I've ever heard,' he said.

'No it's not,' she shoved him away again, and he cursed out loud. 'I've got a lot at stake here too, you know. I don't know why Jim Dryer has connected you with Liza, but your name has been raised and that can't be good.'

He sat down on the edge of the bed and watched her with hooded eyes. 'Look it's no secret that I dated the woman, and if they suspect her of working with me, well, I can't see that as anything but good really. I mean think about it. Dryer is sleeping with you. He's now confiding in you. Coraline Martelli has even let you fill in for he prissy little PA. You're a trusted employee at Martelli. Sowing a few seeds of mistrust in Liza Calendar's direction can only serve us well.' He unzipped his fly, released his cock, and began to stroke. 'And I think I might have an idea of how we can just encourage those seeds to grow into a nice crop of distrust when the time's right.' He nodded down to his erection. 'Let me think about it while you take care of this for me. Oh for fuck sake! You can brush your teeth before you leave.' He offered her a wicked smile. 'You always were a tidy eater.'

Later, feeling much more relaxed, Carl watched as Vera touched up her make-up, and let herself out of the hotel room, then he began to pace. It had been his plan all along to get Liza Calendar to pull a few strings and open a few doors into Martelli for him. But he figured, like most career women, she harbored secret hopes of finding a rich, affluent husband to father her children and raise her status and her income. He really figured he was just the ticket for Liza Calendar, and once she had stars in her eyes, she would get any information from Martelli he needed. But the way the tables had turned, she was going to be even more useful to him, and it would give him the perfect opportunity to get back at her for thinking she could just walk away from him like he was a nobody. Oh, yes. This was going to be lots of fun.

'Put emotion into it, yes, I got that, but how exactly do you think we should go about putting emotion into the new scents?' Paulo asked. Late afternoon sunlight flooded through the window of the break room at the research facility. Paulo stuffed half of a chocolate Milano into his mouth and tossed back the last of his espresso.

'Scent changes with emotion,' Liza replied, then she sniffled and reached for a tissue from a nearby box. 'And certain of those scents added in just the right quantity could really be that little something extra in a fragrance that would transform it from nice to unforgettable, which is what we want. You know, sort of like what happens when chocolatiers add pepper to chocolate. Emotions run high and change fast in, say a club or a bar.' She sniffled again then sneezed.

'Are you alright?' Paulo handed her the tissue box. 'You're not getting a cold, are you, because that would be a disaster right now.'

She blew her nose and sneezed again. 'Your concern is touching,' she half laughed.

He leaned closer. 'Well Blain is definitely not here, and if your nose even considers me making you sneeze, I'll whisk you back to the villa, tie you to the bondage bed, and have my way with you sneezing and all.'

'Oooh, Mr Delacour, I'm all aflutter.' She snuffled, then leaned forward and sniffed his throat. 'Trust me, what I smell radiating off you makes me want to do a lot of things, but sneezing's not one of them.' She pulled away and sneezed three more times into the tissue.

'Maybe it's something the cleaners are using?' Paulo said, reaching out to rub her shoulder.

Just then Jim walked into the room with Vera at his side. He looked all professional, but in spite of her sneeze-athon, Liza could smell the lust swirling between the two of them. Though Jim's herby scent didn't much turn her on, it certainly had never made her sneeze. Vera's scent had never made her sneeze either, though her it always made Liza think of overly ripe peaches on the verge of rotting with just a hint of something acidic. Between both of them, she could smell the slight citrus of nerves, but then Paulo was the boss and he was certainly smart enough to know that Vera didn't really need to be here.

'I thought I'd give Vera the tour,' Jim said with an overly enthusiastic smile. 'She's never been before, and it's nice for employees to see how things work. Gives them a vested interest.' The scent of nervous citrus spiked as they both offered a forced chuckle.

'And what do you think of the place?' Paulo asked.

'Oh, it's amazing!' Vera gushed. 'I'm so excited to finally see where it all happens. A bit disappointed, though, that it took so long to wrangle a tour.'

'Before Liza came along, even Jim didn't get here often,' Paulo said, 'Martelli didn't hire him for his nose.' Liza didn't need the harsh bronze undertone to tell that Paulo was unhappy with Jim. She wondered what was going on.

'Yes,' Vera smiled over at Jim, 'He had other important skills.'

Jim blushed hard and then tugged at his tie and the nervous citrus scent dominated the air once again. 'So how's the research going?' he asked, suddenly all business.

'Making great progress,' Paulo said as Liza sneezed once more.

'You're not catching a cold, are you?' Vera asked, the citrus scent still dominated the olfactory cocktail that she and Jim had brought into the room.

'Nope.' Liza spoke into the tissue. 'Probably just something the cleaners use here that I'm not used to.'

'So what's the plan?' Jim asked, pulling out a chair for Vera and sitting down across from the two of them. Liza sneezed again.

'Liza has something up her sleeve,' Paulo said before Liza could respond. The smell of nerves clashed with the bronze scent of irritation that rolled off Paulo. Something definitely wasn't right. Liza certainly understood men thinking with their cocks, but most of them were careful to keep their work out of it. Work involved power and, if anything, the testosterone was even higher where power was concerned than where lust was concerned. Of course the two were pretty closely connected. Surely Paulo wasn't upset that Jim was fucking Vera, not considering what the two of *them* were doing. Jim wouldn't be in the position he was in if he couldn't be trusted, and Vera, well Vera was an employee in good-standing – as far as Liza knew. Paulo could hardly blame Jim for taking her up on her offer. Though she couldn't say that the two of them smelled right together, if Jim couldn't smell her, and he was getting laid on a regular basis, no harm done, Liza figured. She sneezed again.

'Maybe it's something someone heated up in the microwave that's making you sneeze,' Jim said.

'I suppose that's possible,' Liza replied, blowing her nose. 'But whatever it is, I need to get out of here or my sense of smell will be worthless.'

She and Paulo said their goodbyes and left the break room to Jim and Vera.

'The way you're sneezing, I keep half expecting to run into Blain around the next corner,' Paulo said once they were in the hall.

She was thinking exactly the same thing, and it was really creeping her out. But by the time they got back to the lab, the sneezing had stopped and the possessive, ozone, and desert heat scent of lust rolling off Paulo made the butterflies low in her belly take flight.

Chapter Twenty-two

'Can you smell that?' Liza shouted at Paulo in order to be heard above the music.

He closed his eyes and sniffed hard but all he could smell was watered-down alcohol and sweat overlaid by too much cheap cologne.

She slid her chair around next to his and spoke in his ear. 'The couple behind us. From him, I smell acidic jealousy, and rusty-metal anger. The woman, she smells like female lust, wet earth and sea wind. She's flirting with that guy over there.' She nodded to a man at the bar, who was checking her out. 'He smells like a predator, all copper-sweet and chlorine sharp,' she said. 'He's on the hunt, and he's got his eye on the chick behind us.' She sniffed, then closed her eyes and sniffed again. 'She doesn't smell very faithful.'

'What does faithful smell like?' Paulo shouted back.

'Ah, faithful is a difficult scent to catch sometimes because it's so foundational. It's almost sweet, but not quite,' she said. He could tell by the upward twitch of on corner of her mouth and the way she drew her brow that she was trying to find words for the scent. At last she spoke. 'It's like vanilla or cinnamon, neither is sweet alone, but they always give that intimation of sweetness, like they should be even if they're not. Faithful smells basic. Like it just has to be there for things to work. Sort of like the gasoline smell that goes with cars,' she added, almost as an afterthought. 'There's a slight hint of bitterness, you know? Those things that blend best with sweet are often bitter at their root and uncomfortable, but it's the bitter-sweet anchor that holds them together.' She looked up into his eyes. 'I'm not smelling any of that from the chick behind us. I think faithful is not a part of her makeup right now.'

They both watched as the woman whispered into the ear of the man she was with and headed off toward the bathrooms, leaving him staring into his beer. 'Textbook,' Liza said. The man at the bar followed her with his eyes, then shot her date a glance, downed his drink, and headed in the same direction.

'Come on.' Liza stood and grabbed Paulo's hand. They weaved their way in and out of the crowd, not to the bathrooms, but out the fire escape and into a narrow side street where several people milled around smoking and chatting. They skirted the white haze of cigarette smoke and slipped into the edge of the alley. There she stopped in her tracks, laying a hand against his arm. Cautiously she pulled him out of the reach of the streetlight and into the shadows against the wall just as the woman stepped out of the back door behind the bathrooms. It wasn't more than a heartbeat before the man from the bar joined her. With barely a word, the two were at each other's mouths as though they were starving. The man's hands roamed over the woman's breasts, pinching nipples and kneading flesh like it was bread dough, all the while raking himself against her. Liza had her eyes closed and each breath was subtly drawn out just enough that Paulo could tell she was sniffing. Paulo tried to do the same, but the wet sounds of tongue on tongue and the animal grunts that were getting louder made it impossible for him not to play voyeur.

The man slid his hand up under the woman's skirt and into miniscule panties, and she gyrated and shifted against his fingers once he found her sweet spot. Paulo's cock tightened in response as little whimpers and gasps joined the soundtrack. Next to him, Liza seemed agitated. She sniffed hard and shook her head. Then she grabbed him by the wrist and they moved a few mincing steps closer.

Meanwhile, the man spun the woman around to face the brick wall and she bent forward while he shoved her skirt up over her hips and fingered her open with one hand, the other fumbling with his fly. 'You want my cock, don't you, bitch? You want it up your cunt,' the man said in guttural Italian.

'It's not right,' Liza whispered. 'It's not the scent we need.' Before Paulo could respond, she grabbed his hand and pulled him back out into the street, no longer trying to be quiet.

'What the fuck?' The man looked up from his efforts and the woman gave a little gasp of surprise.

'Sorry,' Liza said. 'Didn't know this place was already taken.' By the time they stepped out into the glow of the streetlight, the couple's attention had returned to each other, and Paulo was struggling to walk around his erection.

'What was it? What was wrong with the way they smelled?' He shifted his hips in an effort to make his cock set more comfortably in his trousers.

'There could be a place for jealousy in the fragrance, and definitely for that sense of forbidden excitement that comes from being sneaky, from fucking where you're not supposed to. We already got that from Ostia Antica. But those two, what they were doing, it's more the moldy bread scent of boredom I smelled on them. It's more calculating ... more, well like that smell of plastic, you know, the smell of something not genuine.'

There was an element in her words that eased the weight in his trousers. Yes, he wanted to fuck her. He always wanted to fuck her, but there was nothing arousing about what she was expressing.

'What then?' He asked.

'I don't know, but boredom is definitely not the message you want in a fragrance.' She ran a hand through her hair. 'Something's still missing.'

'The smell of faithfulness?' Paulo asked, glancing over his shoulder to the alley they'd just left.

'It's not that. It's something else. Something we're just not quite catching.' She stood for a moment, looking up and down the street and biting her lip. Paulo wished he could scent her when she was lost in thought like she was now. It must be an amazing smell. At last she spoke. 'Take me back to the lab, Paulo. I need to check things again.'

It was well after two in the morning when he finally convinced her to give it a rest. Neither of them had slept the night before after their time in the dungeon with Angelo, and they weren't going to make any more progress as tired as they were. Though he'd had hopes of having Liza Calendar all to himself and fucking the woman senseless, what they both needed tonight was rest.

Liza answered her BlackBerry without checking who it was. Early morning light was streaming through the window and she was just out of the shower. She figured it was Paulo calling to say good morning, but her smile evaporated at the sound of Carl's voice on the other end.

'Thank goodness you finally decided to at least forgive me enough to answer my calls, Liza.'

'Carl,' she took a deep breath and hoped he

couldn't hear the nerves in her voice. 'I already returned your call. I thought we were all sorted.'

'I'm sorry, Liza, but I can't just leave things as they are. I need to see you, to apologise face to face. Did you get my flowers?'

'I got them, and you shouldn't have sent them.' When the huge bouquet had arrived, nearly obscuring the deliveryman behind them, she'd torn up the note and had tipped the man to take them to the hospital where he was making his next delivery. She seated herself at the vanity and began toweling her hair. 'I don't need you to apologize face to face, Carl. Everything's fine, it's all good as far as I'm concerned.'

There was a windy-sounding sigh on the other end of the phone. 'Look, Liza, I'm here in Rome and I really would like to see you. At least let me down gently over coffee. My treat.'

'You're here. In Rome?' Her heart did a nosedive and her stomach went cold. 'What are you doing in Rome?'

'Oh for heaven's sakes, Liza, I'm here on business. I'm not stalking you or anything.' The hurt in his voice was palpable, and she kicked herself for the surge of guilt. Why the fuck was she feeling guilty? She wasn't the one who had been caught bare-assed humping a bimbo on the kitchen counter.

'Look, all I'm asking is a tiny bit of your time. Give me a chance to apologise properly at least. Come on, Liza, give me a chance to place my head on the block and offer you my neck.'

'I don't want your neck, Carl.'

'Please. Just coffee.'

'Carl, I don't –'

'You're staying at Bernini Place, aren't you? I could even come there if you'd like.'

‘No. Carl, look,’ she made a face at herself in the mirror. The one thing she didn’t want is him coming here. ‘All right! I’ll meet you for coffee.’ After he’d given her an address for a coffee shop, she hung up and threw the towel across the room. It had been her plan to spend a couple of hours walking in Central Rome today taking in the sights and the smells. It would have given her a chance to sniff around and maybe figure out just what it was that was missing in the sexy fragrance formulas. They were close. The scents could probably sell and do well even as they were, but they could still be better. Even if no one else knew it, she did. Meeting Carl outside at a street café would hopefully keep her from sneezing too badly and messing up her sense of smell. Oh, she could have lied to him, but the one thing she didn’t want was him showing up at Bernini Place, and she knew him well enough to know that he would.

The coffee shop was near the Piazza del Popolo. When she arrived, Carl was nowhere to be found. She was just ready to leave when her BlackBerry rang.

‘Hi Liza, Carl here. Listen, can you meet me in my suite? I’m just across the way at the Hotel de Russie. I’ve already ordered up the coffee. Sorry about this, but I’ve got an important conference call scheduled and it looks like it’s going to be a late start. I need to be here.’ He gave her a room number, but what he didn’t give her was a chance to say no. Damn the man!’ She looked down at her BlackBerry in disbelief. She was now left with two choices, walk out and wait for him to show up unexpectedly either at Bernini Place or, worse, show up at Martelli, or bite the bullet, go up to his suite and say “fuck off” politely in person. She cursed under her breath, shoved the BlackBerry back in her bag, and headed for the Hotel de Russie.

She'd barely finished knocking on his door before the first sneeze came. She'd thought about stopping by the chemist for some allergy pills, but nixed the idea, knowing she wouldn't be able to do her job afterward if she did. Besides she thought she'd be meeting him in a garden coffee shop. The minute he opened the door, looking more like he was off for a day at the races than a business meeting, she sneezed again, and there was no disguising the bronze scent of his irritation, even though the look on his air-brushed face was total and complete contrition. 'Thank you for coming, Liza, for allowing me this one concession, even though I don't deserve any.' Though there was contrition on his face, there was certainly none in his scent. In fact there was anything but. The chlorine of arrogance nearly made her eyes water as she sneezed again and pulled in the smell of cold metal and some wet, swampy scent that she felt more as a warning in her stomach rather than anything she could put a name to.

'Please,' he stepped aside, 'come in. The coffee just arrived.'

She sneezed again. 'There are tissues in the bathroom,' he said. He poured coffee for both of them without asking her how she liked it. 'I took the liberty of ordering some pastries too, since I didn't know if you'd had breakfast or not.'

'I have,' she said, ignoring his offer of tissues and opting for one from her bag. 'And I don't have a lot of time, so I'll say what I've come to say and then we can both get back to work.' She didn't give him a chance to respond. 'I can think of no reason why you shouldn't have sex with whomever you want. The two of us weren't actually in a relationship anyway, and certainly if you felt the need for sex, why shouldn't you have it, since you weren't getting it from me.' She sneezed multiples, and he waited for her to finish.

'If we'd had a relationship, I wouldn't have been tempted. It was you I wanted, Liza. I was just so lonely.'

She was surprised at how easily he lied. Deceit was one of the simplest things to smell, like burnt eggs and rancid cooking oil, and it always made her sneeze or at the very least it made her nose run. How could she have not made that connection where he was concerned? 'But you knew I'd be there in just a few hours, Carl.' Before he could respond, she raised a hand. 'Look, there's no need to lie to me, and believe me, I can tell when someone lies to me. The truth is that it really doesn't matter. We aren't now nor will we ever be compatible.'

He snapped. 'But you're compatible with Paulo Delacour, nice and quick-like.' He raised a hand. 'Oh come on, Liza, word gets around. Delacour is not exactly an unknown around here. What was it rebound? What, were you trying to make me jealous?'

She stepped back toward the door, the hair on the back of her neck rising. 'Paulo Delacour has nothing to do with you, Carl, and nothing to do with why I'm not giving us another chance.'

His hand came down hard on the table, sloshing coffee onto the white linen cloth, making her jump. 'Then why? What's your reason?'

She snapped back. 'You make me sneeze, Carl, and I should have listened to my nose.'

'I make you sneeze? What the hell's that supposed to mean? I make you sneeze, what like you're allergic to me? That's the stupidest thing I've ever heard. That's bullshit. How could I make you sneeze?'

'This was a bad idea.' Her heart hammered in her chest as she fought back another wave of sneezing. 'I'm asking you to leave me alone. Don't call again.

Don't come to my place. Let's just call it even, all right. I'm going now.'

She pulled open the door, but he was in her personal space before she could breathe, shoving it shut hard and pressing her up against the frame. 'You're not exactly a catch, you know? I can have anyone I want. And just how long do you think Delacour will put up with you sneezing all over him? Hmm? How long?'

'Get off me, Carl.' Her voice was barely more than a whisper, and she could barely hear it over her heart. The room was a tsunami of metallic rage and her cold acidic fear.

'Or what? You'll sneeze at me?'

And that's exactly what she did. Repeatedly. When he backed away in disgust, she threw open the door and fled.

Jim watched breathless while Liza Calendar fled for the elevator looking way too nervous for someone who was supposed to be at the Hotel de Russie. Before he could duck back into the room Vera had treated the two of them to as a surprise, he saw Carl Blain disappear back into the suite Liza had just come from and shut the door. 'Fuck me,' he said a little louder than he intended.

'What is it?' Vera called, sitting up in the bed with the sheet pulled over her breasts.

'I just saw Liza Calendar heading down the hall like she was on her way to a fire.'

'What? You think she was here with Mr Delacour?' she asked.

'Oh no, it wasn't Mr Delacour she was with, and that's what worries me.' Immediately he had the feeling he'd probably said more than he should have. He'd certainly seen more than he should have. He had really hoped he'd been wrong about the connection between Liza Calendar and Carl Blain, but seeing was believing. He'd have to tell Paulo. If Liza was not only in cahoots with Blain, but Blain was here in Rome, then something was going down, and it couldn't be anything very good for Martelli.'

'What are you doing?' she asked as he dug through his pocket for his BlackBerry. 'Come back to bed. Business can wait.'

'Just give me a second.' He texted a message to Paulo with shaky fingers.

'What?' she said. 'Jim, darling, what's going on? Who was Liza with?'

'Carl Blain,' he said, absently. 'I knew the two of them had something going on, and I tried to warn Paulo not to trust her, but I'd hoped I was wrong.'

She moved close and looked over his shoulder as he texted. 'That's too bad. I had suspicions myself, though.'

He stopped texting. 'Oh?'

She shrugged and the duvet dropped to reveal a luscious erect nipple. 'Not anything I could put my finger on. You know, just a gut feeling. Some people I don't trust from the beginning, and I'm usually right.'

'Funny,' Jim said, 'I'm usually a good judge of character too, and I didn't pick up on anything until she got a phone call from Blain the other day when we were out at Ostia Antica.' He finished his text and sent it, then he tossed the BlackBerry onto the nightstand and slid under the duvet and in between her open thighs. 'Tell you what,' he reached down between them to rake her clit with his thumb, 'once you and I finish our little business meeting, you can go with me back to the research facility. I have to go there anyway, and this time, I've got permission to take you into the labs.'

Chapter Twenty-three

On the street, it took a while for the sneezing to subside, and even then for a good time longer all Liza could smell was her own fear and anger. How stupid could she be? Why had it not entered her mind that Carl would manipulate her into doing what he wanted her to? Ever since she'd caught him in mid-fuck, he had been trying to manipulate her. In fact, he'd been manipulating her all along. But the bastard was really good at it. And anyway, he was right, she was a nobody. So why did he think it so important to see her in person – just so he could humiliate her and have the last word? How he found out about her and Paulo was beyond her, but still, if he knew, then he knew he was dealing with someone not to be taken lightly. At the end of the day, it was over, and she was pretty sure he'd leave her alone now.

She wandered the streets surreptitiously sniffing and observing, but the unpleasant encounter with Carl had ruined her concentration, so after an hour she gave up and headed back to the lab. Perhaps a revisiting of some of the scents they'd already collected and some of the notes and observations she had taken would give her some ideas. Liza never had problems with olfactory fatigue. That meant she was able to work with and detect subtle differences in scent long after most people no longer could. After a visit to the break room for the much-needed coffee she didn't get with Carl, she headed into the lab with her laptop in tow and settled in to sniffing as the day wore on.

'Any luck with the walk?'

Paulo's voice made her jump with a little gasp of surprise. 'I didn't hear you come in,' she said.

'Clearly.' He gave her ponytail a gentle tug. She could sense the smile in his voice, the affection, and she smiled back.

'No luck. I gave up after a couple of hours.' She didn't mention her little run-in with Carl. It was embarrassing, actually. It made her feel stupid and ugly, and a good dose of Paulo was just what she needed for a cure. She leaned back against him where he stood behind her, feeling the hard ridges of his belly tighten beneath his open jacket. 'Just can't figure out what it is we're missing.'

'They all smell amazing to me. I can't believe you're not ready to send them off for Coraline's blessing.' He leaned down and kissed her behind the ear and a shiver of pleasure crawled up her spine as she breathed in his fabulous scent.

'They smell OK, but not as good as they can. Trust me.'

'I do trust you,' he said, pulling up a stool and sitting down next to her. 'How about a trip out to The Mount this evening? It seems to me if it's sexual scents your looking for, maybe we should revisit the place.'

'Maybe. But I can't help but feel what we need is already here. I'm just missing it.'

'All right,' he stood, pulled off his jacket, and hung it on the back of another chair. 'What can I do to help?'

For the next two and a half hours they went over every sample that they'd collected and the list of corresponding essences that had been associated with those scents. It astounded her that Paulo could be such an incredible distraction on the one hand and yet be as drawn into their efforts as she was on the other. She liked that they could work together side by side and stay focused. She loved the way they smelled when they worked together, like clean sheets and strong tea. Most of all she loved that the power of his nose, was as important to him as hers was to her.

'Can you smell the differences in the two dungeon experiences, I mean other than the obvious that the first one incorporated a lot of voyeurism?' she said.'

'I can,' he replied, sniffing one and then the other, 'though I'm not sure what the smell of voyeurism is.'

'It's curiosity mixed with lust, butter, and cinnamon, but there's also a tiny tang of the forbidden, even a little bit of shame at seeing what normally you know you shouldn't be seeing, like watching that couple at the bar. I don't know, shame is sort of a dairy smell, I think, a little bit sour, a little bit metallic, a little bit muddy.' She could feel his gaze on her as she closed her eyes thinking about the scents that made up the sexual interaction in her inadvertent first visit to the dungeon.

'It does smell … I don't know … more muddy, I'd say.' He laughed, 'probably more dirty because Angelo was running the show.'

'At least until you came into the room,' she said with a little chuckle. 'And then the smell changed, and I'm glad you had the presence of mind to have David bag up samples because you overpowered everything.'

'Thanks, I think.'

For a few moments they worked in silence, then she just had to ask. 'How do you know Angelo?' She added quickly, 'it's pretty clear the two of you have a history.'

A tight, smile played at the corner of his mouth, as though it didn't quite feel comfortable making its presence known. 'Coraline took us both under her wing when we were not much more than boys.' This time the smile moved right in and made itself at home, and his gazed settled on the middle distance as though he were looking into the past. 'Coraline has enormous wings, and to be sheltered under those wings was, well for both of us, probably the difference between life and death. Certainly it was for Angelo. I was more than my mother could handle after my father died. I acted out. I was always getting in trouble. My mother worked for Martelli. Coraline gave me a job when no one else was interested – actually when I was really too young to do very much. But her iron hand was just what I needed. She recognized early on that I had the nose, and clearly Rita wasn't interested. Angelo, well Angelo was living on the streets. He was a runaway. I don't know about his parents. He never said anything. When he speaks English, I've never decided if the American accent is faked or if it's real. He never talks about his past. Maybe Coraline knows. There's not much she doesn't know. Anyway while I had the nose, Angelo had the tech skills. I don't know how he got them. But Coraline saw his gift and put it to good use.' Paulo took her hand where it rested next to her laptop and chafed it with his thumb. His scent changes slightly and she could smell nutmeg and anise. 'We were lovers for a while, as I said earlier.'

Though it hadn't surprise her, she had a sense what he'd shared wasn't common knowledge. 'We were young. Rita had just slapped him down. She wanted nothing to do with anything that was Martelli back then. Me, I was more like a brother to her, so there was never anything between us. But Angelo had a crush on her for a long time. When she made it clear she wasn't interested, he came to me to commiserate after Rita left for Seattle. We got a little drunk and we ended up having sex. We realized we liked it. We were comfortable with it, and emotionally, it was a safe place for us to be at the time. Martelli kept us both way too busy to even think about relationships. That was before either of us joined The Mount. It was good for us then. Later Angelo started doing some work on the side. He invented a bit of very interesting software and before anyone knew it, the man was independently wealthy. He works for himself now, but he's still Coraline's bratty older son in her eyes, and I think in his too.'

'That must be weird, being in the same sex cult with your adopted mother.'

'Not really. Coraline goes elsewhere for sex. She keeps her private life private, and I think it's been a very long time since she's taken a sexually active role in the Roman Mount.'

'And the tension between you and Angelo?' Liza said. 'Over a woman?'

The smile he offered was more of a brief twitch of the lips. 'That obvious?'

'Yup.'

He heaved a sigh and shifted on his chair. 'Angelo took to The Mount much more readily than I did. I've not been an active member very long. When Fidelia became head of security for Martelli and brought in that … little extra you saw, we both went after her. I wanted to date her. Angelo wanted to fuck her.' He grunted. 'Afraid I don't share very well. But like Angelo, Fidelia likes to play with everyone, and Angelo lost interest when I walked away.'

'And that's what the problem is?'

'There's not really a problem. We normally get along fine, but we have too much history between us, and Angelo knows exactly what buttons to push with me, so we enjoy each other in small doses. We haven't been lovers in a long time, and … well I've never seen him react to anyone the way he reacted to you. I'm still not sure how I feel about that.'

She squeezed his hand where it still curled around hers. 'All you would have had to do was tell me you weren't comfortable with what happened.'

He turned to face her and ran a finger down her cheek. 'But I wanted it too. Even though I wasn't comfortable. In some ways, I think I needed what happened between the three of us more than either of you did. I guess I've just got a lot more relationship issues to work through than Angelo does. And really, what happened made me feel good, made me feel almost like … I don't know, like I'd given you a gift.'

She leaned over and brushed a kiss across his lips. 'You did. You did give me a gift, and it was amazing. And I think Angelo and you gave each other a gift as well.'

He pulled her to her feet. 'Come on, let's make some coffee, have a biscuit, and give it a little rest. Then we can come back fresh and figure out just what the problem is.'

As they stood to leave the room she breathed in the summer rainstorm scent of his perspiration, clean and sharp-edged and felt her own scent darken, thicken, and rise up to meet his. As he reached to open the door, she shoved his hand away and flipped the lock. Then holding his gaze, she turned out the light and lifted her arms around his neck. 'I don't want biscuits and I don't want coffee.' She took his mouth, her tongue moving lazily, leisurely against his lips until they yielded, and his scent spiked with ozone and desert heat.

'Make love to me, Paulo,' she whispered. 'I'm tired of waiting to have you to myself, and it's Saturday. We're here alone, and I want you so damn bad.'

His fingers clenched in her hair and he released a long sigh that passed over her lips with the delicious taste of him. 'We'll muddy the waters, you know? If we make love here. Your scent will be all over me, and mine on you and …' he stopped speaking when her hand slid down to stroke his growing erection through his trousers.

'And right now, I don't give a fuck,' she said, biting his lip as she pulled back. 'Everything's bagged, everything's sealed, and the preliminary scents aren't even in this room. It's you I want to smell, Paulo, you and me together and no one else.' Her words came in staccato gasps with her efforts to breathe in the thickening and changing dance of their scents. 'No one else.' She rubbed herself against him and he sucked a deep breath. He gave a quick look around, then ran both hands down to cup her bottom, lifting her. Her flip skirt slid up her bare thighs as she wrapped both legs around his waist and went back to eating his mouth.

The apricots on toast smell of anticipation washed over the bloom of heat as he settled her ass onto the high stainless steel table at the back of the room, shoving bagged shirts and underclothing off onto the floor in a rustle of plastic on plastic.

'I need to smell you, I need to smell you, I need to smell you,' the words came out like a desperate chant as she ripped open his shirt and shoved it off his shoulders, burying her nose in the striations between his pecs. Then she trailed kisses across a taut nipple and around until she nuzzled into the soft down of his left armpit, making him squirm and scrunch, trapped in the shirt, struggling to unbutton the sleeves. Being trapped at the mercy of her sense of smell made his cock even more anxious in his trousers, sharpening his scent to a black pepper and ozone edge.

She shoved and pushed and slid her way off the table, practically falling on her ass before she grabbed onto his belt to steady herself, nearly pulling him over on top of her. Then she undid the buckle and went to work on his fly, sniffing and nuzzling as she went.

'Liza … Christ, Liza …' He finally managed to shrug free of his shirt and then went to work helping her with the trousers, shoving down his boxers until his cock bounced free. She didn't immediately take it in her mouth. Instead, she rubbed her face over his cock, then over his heavy sac and his pubic curls, and again he was squirmy and ticklish, resting one hand on the top of her head while the other shoved his trousers and boxers down over his hips.

'Oh God, Paulo, if I could only just bottle your scent, then I'd never get out of bed, never stop touching myself, never stop being right on the edge of coming every time I smelled you.'

He dropped to his knees onto the floor and pushed her back, his hands sliding up her thighs until he could grab her panties. With a finger hooked in each side he yanked them off. She didn't protest as he shoved into her without foreplay. Her growl matched his at penetration, and she wrapped her legs around him and dug her heels into his kidneys. 'I have to have you, Liza,' he gasped against her ear. 'Surely you can smell how badly I need to have you. I've wanted you all day long. I've needed to come so badly,' he thrust hard and they both slid on the tiled floor, and she cried out and cursed. 'I've needed to come so badly, but I've held it, Liza, I've held it for you because I want there to be plenty for you to smell when I unload, when we come together and rub our scent all over each other.'

Her body quaked beneath him, the scent of honey and butter and seashore pressed against desert heat and ozone, and the spiced, hot pepper scent of their desperation spread over it all. As she drew breath after heavy breath of their scent, dragging it into her sinuses, into her lungs, into her belly. She wasn't exactly sure when the orgasm started, but she had the feeling it might have begun as a tremor of soft fruit anticipation the moment she scented him, the moment she pulled him into the first kiss. And all this time it had been building with the rub of his cock against her clit, the rake and press of his balls against her perineum, the friction of his skin against hers, flint and steel igniting the spark until her whole body shook with it and then rose to a smell that she could barely take in. It was opium, it was strong wine, it was every drug at its sweetest, when the ride was most euphoric. It was that and more, and still she came.

She felt him tense, heard him grunt, smelled the sharp spark of his orgasm ready to burst like the fountains at the villa. Then he erupted inside her, thick and heavy with scent, laced with her own – smell still changing and evolving as it filled her, flooded her, and ran down her bottom onto the white-tiled floor.

Then, while he was still vulnerable, still gasping for breath, she shoved her way free, and squatted on top of him open-legged, open-pussied, rubbing and shifting up and down against his cock, against his damp pubic hair, then up over the soft down that led to his navel. She slipped and slid and gyrated, covering him with her scent while reveling in his. Then she fell forward on top of him, forcing a harsh grunt of a breath from his oxygen-starved lungs. 'Can you smell us? Can you smell us, Paulo? My God, we smell brilliant! We smell better than anything. We smell like everything that counts. We smell … we smell …' She sat up, hand still stroking the silky heat of his semen between her legs, nose still pulling desperately at every nuance of scent. 'Paulo …' She froze, her heart feeling like it would beat its way out of her chest.

'What? What's the matter, Liza?' He rested and hand on her hip. 'What is it?'

She locked onto his dark gaze. 'Paulo, we smell like everything that counts.' With all the grace of a floundering moose, she pushed and shoved her way to her feet. He gave a muffled 'umph' when she stumbled and elbowed him in the ribs, but he scrambled to stand right behind her.

'Your handkerchief. Give it to me.' He already had it out of his pocket. She went to work cleaning his semen and her juices in a task that would have made her incredibly horny all over again if her heart hadn't been hammering for other reasons – reasons she could see by the dark spark in Paulo's eyes, by the rapid beat of his pulse in his throat that he completely understood. 'This is it, Paulo. This is the missing part of the puzzle. It's us, it's basic like vanilla and cinnamon, it's the binding, it's something that's not the scent of the dungeon, not the scent of kink or voyeurism or a good spanking. All of those things are apart of what Martelli's trying to create in this new line, but there's nothing as basic as a man and a woman who can't get enough of each other, a man and a woman who can't resist the need to be together even in the most inopportune place. It's magnetism, it's connecting, it's primal. Animals are attracted to each other by scent all the time. Why should humans be any different, and for all the kink, and all the emotions that accompany the Dom/sub relationship or a night in the dungeon with an audience, it's that basic scent, as simple and basic as two people who lust for each other, two people whose chemistry is explosive and magical. Paulo, I promise, this is the missing ingredient.'

Chapter Twenty-four

'Didn't you get my text?' Paulo barely made it out of the lift before Jim was on him. 'We need to talk.' He glanced around as though he feared they were being spied on.

Paulo shot an exaggerated look at his watch. 'I'm off to Milan in just a few minutes, Jim. Can't it wait?'

'No, it can't. Didn't you get my text?' He asked again.

Paulo let out an exasperated breath. 'I got your damned text, Jim, and frankly I don't know what got the bee up your ass about Liza, but I don't want to hear it. I talked to her about Blain, and if you'd bothered to check it out, you'd have known his call was nothing to do with Martelli.'

Jim grabbed Paulo by the arm. 'And her being in a room at the Hotel de Russie with him? What about that?'

Paulo froze in his tracks. Instantly the man moved his hand away from his boss' arm and stepped back, but he held his gaze.

Paulo nodded to his office and stormed in that direction without look back. He knew Jim would follow. Inside he motioned him to shut the door, then he turned on him. 'Tell me, Jim, how do you know that Liza was in a hotel room with Carl Blain?'

Jim's face reddened and he raked his teeth over his lower lip. Then he squared his shoulders and said, 'I was there with Vera.' He waved a dismissive hand. 'It was her treat, sort of a surprise for me. I stepped out the door for a second and saw Liza Calendar coming out of a room several doors down. She didn't see me, but I did see Carl Blain sticking his head out before he shut the door behind him.'

'How did she look?' Paulo ask, trying to keep his breathing even.

'What do you mean how did she look?'

'Did she look disheveled? Did she look smug? Did she look sneaky? And what about Blain? Was he dressed? Was he in a robe? Was his hair well combed?'

'She was dressed smart casual, so was he. And neither of them were disheveled. Look,' Jim said raising a hand, 'I never said she was fucking him. That would certainly simplify things if she were. I don't think it's about sex and I told you that from the beginning. If it's business, though, if they're in a working relationship that involves infiltrating Martelli Fragrance, then the whole thing makes a lot more sense. And knowing Liza Calendar, if it's business, she wouldn't be fucking him.'

Paulo folded his arms across his chest and glared at Jim. 'So what the hell do you think her plan is, then? You think she's a part of Blain's hostile takeover plot?'

Jim ran a hand through his hair, leaving it standing on end. 'Well she's certainly in a position to be, isn't she? And she could do him the most good where she's at, don't you think?'

'She doesn't like him and he makes her sneeze.' The words slipped out before Paulo could stop them.

'Makes her sneeze? Seriously? You believe that?'

Paulo didn't answer. In truth, he didn't know what he believed, but he just couldn't believe that Liza was in cahoots with Blain, and whatever reason she had for being at the hotel with him, well he'd take Angelo's advice once again and ask her.

Jim blew out a harsh breath. 'Look, I'd be remiss in my duties if I didn't tell you this. Even if you don't want to hear. I'm just saying keep her close. Keep your eye on her, and maybe put security on the alert. Also, if her work's done here, then send her home, or better yet, if it'll make you feel better, take her somewhere, you know, just the two of you, somewhere where you can keep an eye on her. She doesn't have to know that's what you're doing. She could just think it's a romantic getaway. You know, something you'd both enjoy.'

It was early afternoon when Liza got back to the Martelli offices. Paulo was at meetings in Milan, so she had been at the labs with Coraline checking the final formulas. The scents that would launch this fall as the *Innuendo* line would be the most amazing, cutting-edge fragrances Martelli had ever launched. The money thrown at the line before Liza came on board was boggling, but it had cost little on the whole, for what she had managed to do in a short amount of time. There was very little technology involved in using her nose, and she was happy to do it. The cost to get the scents ready by autumn, however, would not be small, though it would be well worth it to launch a line that would blow the lid off the market. Coraline had hinted at a permanent position for Liza with Martelli. Her head was spinning with possibilities. Though Paulo would be away from the office for the rest of the day, a celebration dinner had been in the works for the evening, until he had texted to say the meetings in Milan were running longer than expected and he wouldn't be back until tomorrow evening. That being the case, she was thinking maybe she'd enjoy a quiet night. She hadn't had one in ages. She hadn't really had the chance to enjoy the Bernini flat. A nice long bubble bath, a good Skype session with Addie and maybe Rita, then maybe she would curl up with a raunchy novel and crack open that bottle of primitivo Coraline had so highly recommended. Yep! That would do nicely. Then when Paulo got back – her insides tightened and tingled with anticipation – she'd be ready for him.

'I know, Jim. I know. It worries me too. I told you, I've never thought Liza Calendar was trustworthy.'

Liza stopped in her tracks at the sound of Vera's voice coming from the open door of the break room. A peek around the corner showed that she was alone, talking on her iPhone.

Liza held her breath and listened, struggling to hear around her pounding pulse.

'So you talked to Paulo about her?' There was a pause. 'Well that's good. What did he say? I agree. Keep your friends close and your enemies closer.'

Liza couldn't breathe. The cloying reek of her own sense of betrayal threatened to choke her.

Vera's laughter seemed loud and grating in the silence. 'Well he's certainly doing a great job of keeping her close, I'd say.' Her chuckle sounded vicious. 'It's a dirty job, but I suppose someone has to do it. I would have thought the connection with Blain would have been obvious from the beginning. Does Ms Martelli know about her? … I see … So she has her doubts too. Well that's good, good that they're keeping a close watch on her. I mean, hey, if she can do Martelli some good while she's here with that magical nose of hers, and Mr Delacour gets laid and we all get a better Christmas bonus, then I say so much the better.'

There was more silence while Vera listened to what

Jim was saying. 'Well I can't see her pulling anything when Mr Delacour's between her legs every chance he gets. Still I suppose it is worrisome, her coming out of Blain's hotel room and all. Mr Delacour seems like the jealous type to me. But, hey, he's getting some, so win-win, the way I see it.'

Liza reached out for the wall, feeling as though her legs might give from under her, feeling like she might be sick.

'Listen, Jim, I have to get back to work. Alessandro is off tomorrow so it'll just be me at the queen bitch's mercy. I need to meet with him and find out what I'll be up against.' As she disconnected and made one last check of her email, Liza fled down the hall to her office.

She dropped into her chair barely able to breathe. With trembling fingers, she started to call Paulo. Then she changed her mind. Her work here was done. She had plenty for an article about her experience in the perfume industry and Martelli now had what they wanted. She wouldn't take their fucking money. She'd never done the job for money, and it felt like her insides were on fire every time she thought that they could believe such a thing of her. But then she supposed that's the way big business worked; no one could possibly think that someone might do something because it pleased them, because it excited them and made them happy. She wiped viciously at her eyes as she thought of how happy she had been these past few days with Paulo. Well she was just being stupid, wasn't she? She forced back the tears and packed up her computer bag, checking around the office for anything else that was hers. Her nose had been wrong this time. Her nose that she had always counted on to be right about situations. About people. She slipped out of the office unseen and held herself together through the walk back to the flat, oblivious to Bernini's Angels gracing the Ponte Sant'Angelo, oblivious to the scents of coffee and traffic and tourists and harried Italians, oblivious to everything but the scent of her own betrayal. Once she was safely locked in the flat, she tossed her bag on the sofa, threw herself on the bed, and wept.

It felt like she'd cried forever. The long shadows of early evening were creeping into the bedroom windows when she sat up red-eyed and drained. In the bathroom, she blew her poor beleaguered nose, drank a large glass of water, then went back to the den and booted up her laptop, logging into the site she used for travel. It was high tourist season and without flying first class, the earliest flight she could book was for tomorrow evening. Still, Rome was a big city. She was sure she could make herself scarce until flight time. If she had to she'd wait in the damned lounge, and there were plenty of hotels. She'd find some way to stay away from Paulo. When she calmed down a bit she would send an email to him and to Coraline. Nothing personal, because clearly it hadn't been, at least not to them. She would simply tell them now that her work was done, she saw no reason to linger. Clearly Paulo hadn't believed her when she told him what had happened between her and Carl. She wondered now why he'd even bothered to ask. Well, best she get away as soon as she could and get on with her life.

Once her flight reservations were made, she pulled her bag from the closet, flung it on the bed, and began to pack. She was randomly tossing underwear in the bag when Skype sounded on her laptop. She would have ignored it until she saw it was Rita. Suddenly she was completely empathetic with Rita for not wanting anything to do with Martelli Fragrance, and though she didn't want to talk to anyone, she really needed a friendly shoulder.

Chapter Twenty-five

The delays had been maddening. The meetings had run long, he'd missed one flight, and another was cancelled. Paulo wanted desperately to be back with Liza. They still hadn't had the chance to properly celebrate the new line that would be so much more amazing than anyone could have imagined thanks to her. But at the moment, it wasn't anxiety over the future celebration with Liza that was making him crazy. He texted her again from the queue at passport control in Fiumicino. The knot in his stomach tightened further when there was still no response to any of the previous texts he'd sent nor to any of his calls. The last message he'd gotten from her was to say that Coraline had been elated over the new line. As soon as he was through passport control he tried to call her again, but again her BlackBerry rang over to voicemail. 'Hi, I'm at the airport. Looking forward to seeing you soon.' As an afterthought, he added, 'is everything all right?'

He knew it wasn't, he sensed it wasn't, and yet he still held out hope that maybe something was wrong with her BlackBerry. He broke as many speed limits and traffic laws as he could to get him home faster. Once there in the lift, he checked his BlackBerry one more time for a text he hoped for but felt certain now wouldn't be there. When it wasn't, he stuffed the device into his pocket and shoved his way into his flat.

'About fucking time you got home!' He recognized

the voice before he actually looked up to see Rita standing in front of him, hands on hips, eyes blazing fire and ice.

'Nice to see you too, sis,' he said, closing the door behind him. 'What are you doing here?'

She ignored his greeting and followed him into his bedroom where he dropped the garment bag on the floor. 'Are you out of you mind, or are you just being an asshole, because the first I might be able to forgive, might. But if the second is the case, I swear I'll kill you and dump your body in the Tiber for the fish to eat.'

'Rita, what the –'

'She's my best friend, you bastard! My best friend!' she gave his garment bag a vicious kick with the toe of a very wicked-looking black leather boot. 'And don't tell me you didn't know, because I know you did. I can't find Mom, and if she knows, if she's in on this stupid shit, then I'll kill you both. The two of you deserve each other.' Suddenly her eyes teared and she ran a hand through her hair. 'Paulo, how could you? How *could* you?'

He took her by the shoulders – carefully, for his own protection. 'Sis, I have no idea what you're talking about, and if you're going to feed me to the fish, I'd at least like to know why.'

She jerked away and began to pace at the foot of his bed, kicking the bag once more for good measure. 'Keep your friends close and your enemies closer? Ring a bell? Hmm?'

He shook his head. 'No. Should it?'

'Is that what it was all along? You were toying with her because you didn't trust her? But in typical Martelli fashion, just because you don't trust someone doesn't mean you can't use them to get what you want, does it?' This time as she passed him, she gave him a hard shove on the arm that nearly sent him off balance. 'How the fuck could you not trust her? How the fuck could you possibly think she was in cahoots with Carl Blain?'

'What?' He dropped onto the bed, suddenly unable to stand, barely able to hear her over the sudden beating of wings in his ears.

'Check you goddamned email. She said she sent you and Mom both a letter of resignation.'

'Liza? Liza did? Why?' With hands no longer steady, he checked his BlackBerry. Sure enough a message had just come through that must have been held up in the ether somewhere while he was flying and had only now caught up with him. It was polite, distant, and professional. Liza Calendar had done what she'd come to do, she'd enjoyed the work. She didn't want Martelli's money, and she was catching a night flight back to the States. She wished Martelli all the best with the new line. That was it! All professional, nothing personal.

The room tilted, and it felt like he was breathing cotton wool. 'Why?' he managed a strangled plea.

Rita plopped down next to him. This time she took his hand. 'Paulo, she thinks the only reason you made love to her was because you thought she might be working for Carl Blain, and you were keeping your enemies close.'

'Why the hell would she think that? I mean I know what Jim thinks, but Jim's wrong about her. She would never work for Carl Blain. Never, no matter how it looks.' Then, for some reason that made more sense to him than it would to anyone who didn't know Liza, he added, 'Carl Blain makes her sneeze.'

Rita's laugh came out a little sob and she wiped her eyes with her fingertips and gave him a half-hug. 'She told me that. She would never be in cahoots with anyone who makes her sneeze,' then she held his gaze, the fire in her eyes bright again. 'She can smell what a person's like, Paulo, she can smell their heart, and nobody has ever smelled good to her until you came along. Don't fuck it up.'

He sprang to his feet. 'Do you know her flight number? When she's flying?'

She nodded. 'I know more than that, bro.' She pulled out her own BlackBerry and texted him the information. 'She's probably on her way to the airport now. You text her and so will I.'

Their efforts were interrupted by the ringing of his BlackBerry. He answered it without thinking, not minding that Rita moved close enough to hear the conversation.

'Paulo, this is Jim.' The man didn't take time for niceties. 'Someone's stolen the formulas for the new line. Police have taken Liza Calendar to the station. They caught her at the airport.'

Paulo exploded. 'What the fuck do you mean they caught her at the airport? You can't really believe she'd do such a thing! That's bullshit and you know it!'

'What the hell? Are you out of your fucking mind!' Rita yelled into the phone before Paulo could shush her. She immediately pulled up her BlackBerry and he could hear her calling the Martelli lawyers.

Jim heaved a hard-put-upon sigh into Paulo's ear. 'I know how you feel about her, Paulo, but all the evidence points to her. Who else could have done it? And why would she have slunk away to the airport without telling anyone if she didn't? She had us all fooled and –'

Paulo hung up on him, and motioned Rita to follow. 'I don't know who it,' he said, 'but I know as sure as I know my own face in the mirror that she didn't.'

'I'm calling Mom,' Rita said. 'She needs to know what's going on.' Paulo was already out the door with Rita right behind him.

Chapter Twenty-six

It probably wasn't the smartest thing to do in a police station, but it sure as hell felt good to land a fist in the middle of Jim's smug face. Rita made no attempt to stop him, but then Paulo figured he'd beaten her to the punch by microseconds. Jim waved off the police and wiped his bloodied nose on a white handkerchief. 'I'm sorry, Paulo, but it is what it is.' He stepped back as he said it, putting a little more space between him and his boss. Rita growled at him, and he took another step back for safety. Just then Coraline walked in and, Paulo could swear, the whole police station went quiet with her arriving like the queen of the world in her usual haute couture, looking as good in the evening as she did in the morning. All heads always turned, and he was sure more than a few knees were tempted to bend. She took in Jim's bloody nose and Paulo's fist and gave her daughter a hug. 'You took the Martelli jet from London?' She asked.

Rita nodded. 'Might as well, it was there, wasn't it?'

'That's what I left it for.'

Coraline turned to Paulo, her arm still around Rita's shoulders, and gave him the smile of a woman in control. 'The lawyers are with her, and she should be released …' she looked down at her watch '… any minute now.' The Martellis were a formidable lot, and Paulo was proud to be considered a part of the family. 'You,' Coraline focused a withering gaze on Jim

Dryer, 'are a very poor judge of character, Mr Dryer. I'm very disappointed.'

Before he could do more than make a couple of fish gasps, the door opened and Liza was escorted through by Martelli's lawyer, the legendary Mr Serrano, not one of the underlings, but the main man himself. Rita or Coraline, whoever had gotten there first, had called in the big guns, a sign that Liza was of value to the whole Martelli family.

Liza's eyes ignited as her gazed locked on Paulo. She stepped back and slapped his arms away when he tried to hug her. 'They arrested me at the airport. At the airport! In front of everyone, Paulo, and all I'm guilty of is helping you find a formula for your damned perfume.'

'I know that, Liza. You've done nothing wrong. We all know you didn't do it. It was a stupid mistake, you being brought here.' He shot Jim an incinerating glance. It was all he could do not to pull her into his arms and hold her until she stopped fighting him. Rita gave his hand a reassuring squeeze. He still held Liza's gaze. 'I'm so, so sorry. I don't know what happened, but I'm sure as hell going to find out.'

When she saw Rita take his hand, she softened slightly and gave him half a nod of acknowledgment, then she bit her lip and swallowed a shaky breath. 'If you take me to the lab now, I can find out for you. Who took the formulas, I mean.' She touched her nose. 'If the police haven't contaminated the scene too much.'

'Oh for fuck sake! You can't be serious,' Jim said. But he raised his hand and moved back out of range when Rita took a step in his direction, fists clenched. Coraline was already on her BlackBerry calling the lab to tell the police to take a break. As if anyone would argue with Coraline Martelli. Then she slid her arm around Liza and nodded toward the door. 'Don't worry, darling. We'll get this sorted out.'

Paulo had driven the Land Rover to the police station with every intention of bringing Liza home with him, but when he opened the door for her to get in next to him, she ignored it and got into the back with Rita. 'Liza, you've got to know that I wouldn't, that I didn't –'

Rita shook her head and slipped her arm around her friend. 'Not now, Paulo. Just get us there.'

His heart twisted. He hoped, God he prayed, that Liza could smell how he felt. He didn't have to scent her to know how hurt and betrayed she had to be, and he would give anything to make it all better for her.

When they arrived at the research facility, it was dark. Coraline had a driver deliver her to the police station and then on to the research facility. Paulo neither knew nor cared how Jim had gotten there. Every time he saw the man, he fought the urge to punch him again. At the facility, everyone had long since gone home except for the police, who were now all congregated in the break room having coffee.

The click, click of their shoes echoed in the empty hallway as they moved toward the labs where the scents had been stored. Paulo didn't have to listen to know that Liza was already sniff-sniffing. She'd started in the break room, and he figured it was so she could separate the scents of the policemen from the scents that were there before. He tried to catch her gaze before he punched in the code to open the door, but she kept her eyes forward, concentrating.

Once they were inside, the door slid shut behind them and he motioned them all to stay back, knowing that she wouldn't want their scents, and the emotions, of which there were a lot right now, to interfere with the smells that were left in the room. They all watched her, holding their collective breath, as she walked around the lab sniffing, then cocking her head, then sniffing and closing her eyes. She was fierce. God, she was fierce! When she was like this, with her nose leading the way, she was breathtaking. She was wild and untouchable. But she had certainly touched him, more deeply than he would have ever thought possible, and God, he wanted to believe that he had returned the favour. He wanted her to trust him again, to be with him again, as no one else ever had.

In the middle of the room she stopped, stood dead still, closed her eyes, and inhaled deeply. The look on her face went from questioning to a deep frown.

'What is it?' Coraline said in half a whisper. 'What do you smell?'

She opened her eyes and looked at the Martelli matriarch. 'Does Vera have access to this room?'

'Not that I know of,' Coraline replied.

All eyes were suddenly on Jim. 'I brought her in here, yes, but I had permission, and I was with her.' He thrust his hands on his hips. 'Oh come on, you can't really believe –'

'Shut up, Jim,' Paulo and Rita said at the same time. All eyes were back on Liza.

She sniffed again and moved around the room. 'You were in here with her, yes, I can smell that. But that's an older scent, faint. When was that?'

'Two days ago. Surely you can't –'

She shook her head and raised her hand. 'You, yes, you were in here with her two days ago. I can smell that, but her. She's been her more recently. She smells like wet vegetation. She smells different.' Liza shook her head again as though she were clearing away spider's webs. 'At first, I can smell lust. Hers and yours.'

Jim blushed and shifted from foot to foot.

Liza continued without noticing, or probably caring, about his discomfort. 'But there's more. Cinnamon curiosity and … deception, like sour milk.'

'Oh give me a break,' Jim said. Though this time he didn't sound so sure.

'But the scent of her the second time is different. There's fear, along with the deception. There's excitement.'

'This is ridiculous,' Jim said. 'Look I know you don't like her, but this is just too much.'

Her gaze turned on him. 'I like her just fine. I just don't like the way she smells.'

'There's nothing wrong with the way she –'

'Shut up, Jim,' Paulo repeated.

Rita erupted like a Vesuvius. 'This is my best friend you're talking to, you asshole.' Then she turned her attention to her mother. 'How the hell could Martelli hire such an idiot? He brings the woman he's fucking in here, in a place she wasn't supposed to be and –'

'I had permission, and all of the evidence points to her.' Jim stabbed a finger in the air toward Liza and the room erupted in chaos just as Paulo's BlackBerry rang.

'Hey, bro,' Angelo's voice filled his ear. 'You know that little research project you had me on?'

Paulo covered the phone, made a shrill whistle with his fingers in his mouth, and the room went silent. 'Go on,' he said into the device.

'Well, the connection with Liza to Blain may be documented, but it looks to me like it might be the connection with a Vera Bellini you need to be checking out. She works for Martelli, right?'

'Yes.' Paulo switched the device to speaker. 'Go on.'

'Claims she has a degree in chemistry?'

'That's right,' Jim said.

There was a grunt and a curse on Angelo's end of the conversation. 'Well, there is no degree in chemistry. I checked her out. She's had an on again off again relationship with Blain for ten years, and whenever Blain pulls a dirty buy-out, she's never far away.'

Suddenly Jim looked a little green around the gills, as he grabbed onto the counter for support.

'Bro?' Angelo said, sensing the tension in the air. 'What's going on?'

'Someone's stolen the formulas from the lab, and I think you might have just found our culprit.'

'She hasn't been answering her phone.' Jim's voice was barely audible. 'I thought maybe she was just busy. I … I didn't think it was strange that she kept wanting to see the research facility. I mean it's an interesting place.' His mouth was a hard line. Paulo didn't want to know what was going through his head at the moment, and as much as he deserved it, he couldn't help but feel sorry for the dumb bastard.

'She's probably on her way to the airport,' Angelo said. They could all hear the tapping of computer keys over his phone. 'Yup! Blain's private jet is there and due to depart in … an hour.'

Paulo didn't want to know how Angelo got his information. He was just glad he did.

Coraline was already calling the police.

'This time,' Rita said, slipping an arm around her friend, 'maybe they'll get the right person.'

'If Blain gets those formulas, and we've got nothing more to go on than Ms Calendar's sense of smell, then he can pretty much do what he wants,' Jim said, unable to meet Liza's gaze, or anyone else's for that matter. 'As heavily invested as Martelli is in this project, a hostile takeover is pretty much a given.'

Coraline clucked her tongue. 'Oh there was not going to be any hostile takeover, Jim, darling, in spite of your stupidity.'

'What? How can that be?' Jim looked as though he was about to pass out. 'I know how much money Martelli invested in those scents, and it was a lot. A helluva lot.'

'Oh I know exactly how much money it was.' Coraline took out her compact and powdered her nose. 'But you don't have a clue of the depth of Martelli's resources. You haven't been here long enough to understand.' She snapped the compact shut and stuffed it back in her bag. 'Carl Blain is no more likely to succeed at a hostile takeover of Martelli than his father was in his attempt back when I was the new CEO. You see, Jim, Martelli is family owned with deep pockets. Very deep pockets.'

'I don't understand,' he managed.

'Martelli's family is worldwide. Oh for heaven sakes,' she said when she saw the direction his mind was headed. 'Not mafia, though there are times when I suppose it might feel that way. The Mount, you silly man. The Mount is worldwide, and The Mount has been heavily invested in Martelli for, well for as long as there's been a Martelli. Carl Blain couldn't have touched us even if he had stolen the formulas.' She looked at Paulo. 'The right formulas, I mean.'

'Wait a minute.' Jim's eyes darted to Paulo, then to Coraline and back again. 'What do you mean the right formulas?'

'In spite of your stupidity, Jim,' Paulo said, his eyes locked on Liza, who looked as though she were in shock, 'I can promise the formulas are quite safe. Surely you didn't think I'd risk all of Liza's hard, brilliant work, did you?'

There was a murmur among the troops. Liza shifted

slightly and half whispered, ‘I don’t understand.’

‘You sneezed the other day while we were here, remember? That was after Jim told me Carl Blain might be planning something.’ He stepped closer and risked life and limb by touching her arm. When she didn’t pull away, his pulse danced against his throat. ‘Do you really think I’d risk all of your hard work, all of your brilliant efforts, knowing that bastard was around?’ He shrugged. ‘Granted, I didn’t know about Vera, but I still wasn’t taking a risk. Blain can do what he wants with the formulas that were stolen from here. They aren’t worth anything without our secret ingredient, and the only samples that have that secret ingredient are locked away somewhere safe. We’d never leave them here in the lab unprotected.’

Liza’s knees went loose and this time she allowed Paulo to slip his arms around her. ‘Then you mean …’ She swallowed hard, unable to finish her sentence, and her eyes misted slightly.

‘I mean I know you, Liza Calendar. I know your scent. Weren’t you the one who told me that the nose never lies?’

Chapter Twenty-seven

A Week Later

Liza chuckled as she got onto the lift in Bernini Place, checking the text from Coraline. Apparently a very repentant Jim Dryer was taking his much-deserved punishment from Fidelia, though Coraline worried that they were both enjoying it way too much. Still, the man made a mistake, and men often think with their cocks. It was biology. All things considered, everyone was convinced that it wouldn't happen again.

Like his father before him, Carl Blain had made the fatal mistake of underestimating Coraline Martelli. It was a mistake he'd not get the chance to make again. Coraline had connections, powerful connections, and very, very old money. Carl's plane was grounded and the missing scents were found. Even though they were useless, the plot was exposed along with the break-in in order to get the scents, and there were enough people who knew about the hostile takeover plans that the plot was obvious. As much as the new line had cost Martelli, it was nothing compared to the expense Carl Blain had gone to in order to try and guarantee his success where is father had failed. Blain Holdings was ruined, and Carl would be doing time. *High Rising* magazine had way more of a story than it had bargained for, and there was an influx of new advertisers. Addie was already looking to hire a couple of people and Liza would then become the silent partner – the one with the Nose. She smiled to herself.

The fact that Carl had actually planned to use Liza in his scheme when he found out she would be doing a story on Martelli Fragrance showed how little he knew about her. She was never the type who went all starry-eyed over celebrities and important people. She trusted her nose, and as she approached the door to her flat, her nose smelled something yummy – two somethings yummy, in fact.

Inside, she sat her computer bag down, kicked off her shoes, and followed her nose past the kitchen and living room and down the long hallway to the bathroom where the smell intensified and mixed to a pussy-drenching cocktail of male heat. Beneath that she could smell the soft scent of lavender and geranium. On tiptoes, she peeked around the corner of the bathroom door and let out a squeal of surprise as Paulo, completely naked, pulled her into a deep, tongue dance of a kiss, bending her back until her feet nearly lost contact with the floor. She didn't know how he'd managed it, but he had her blouse unbuttoned and pushed off her shoulders before the kiss ended in a trail of nips and licks down into her cleavage as he righted her and undid her bra in a single smooth move.

'Congratulations to Martelli Fragrance's newest exec and The Mount's newest recruit,' this time it was a very naked Angelo who knelt in front of her and set to work on her skirt, lingering to tongue her navel and nuzzle down into her panties until his hot breath brushed against her tight curls. Paulo moved behind her to keep her from tumbling backwards, nipping and nibbling her neck and cupping and stroking both her breasts as she leaned back against him. She could feel his erection pressing against her lower back. Angelo hooked his fingers in her knickers and dispatched them efficiently. It was then she noticed the bottle of Moet et Chandon peeking out from the bucket of ice on the marble counter.

The two men nudged and manhandled her until she was in position, then Paulo stepped aside just enough that Angelo could lift her until her bottom rested on the cool, polished surface of the countertop. Without a word, he shoved her legs open wide and stood in between, his cock rubbing maddeningly close to her pussy. Then the two men nodded to each other, and Paulo opened the bottle of champagne with a pop and an eruption of cold bubbly foam cascaded down over Liza's breasts and belly, just as he tilted her head back and primed her mouth with a wet tongue kiss. Then he tipped the bottle a few inches above her lips so that its sparkling contents cascaded into her mouth and down her chin. She yelped and gasped and nearly choked, then she smacked her lips and drank sloppily. Both men moved their mouths to catch their share of the downpour, taking turns lapping and sucking from her fizz-drenched breasts and belly. As she drank, Angelo hooked his hands beneath her knees and pulled her closer until her butt was off the edge of the counter and her shoulders rested against the mirror. Then he knelt, lifted her feet onto his shoulders and ran his tongue down to part her pussy lips, causing her to shudder. There was barely time to catch her breath before Paulo moved the champagne bottle and the flow pooled in her navel, then ran down over her pubis. It flooded over her hard clit and sluice between her pouting labia right into Angelo's waiting mouth, which lapped and slurped noisily. Between the tickle of the bubbles and the nibble and suck of Angelo's very impressive mouth, she came, bucking and grinding against the marble. 'You gotta taste this, bro,' Angelo gasped, smacking his lips, his breath cool against her fizz-drenched slit. 'Liza's pussy makes champagne taste so damn good.'

And the men changed places, making sure to dribble plenty in her mouth before flooding her pussy with another deluge, as Paulo drank deeply from her cup. She wasn't sure she'd ever actually quit coming when Paulo pulled away, took his cock in his hand, and pushed it up into her. Angelo chose that moment to climb onto the counter and drizzle Moet et Chandon onto his cock before he offered it to her. The smell of desert heat and ozone, the scent of evergreen and hot earth mixed with the sour-fresh scent of the fizz, and the taste of it all mixed with the cream of his precum was enough to keep her on the edge, as the two men passed the bottle.

There was another nod of a message between the two and Angelo produced another bottle of fizz from the small refrigerator next to the tub. This time she barely heard the pop of the cork above her own moans. Another nod and Paulo cupped her bottom and pulled her off the counter and onto the tile floor on top of him, still fully impaled.

Angelo followed them down drizzling champagne over the slope of her back, the bubbles cascading down to tickle and stimulate her anus. Before she could respond with more than a gasp, Paulo pulled her forward against his chest and there was another cascade of champagne against her back hole. This time when she gasped, Angelo went to work on it with his tongue, and then slid a finger inside the tight sphincter, massaging and caressing and rimming. She knew where this was heading, and as though the two men could sense her nerves, Angelo handed the bottle to Paulo, who offered it to her. She drank liberally, then handed it back, raising her ass as much as she could while still riding Paulo mercilessly against the tiles. Both men took a long draw on the bottle, then Liza felt another drizzle on her ass and Angelo scissored two fingers up into her. 'Relax,' he whispered against her neck. 'You're gonna love this.' He pulled back just enough that she could hear him pouring champagne. First she felt it against her open hole and then onto his cock. The bubbles tickles and stimulated the sensitive anal tissue and she bucked and shivered and came again. It was that moment that Angelo chose to push his cock up into her tight asshole. The tickle, of fizz and the delicious feeling of being so well filled, along with the thrusting of Paulo beneath her overwhelmed her senses. The fact that her body was so full and the scent of the two men impaling her mixed with her own was so multifaceted catapulted her into an orgasm that threatened to break bones and bruise tender bits. Both men held her tightly and found a rhythm that kept her feeling as though her whole body effervesced just on the edge of another convulsion and another. With Paulo eating her mouth like it was candy and Angelo doing the same to her neck and shoulders, they all three came together. The raw cries of pleasure echoed off the bathroom walls and then muffled themselves against flesh, lips against breasts, against lips, against shoulders and bellies. It was an altered state. She was sure of it. Either that or they'd completely left the planet. Her mind stopped registering anything beyond pleasure and scent, beyond the fact that she was wrapped in the arms of two men who smelled so right, two good men who smelled as good as they really were. God, could it get any better? Then she came again. And again.

At some point there was a bath, then there was a very messy, very sexy meal, a good bit of which was eaten off each other's bodies. Then there was a shower and then they did their best to destroy the mattress and the bedding before they all collapsed into a comatose sleep.

Dawn was just painting the room in shades of silver grey when Liza awoke sandwiched between Paulo and Angelo, who both held her to them possessively. They were both hard, and that realization made her pussy quiver with the anticipation of their awakening. But for a moment she simply lay there, breathing in the scent of desert lightning and evergreen and forest floor, and her own honey butter scent sharpened and deepened to blend. For the first time in her life she was thankful for her sensitive nose. It had kept her out of a lot of relationships, kept her on her own for a long time, but in the end it had guided her flawlessly to a perfect vocation and to a new life and new loves she would have never found if she hadn't been willing to follow her nose.

The Mount Series

For more information about **KD Grace**

and other **Accent Press** titles

please visit

www.accentpress.co.uk

For news on Accent Press authors and upcoming titles please visit

http://accenthub.com/

Printed in Great Britain
by Amazon

84015666R00161